MALE REVUES AND SUBTERFUGE

HEATHER WEIDNER

Male Revues and Subterfuge

Sleazy strip club owner, Chaz Wellington Smith, III is at it again with an all-male revue called the Cheeky Monkey, catering to girls' nights out and bachelorette parties. Recently, his new venture has been plagued with annoying pranks that have turned costly, and of course, private eye Delanie Fitzgerald is the one he calls to find out who is center stage for all the mayhem.

In this fast-paced mystery, Delanie and her computer savvy partner, Duncan Reynolds, are hired to uncover the culprit who ordered five hundred mattresses for Chaz's new club, the origin of a creepy, child-sized cowboy doll, and the instigator of rowdy mob protesting false claims of human trafficking. And if Chaz's problems aren't enough, Delanie has two attractive men vying for her attention and distracting her from signs of impending danger.

The team from Falcon Investigations has to connect the dots before it's lights out for Delanie, and someone closes the curtains on Chaz's new business.

Praise for the Delanie Fitzgerald Mysteries

"If you mixed Kinsey Millhone and Stephanie Plum with the latest in stakeout technology, you'd end up with Delanie Fitzgerald."

Kelly Brakenhoff, Author of the Cassandra Sato Mysteries

Praise for Glitter, Glam, and Contraband

"Drag queens and pawn stars and snakes! Oh my! Throw in other intriguing cases for P. I. Delanie Fitzgerald to solve, sprinkle with some old-fashioned sleuthing, toss with interesting and well-researched history on Edgar Allan Poe, and you've got yourself a recipe for an honest-to-god page turner!"

Jayne Ormerod, Author of *Goin' Coastal* and Other Cozy Mysteries set along the Shore

"Heather Weidner has once again written a must read with this work. Delanie Fitzgerald, the P. I. heroine created by Weidner, engages readers with her snappy, sassy, intelligent attitude and wicked one-liners."

J. L. Canfield, Author of *What Hides Beneath* and *Icy Roads*

"*Glitter, Glam and Contraband* is fast-paced and humorous. P.I. Delanie Fitzgerald's investigation into a series of thefts at a gentlemen's club introduces her to a world of drag queens with fanciful stage names like

Tara Byte and Anna Conda. But there is nothing funny about the illegal sale of exotic reptiles or antiquities that she uncovers. Delanie juggles a number of interesting cases with real world settings. Great read!"

Charlotte Stuart, Author of *Survival Can Be Deadly*

Praise for The Tulip Shirt Murders

"Smart, sassy Delanie is back for more murder and mayhem, and readers will enjoy every twist of Weidner's cleverly plotted mystery."

LynDee Walker, Agatha Award-Nominated Author of *Lethal Lifestyles*

"Weidner's latest Delanie Fitzgerald mystery delivers everything her fans have come to expect—a spunky P.I., a fast-paced plot, and a supporting cast of deliciously sleazy characters."

Mary Miley, Author of *The Impersonator*

"The intrepid Delanie Fitzgerald once again teams up with a computer geek and an English bulldog named Margaret for a hair-raising adventure in *The Tulip Shirt Murders*. You'll be hooked from page one."

Maggie King, Author of The Hazel Rose Book Group Mysteries

"In Heather Weidner's latest mystery, *The Tulip Shirt Murders*, feisty private investigator Delanie Fitzgerald proves yet again that she can handle everything from bootleggers to murderers to strip club owners. Never shying away from dangerous situations, Delanie doggedly chases down clues until she flushes out the bad guys and solves the crime. *The Tulip Shirt Murders* is a fun read that will keep you laughing...and guessing...until the very end."

Frances Aylor, Author of *Money Grab,* A Robbie Bradford Novel

"Stakeouts, disguises, and surveys lead PI Delanie Fitzgerald on the road to catch the Tulip Shirt Murderer."

Teresa Inge, *Virginia is for Mysteries* & *50 Shades of Cabernet* Author

Praise for Secret Lives and Private Eyes

"Move over Kinsey, there's a new sassy PI in town – Delanie Fitzgerald. *Secret Lives and Private Eyes* is an impressive debut for Heather Weidner."

Debra H. Goldstein, Author of *Should Have Played Poker*

"If you like spunky sleuths and mysteries brimming with local color, then you'll love Heather Weidner's fun debut set in Richmond, Virginia!"

Meredith Cole, Award-winning Author of *Posed for Murder* and *Dead in the Water*

"Delanie is masterfully written. She's the strong woman readers cheer for."

Lyn Brittan, Author of The Mercenaries of Fortune Series

"Watch out Stephanie Plum. Delanie Fitzgerald has arrived. And she doesn't take 'no' for an answer."

Betsy Ashton, Author of the Mad Max Mystery Series

To Stan,
thanks for being my photographer, roadie, and biggest fan!

Prologue

Delanie Fitzgerald picked up her iced coffee from the counter at Sacred Grounds, an eclectic hangout for students and creative types near Monroe Park and the Virginia Commonwealth University campus. She found a lemon-yellow straight back chair at a homey table in the corner and settled in to wait. Brightly colored paintings of cows and hedgehogs dotted the lime green walls. She chose the chair that faced the door and large glass windows. Setting her purse on the table next to her, she wiggled out of her coat, located her phone, and pretended to be engrossed.

Half-way through her drink, a gangly millennial opened the front door and glanced around. Delanie pushed the button that activated the hidden camera in her purse. He ambled over and dropped a black messenger bag in the lavender chair across from her. "Hi, Kelly. It's good to finally see you in person. I'll be right back."

Delanie nodded, acknowledging the name she had given him online, and returned to her phone while he ordered. She glanced at a local news alert. Another creepy doll had been found in the Richmond metro area. That is the fifth or sixth one in two weeks. Odd, child-sized dolls in a variety of costumes, had been spotted at intersections and area businesses. Half the town was curious to find the perpetrator, and the other half seemed to be spooked.

She looked up as the man approached again. Turning on her best smile, she pocketed her phone. "Hi, Donnie. It's nice to finally meet you, too."

"Yeah." He pulled out the aqua chair and sat down. "I feel like we're old friends. We've talked for days online. I feel a connection. We're on the same page with our dreams and goals and stuff."

Delanie smiled again. "I've enjoyed our chats. So, what news do you have for me?"

He blew on his coffee. "I've thought this over. I'm in. I'm not happy with where my job is going. When I joined, it was a startup company with a mission to make a difference. Kip, the owner, had all these lofty plans of doing pro bono work and donating large amounts of the profits from the regular work to social groups. He got us all hyped up about being the change. We didn't mind giving up our lives and working round the clock for a cause. Tons of dollars later that hasn't happened." He took another sip of his drink and wiped his mouth with the back of his hand. "And now there are rumors that he's looking to sell the company and retire early. He's going to pocket bazillions and trade us all like commodities. That's not what I signed up for. I gave my blood, sweat, and tears to this, and all I got were broken promises." He had a lost-puppy look in his eyes as he stared at her across the table.

"I think our relationship can be mutually beneficial. And I hope it helps you find your center again." Delanie flipped her long, red curls over her shoulder and flashed a toothy smile.

Donnie leaned forward and pulled something out of his pocket. "Here. This should give you enough to start with. You'll get more after I receive payment." He pushed a black thumb drive across the table.

Delanie picked it up and waved it around in the air in front of her purse. "It's amazing that something so tiny can hold something so important. This will be extremely helpful to my client."

He snatched the thumb drive from her grasp. "I'm not doing this for the money," he whispered. "It's my way of righting the wrongs of corporate America. But the money will provide me a cushion when the job comes to an end. Maybe with your help, I can strike out on my own and do consulting work. You can have this when the funds reach my account."

"I'd like for us to work together again." Delanie licked her lips. "I'll make sure the bitcoin is transferred to the account you gave me. You should have confirmation this afternoon. Let me know and then we'll talk about some future work. But I kinda need that now, or you're going to have to meet me this afternoon to do a handoff."

Donnie's gaze darted around the room. "I guess I can trust you. We're friends, right?" He dropped the thumb drive on the table and picked up his bag and coffee. "Okay. I'll be watching for my money. I'll text you when it lands. I have to get back to work."

"Thanks," Delanie replied. "I'll let my client know immediately. He'll be pleased to get this."

Donnie nodded and rose. "I'm available and interested. I am the change." He pumped his fist in the air as he walked out.

Delanie turned off her camera and texted her client about the encounter. The video and thumb drive were enough to confirm Kip Thornhill's suspicions that one of his employees was stealing his corporate data.

Chapter One

Delanie Fitzgerald reached for her credit card and bag of books. "Thanks, Mary." She left the Little Bookshop with a variety of books for her nephews and niece. On her way down the steps, her purse trilled, and she fished through it for her vibrating phone.

"Hey, Chaz. What's up? I haven't heard from you in a while." Chaz Wellington Smith, III, was her private investigation firm's best cash-paying client and a local strip club owner. He had called on her in the past to clear his name when he was charged with murdering the mayor, to shut down a blackmailer, and to uncover a time capsule in a statue that contained historic valuables. *Wonder what he wants this time?*

"Hey, can you meet today or tomorrow? I have a job I want to talk to you about." It sounded like Chaz was chomping on something.

"Sure. What about this afternoon? Are you downtown?"

"Yep. I'm at the Treasure Chest now. How about you meet me in an hour or so at the Cheeky Monkey? See you then." Chaz disconnected.

Delanie fired up her black Mustang and glanced at the clock on the dash. She had enough time to grab lunch and head to the West End to Chaz's new club that featured an all-male revue.

After balling up the wrapper from her lunch in a bag, she pointed her car toward Route 288 and told the radio to call her partner, Duncan. Duncan Reynolds, who had the uncanny ability to get computers to cough up information, worked with Delanie and did web design on the side, often his euphemism for white-hat hacking.

"What's up on this fine afternoon?" her geeky friend said in a sing-song voice.

"Hey, Dunc. Guess who I got a call from?"

"Tell Chaz that Margaret and I said hi."

Delanie smiled at the mention of Duncan's rotund sidekick and shadow, Margaret the English bulldog. "I'm headed to his new club now."

"Let me know what he wants. With Chaz, you never know. At least he's a regular source of income."

"I'll call you later with details. In the meantime, I wrapped up the work for Kip Thornhill. Can you make the social media stuff for my alter-ego Kelly vanish?"

"I'm on it." Duncan disconnected, and Delanie merged onto the interstate.

About twenty minutes later, she exited and found a spot in front of the Cheeky Monkey's main doors, next to Chaz's black Mercedes. She grabbed her purse, hip-checked the car door, and looked around the parking lot. A large white ragdoll, about the size of a small child, stood with its arms wrapped around Chaz's huge neon sign of a monkey in a cowboy hat. The doll sported a cowboy hat, jeans, and a red-and-white checked shirt with black "Xs" where the eyes, nose, and mouth should have been. Delanie snapped several pictures with her phone. Whoever was planting them around town took time to match them to their location. This couldn't be what Chaz wanted to see her about.

Delanie pulled on the brass bar of the glass door, and it swung toward her although the club didn't open until seven in the evening. *Interesting*. Delanie made her way through the lobby to the main bar, which was decked out in a kitschy cowboy motif. The dining room with the stage was fairly dim except for the emergency lighting. A red and yellow neon monkey sign blinked on and off over the bar. Delanie searched the bottom of her purse for her phone at about the time a tall blond man in a form-fitting athletic shirt came from the back, carrying several crates of glasses.

"Oh, hi. I remember you from Chaz's club downtown. Is he here? I'm Delanie Fitzgerald."

"I'm Sven. He's in his office. Just a sec. I'll take you back there." He set the crates behind the bar and dusted his hands off on his jeans. "This way."

Delanie followed the bartender down a narrow dark hallway past the kitchen. He knocked on the door and waited for a "Come in" before he opened it.

"Hey, Delanie." Chaz jumped up from his desk and hurried around to hug her. "Thanks for coming over so quickly. Can I get you anything?"

Delanie shook her head and shed her ski jacket before settling in one of the dark chairs across from Chaz's black lacquered desk. The furniture looked exactly like what was in his office at the Treasure Chest. The only difference was that this office didn't have a jumbo-tron-sized flat screen TV and a bar.

"I'm having some issues here at the Cheeky Monkey that I'd like for you to look into."

Delanie suppressed a giggle at the mention of the name of his latest entertainment venture in Goochland County, west of the bustling Short Pump area. "Definitely a hit for girls' nights out and bachelorette parties. I heard the food is really good."

"It is. Business has been off the charts, but we've had some weirdness going on lately. Have you heard about those blasted dolls that keep showing up in town?"

Delanie nodded. "I saw it on the news. And out by your sign."

"The place was crawling with people taking pictures of it and the news cameras have shown up a couple of times. I think this one was the sixth one found in the last month."

"Any idea of why it was left here or by whom?" Delanie leaned forward.

"No. That's just another annoyance. This place seems to be jinxed. The latest problem is that the internet was down, so the cameras here didn't work. I think this is part of a bigger effort to sabotage my business. I mean the free publicity from the doll has been good. It's creepy, and it's the cherry on top of a whole list of other weirdness."

Delanie pulled out a notebook and pen from her purse. "What else has happened?"

"It's all been in the last few weeks. The computers go down for no reason, and we can't take credit card payments. The internet was down, and that knocked out the security cameras. Oh, and last week, we got a huge booze order. It was over ten thousand dollars, but it wasn't what we ordered. The distributor insisted it was the order we placed." Delanie raised an eyebrow and he continued, "Our normal order is wine, champagne, and vodka. I was charged for cases and cases of whiskey and bourbon, not this clientele's preference. It took Violet, my manager, a couple of days to get that straight and smooth over hard feelings with the distributor." Chaz rolled his eyes and ran both hands through is blond hair, cut to look hipster cool, even though he had aged out of that demographic years earlier.

"Sounds like someone's playing dirty tricks. Any ideas?"

"Nope. That's why I called the experts, you and your computer whiz partner." Chaz pulled a thick white envelope out of his drawer and pushed it across the desk to her. "Here, start with this and let me know if you need more."

"Can I get a list of employees and contractors who have access to this facility? And any that have left recently."

He nodded and picked up his phone. "Hey, Violet. Run me a list of all the active employees with their info and a list of any that have quit, or we canned. Thanks. Uh, now."

Delanie heard the woman say something, but Chaz disconnected the call.

"Duncan and I'll get to work. Anything else I should know before I start poking around?"

Chaz furrowed his brow. "Marco runs security for both places. Since he's downtown, he hired Gwen for this facility. She's ex-Army and has two or three contract security people each night, depending on what's going on. Sometimes she has to break up girl fights. Violet is my operations manager. She runs the day-to-day stuff. We have three or four bartenders, either full-time or part-time. There's probably another fifteen people when you add waitstaff and kitchen prep. I have an outside cleaning crew, but they don't come in until mornings. Oh, and there are five to ten dancers at any one time. And if they aren't scheduled for a show, they often wait tables or tend bar."

A steady rat-a-tat-tat on the door interrupted him. "Enter," Chaz bellowed.

A rail-thin woman with angular cheekbones strode in the office and handed Chaz a folder. "Thanks. Violet, this is Delanie Fitzgerald. She's my private investigator. She'll be here for some time doing some research work for me. Please give her whatever she needs."

Violet looked Delanie up and down and nodded. "Okay, Chaz, do you need anything else? I'm training new waiters."

"Is Easton in his office?" Chaz asked.

The woman paused and pursed her lips. "He's still at lunch, but he should be back soon."

Chaz handed Delanie the folder as Violet slid out the door and closed it with more force than needed.

The noise didn't seem to bother Chaz. "Easton Marsh is my cousin. He moved back to town and needed a job, and I needed someone to oversee this place. Right now, he's doing marketing for us and acting as a director. If he does a good job, he'll run this venue eventually. But for now, Violet does all the heavy lifting, and I sign off on the business decisions."

"I'm going to see what Duncan can dig up." Delanie dropped the folder and Chaz's envelope filled with cash in her purse. "Thanks for calling us."

Chaz made a face like he had licked a lemon. "Who else would I call? You and Duncan are almost family. You've kept my butt out of trouble so many times."

Delanie rose.

"Come on," he said. "I want you to meet Easton if he's back."

Chaz strode out of his office, and Delanie had to pick up her pace to keep up with the taller man. He stopped suddenly in the narrow hallway, and Delanie almost plowed into the back of him. "Hey, Easton. When did you sneak in?"

"I've been back for a while," floated out from an interior office.

Chaz stepped across the threshold, and Delanie followed. The office, more modest in size and décor than Chaz's, sported a wooden desk with a laptop and a leather office chair. A pine green ginger jar lamp looked small on the empty credenza behind the desk. Two guest chairs faced the desk in front of two empty bookcases.

A tall man with wavy dark hair and piercing blue eyes stood when he saw Delanie. His megawatt smile reminded her of a make-believe Disney prince.

"Easton, this is Delanie, my private eye. She's going to get to the bottom of all this nonsense. Give her whatever she needs."

"My pleasure. Please let me know if I can assist you in any way. I'm at your service." He shook her hand longer than customary.

Delanie hoped she didn't roll her eyes. He did everything but bow and kiss her hand. "It's nice to meet you. I don't think I've ever met any of Chaz's family before." Delanie looked Easton over. He was the anti-Chaz with his tailored charcoal gray suit and crisp white dress shirt. Easton's red tie and cuff links made him look like a banker or a stockbroker, while Chaz's shiny, rumpled suit looked slept in.

"My door is always open." Easton winked. "Just let me know what you need."

Delanie nodded and followed Chaz out in the hall. "Call me when you find something. This is making me nuts. Delanie, I'll give you a quick tour of the place before you head out."

"It was nice to meet you," Easton yelled out the door.

Chaz stopped abruptly at the next office. "This is Violet's office. She's always here and knows everything." Delanie looked inside the empty, dark office.

A few steps later, Chaz stopped again at a T intersection of three hallways. "The dressing room is back here along with the prop room, and this hallway leads to the back of the stage. That one goes to the kitchen, prep area, and the main dining room." Chaz turned on the heels of his pointy-toed gray shoes and walked down the hallway to the main dining room. "This is where the magic happens. We do one show daily, and a special brunch show on Sunday. Easton wants to open up for lunch, but I'm not sure the numbers are right for that yet. Our audience wants an evening of fun. They don't want to have to rush back to work after their lunch hour. Anyway, business is great. I need these annoying pranks or whatever they are to go away before they damage my bottom line."

Delanie nodded, taking in the darkened dining room filled with rows of tables in front of an elevated stage. A glass booth, opposite the stage, looked like the sound and lights area. Western gear and memorabilia covered every inch of space.

"It looks like a fun place. I'll be back tomorrow. What time do they start their prep work?"

"Around four."

"If you think of anything else, let me know. In the meantime, I'll get with Duncan and see what he can uncover."

"Appreciate it. The pranks are stupid, but the other stuff costs me money. And that sends me into orbit, especially if someone is doing it on purpose." Chaz furrowed his brow.

"We'll see what we can find." Delanie patted him on the arm.

After stepping out on the sidewalk, she zipped up her jacket against the January chill. The temperature had dropped since she'd been inside. Chaz saluted and waved to her from the front door.

Delanie pushed the button for her heated seats and told the car to call Duncan. "Hey, there. What are you and Margaret up to?"

"We're packing up. I've been doing a website for an art gallery. It's game night, and Evie and I are bringing the food. How's the Cheeky Monkey?"

"It's over the top with its cowboy motif. I've got a list of names of current and former employees for you. Chaz had one of those creepy dolls left by his sign. I'll send you photos."

"Ha. Central Virginia's wild, wild west. I guess Chaz is playing off of the fact that it's in the West End with all that cowboy stuff." Duncan laughed at his own comment. "I'll be in early tomorrow morning if you want to brainstorm. And those dolls are weird. According to the news, no one has a clue who keep leaving them all over town. I guess it's harmless."

"It didn't look at all that threatening to me. He said he's had other problems, too. Have fun at game night. Tell Evie I said hello." Evie Hachey had been Duncan's girlfriend since they hit it off at a local

Comicon. She was the perfect match for the computer geek who liked to fly under the radar.

"Will do." He disconnected the call.

Delanie made a quick stop at Kroger and picked up a salad and iced coffee for dinner. She would plow through the list of names since her evening was wide open. She hadn't had anything resembling a date on her social calendar since Eric Ellington, the FBI agent she had been seeing for the past few months, was away in Boston on assignment He was fun to hang out with on the rare occasion that he was in town. When he was on a case, the phone calls and texts were few and far between.

Chapter Two

Delanie managed to unlock the front door of her office, while balancing two coffees, her purse, a messenger bag, and a box of doughnuts. She set her stuff on the empty receptionist's counter and relocked the door. Falcon Investigations inhabited a small suite in a strip mall. She picked up the load and walked past the darkened kitchenette. Following the sound of voices past the empty offices, she headed to the conference room at the end of the hall. Duncan had his feet on the large oak table as he talked to someone on Zoom. He waved. Margaret, the Wonder Dog, who had taken up residence beside her pal sniffed the air as Delanie put the doughnut box next to Duncan's laptop.

Duncan smiled and raised a "wait a minute" finger. "Okay. I'll get the files to you today. Gotta go. Got another meeting." Pulling off his headset, he opened the box. "Good morning. Thanks for bringing these."

"I thought the sugar and caffeine would help." Delanie rooted through her messenger bag and pulled out Chaz's list. "I went through this last night and made a spreadsheet of all the players. I was hoping you'd be able to find more in the secret places you traverse on the dark web. Chaz thinks someone is sabotaging him and the creepy doll was the latest antic." Delanie filled Duncan in on the weirdness at the Cheeky Monkey as he reached for a doughnut.

When she finished, Duncan tapped his lip with his finger. "Give me a bit to see what I can dig up. I did some quick research on the dolls last night. It's pretty interesting. The phenomenon started in in the midwest in the nineties. Someone left decorated dolls around town for about three years. No one knew who did it or why. In another town at about the same time, someone left creepy clowns. Those spooked a lot of people. Around here, no one has caught the culprits on camera which is odd. Everyone has cameras these days. But the dolls have an almost cult-like following on social media. People drive around and take pictures of them. They have their own Facebook page."

"I've seen pictures of them at businesses and in intersections. Chaz's is hugging the monkey sign in the parking lot," Delanie said.

"Someone's putting some time into these. Look at these pictures." He turned his laptop around, so she could see dolls with wigs, hats, and costumes. All of them had an X for the eyes and mouth.

"They don't feel threatening. It's like a joke or those lawn decorations that people used to have years ago. Now the clowns would creep me out." Delanie turned on her laptop.

"Me too. I've seen too many horror flicks." Duncan shuddered and stared at his screen.

"I put the spreadsheet on the server, so we can share it. I'm going to call my friend to see what she knows on the dolls. She's usually got her finger on the pulse of what's going on here in River City."

Delanie picked up her phone and walked down the hall. Margaret raised her head but stayed put since the doughnut box remained in the conference room.

Settling in her office chair, Delanie punched her contact for Ami Lawrence at *Essence Weekly* magazine.

Ami answered on the first ring. "Hey, girl. What's up? I haven't heard from you in ages. We need to get together soon."

"It's been all work here. How are things with you?" Delanie cradled her phone with her shoulder and picked up a legal pad.

"It's been crazy busy, but at least I have a job. So many papers can't make it these days."

"You've found your niche. I see people reading it all over town. I'm glad things are going well. Hey, the reason for my call is that it seems that one of my clients found a creepy doll outside his business. I wanted to see what you knew about them since you always know what's going on in RVA." Delanie sifted through the pile of mail on her desk.

Ami laughed. "Yeah, for a girl who has no social life, I know what everyone else is doing. Let me see here." Delanie heard papers shuffling. "We did a story on it a few weeks back. The first one was at a bowling alley on the southside. The doll was dressed in a bowling shirt and jeans with a ball hat. Then there was a boy doll, dressed as a kid, on Boulevard. He had a helium balloon. Then there was a girl in a sunhat at a nursery off Forest Hill Avenue. Oh, and another female doll in a dress at an intersection off Granite near Libbie Avenue. And then of course, Chaz's."

"It's at the Cheeky Monkey in Goochland near Short Pump. It was dressed as a cowboy, and it was hugging Chaz Smith's sign for the all-male revue."

Ami snorted when she laughed. "At least it wasn't one in the buff at the Treasure Chest. We'll probably do a follow-up next week. The dolls are a hit on social media. They've spawned their own hashtag, #creepydollsRVA."

"Any idea who's doing this?" Delanie asked, doodling on a notepad.

"Nope. So far, they've successfully evaded being caught. They seem to know about the areas where they leave the dolls. I don't think it's politically motivated. And who knows, it could have caused copycats to try their hand. I'll send you our articles."

"Thanks. Duncan found articles from Missouri and Kansas about other creepy doll and clown sightings," Delanie said.

"Not sure the reason, but the doll's have done a good job of creating a buzz. I think some of the local TV stations have kept the stir going." Ami's voice trailed off.

"We need to find a day to get together soon. Miss you."

"Sounds good. Miss you, too." Ami clicked off.

Delanie stared at the legal pad filled with squiggles and weird drawings. It didn't seem like the doll was targeted at Chaz or his business specifically, but the other pranks were. She started a timeline of what Chaz had told her. She'd fill in more details after tonight's visit.

§♠

A LITTLE AFTER FOUR-THIRTY, Delanie parked near the front of the Cheeky Monkey and shrugged off her jacket. Pocketing her phone and keys, she locked her purse in the Mustang's trunk. She pulled on the club's front door, but it was locked. Not seeing anyone inside, she wrapped her arms around herself and tried to warm up. She hiked around the shopping center to the back. The chilly afternoon air made her wish she hadn't left her jacket in the car. The door, near the blue dumpster, stood open. Slipping inside, her eyes adjusted to the interior darkness. Muffled voices echoed through the empty corridor.

Delanie walked toward the noise and paused at the intersection. Deciding whether to make the dining room her first stop, she looked toward the dressing room. She heard footsteps, and someone put a hand on her shoulder. Delanie yelped and swung around.

"Hey, hey. I didn't mean to startle you. Welcome back. Is there anything I can help you with?" Easton stood a little too close.

Delanie exhaled to try to calm her heart rate. "Yes, do you know where Violet is?"

"Here, I'll show you. She and Javi are training the new waitstaff. Follow me." Easton, sporting another designer suit, squeezed past her in the narrow hallway. He brushed against her, and a whiff of his cologne tickled her nose.

Delanie wasn't sure if being caught unawares or Chaz's cousin gave her a spark of adrenaline. *Nah, he's not my type.* Taking another couple of deep breaths to ward off the jittery feeling, she followed him to the spot where the hallway opened into the main dining room. This time, the stage and the red and yellow neon lights around the bar made the almost empty room seem more alive.

Violet looked up from the cash register as Delanie followed Easton. Three waiters who could have been bodybuilders in previous lives, leaned over her shoulders to see what she was demonstrating.

"And that gentlemen, is our point-of-sale software. Food and drink orders need to go in as soon as you can. The sooner in, the faster you'll be able to serve your clients. Be accurate. Be beautiful, and the tips will flow. Any questions?"

A puzzled look flashed across the blond's face. "I wanna try it before I have to do it for real," he said in a heavy Boston accent.

"Not a problem," Violet said. "You go first. I want cheeseburger sliders, well done with no pickles, fries, and a Diet Coke."

The would-be waiter moved closer to the screen and stared at the buttons.

"You need to put your code in first," the dark-headed guy behind him said.

"Oh, yeah," the blond replied. He used one finger to type in a code. Then he stared at the screen. "What did you want again?"

Violet rolled her eyes and repeated her order in a sharper tone.

"Come on," Easton said. "She's going to be tied up here for a while. I'll show you around while you wait. Would you like something to drink?"

"I'm good for now."

Easton looked her over and grinned like a four-year-old with a secret. "This way, then." He pointed toward the other hallway.

"This is the prop room." He pushed the door open to reveal a room with floor-to-ceiling racks on one side and shelves on the others. Chaps, sequined outfits, and every kind of cowboy prop imaginable covered the room.

"Wow." Delanie marveled at all the hats and gun belts.

"It's probably a fire trap in here, but we definitely have the costumes. And this is the dressing room." He held the door open, and she peeked under his arm. "The guys should start getting ready around five-thirty."

"Interesting." It reminded Delanie of the backstage area at Freeda's, a downtown drag club where she'd gone undercover last fall to find out who was stealing from the entertainers. "Is Gwen here?"

"Uh, yes. You sure you don't want anything while you wait for the entertainers."

"I'm working but thank you. Gwen's office is back here?" Delanie pointed behind her.

"Such dedication. I'm sure that's why Chaz speaks so highly of you. Yes, her office is right this way." He stepped in front of her and blocked the hallway.

When he didn't move, she asked, "So how are you kin to Chaz?"

"My mother and his father are siblings. Chaz and his brothers visited us a lot growing up. We lost touch as we got older." He turned and led the way to the security office.

"Chaz is an only child," Delanie said.

"Huh?" Easton stopped to look at her. "No, I meant Chaz visited with me and my brothers." He shook his head and proceeded down the hall. He stopped abruptly in front of an office that could have doubled as a broom closet. There was enough room for a metal shelf, a folding guest chair, and a tiny desk.

Gwen looked up and hung up the phone.

"Hey, there." Easton turned on his dazzling smile. "Delanie's here to see you. I've been giving her a tour."

"Come in." Gwen, who sported a Cheeky Monkey polo shirt and braids pulled back into a tight bun, stood to shake the private eye's hand.

"I'll be in my office if you need anything." He patted Delanie on the shoulder as he retreated down the hallway. Both women waited until Easton was out of earshot.

"I'd say close the door, but it gets a little claustrophobic in here. I usually leave it open. What can I help you with? Marco said you'd be by."

"Marco's the best. He said you've been having some issues lately." Trying to get comfortable, Delanie fidgeted in the aluminum chair.

"He's a good boss. He raved about how good an investigator you are. I could use your help. Most nights, it's all I can do to keep everything running smoothly. You'd think that women would be easier to manage than a bar full of drunk men, but it has its own set of problems. I don't have the time to watch security feeds, look out for pranksters, and keep an eye on the clientele, too."

"Chaz said that you are former Army."

Gwen smiled. "Yep, but MPs are armed. Usually, if I had issues with a drunk GI, I could go to his commanding officer. Here, I'm finding lost purses, breaking up girl fights, dragging women out of the dressing room, and calling Ubers for those who had too much fun."

"What can I help you with?" Delanie pulled out her notebook and pen.

"Let's see. I've been here almost two weeks. In that time, someone stole half the costumes for the big finale. We found them the next day in the dumpster." Gwen paused and raised a finger to highlight each point in her list. "The internet has gone down at least twice, taking the security cameras with it. The server went down, and they couldn't take payments, and the weird doll appeared out front. When the computer guys came each time, it was a loose wire, or something had been unplugged. Oh, and I forgot about the mixed-up alcohol delivery."

"Can you get me dates of each of these events?"

Gwen nodded. Delanie passed her a business card. "You can text or email me."

"Thanks. Marco and Steve are working on redundancy for the cameras, so they can monitor them from downtown."

"That's a good start. Is the computer room locked?" Delanie asked.

"No. The sound guy has to get in there during the shows."

"You may want to get Marco to put a lock on it and limit the number of keys."

Gwen nodded again. "I feel like I'm putting out fires all the time. Marco's coming over tomorrow. I'll add it to my long list of stuff to talk about with him." She sighed.

Delanie looked up from her notes. "I'll be around tonight. Let me know if I can help with anything. The doors will be opening soon. Where's the best spot to be unobtrusive?"

"In the back near the sound booth." Gwen's phone rang, and she reached for it.

"Thanks for all of your help." Delanie rose.

"Ditto. I'll send you the list of dates tomorrow."

Delanie slipped out and made her way to Violet's office. The light was on, so she knocked and stuck her head in through the open doorway.

Violet looked up from her laptop and glared at Delanie.

"Hi. I just stopped in to talk to Gwen, and she's making a list of the problems that Chaz talked to me about. Do you have copies of the recent work schedules?"

"Of course." Violet pinched her lips together like she was trying to keep words from escaping.

"Could you send me the work schedules for the past month?" Delanie slid her business card across the table.

"No."

Delanie stared at Violet.

"Not tonight," Violet said. "I'll put it on my list of to-dos for tomorrow."

"That's fine. Thank you for your help." Delanie stepped out in the hall and walked toward the dining room, trying to dodge the clingy Easton. His office door was closed, so Delanie hoped he was preoccupied.

She found a table for two next to the sound booth and chose the chair that backed up to the wall with a good view of the lobby, bar, and stage. Pulling out her notebook and pen, Delanie doodled until the doors opened a little before seven. Groups of women in casual outfits trickled into the bar area where large reservation signs blocked the three tables closest to the stage. It was hard to hear anything above the music and the din of what sounded like hundreds of voices. Waiters in unbuttoned western shirts, tight jeans, and cowboy hats buzzed back and forth from the packed tables to the bar.

When the lights flashed, the audience squealed and whistled. Easton bounded on stage. "Welcome, welcome to the Cheeky Monkey. Who's ready for a good time?" After the shrieks calmed down, he continued, "Well, you're in for a treat tonight. The West End Rowdies are here to show you something you'll never forget. So, without further ado, let's start this rodeo."

The music pulsed, and Delanie could feel the bass in her chest. Lights pulsed, and a disco ball dropped from the ceiling.

Delanie kept one eye on the show and the other on the audience. Nothing seemed out of place. Lots of women drank fruity cocktails and put dollar bills in the dancers' chaps. Around eleven-thirty, Delanie rose and stretched. She picked up her notebook and purse and wended her way through the crowds.

The temperature and the sound level dropped in the lobby. It felt almost like air conditioning. Delanie waved to Gwen, who stood at the door talking to a uniformed security guard.

"Had enough for tonight?" Gwen asked. "I'll make sure to get that list to you."

"Thanks. I'll be back later this week. Tell Marco I said hey."

Delanie shivered when she stepped out into the night air. The temperatures had dropped below freezing. She jogged to her car and immediately turned on the heated seats. Lots of activity at the Cheeky Monkey, but nothing stood out as unusual. *Hopefully, Duncan will have better luck with his research.*

Chapter Three

Not having any bright ideas about Chaz's latest dilemma, Delanie did laundry, emptied the dishwasher, and made her bed in her quaint 1939 Yates model Sears Catalog House. Her cottage had character, and she loved that some of the boards and the flooring still had the original model numbers stamped on them. Before World War II, the mail-order kits could be ordered, picked up at the railroad station, and assembled by the purchaser. The perfect business offshoot for the catalog retailer that sold furniture and household goods.

Not finding anything interesting in the pantry for breakfast, she made a quick stop and polished off her asiago bagel before grabbing a coffee and hustling through the front door to her office suite. No sounds except the hum of the heating unit. No Margaret or Duncan. She flipped on lights as she walked down the hall to her office where she settled in to check email. Violet had sent over the work schedules. Nothing yet from Gwen.

After comparing the schedule with the list of employees, Delanie searched online for the creepy dolls. What she found matched what Ami had told her. She made a list of all the appearances around town. If she had time later before heading over to the Cheeky Monkey, she'd see if any of the other dolls were still at their locations. On a whim, she texted Duncan the names of the people who were interviewed about the dolls. Though it really may not be related to Chaz's other problems.

Delanie's phone dinged with a text. **Be there in a little while. M. is being stubborn.**

She returned Duncan's text with a string of smiley emojis and a dog one for Margaret.

Delanie padded down the hall for a second cup of coffee. While the machine spewed steam, she thought of all the pranks Chaz and Gwen mentioned. *It has to be an inside job. Who else would have that much access to the place to cause trouble multiple times?*

After that last sputter from the coffee maker, she filled her mug and returned to her office. Gwen's email popped in at the top of her inbox. Delanie created a timeline by date and filled in the staff who were working on those days. As she highlighted names who were present at each event, she heard Duncan come in through the front.

"Hey, I'm in here," she yelled.

"Good to see you." Duncan poked his head in her office. "I'm going to set up in the conference room after I get some caffeine and finish my sausage biscuit."

"I'll be right there. I was able to find a little information last night." Delanie gathered her notes.

"Have fun at the Cheeky Monkey?"

"Loads. The flashing lights and pulsating music gave me a headache."

"That's a sign of getting old." Duncan grinned.

Delanie threw a stress ball at his back as he ducked out of her doorway. She picked up her laptop and papers but couldn't find the yellow squishy ball anywhere on the floor. She headed to the conference room where Margaret was under the table, chewing on it.

"How was game night?"

"Fun. Evie and I did make-your-own nachos. It was good, but it gave me heartburn. I should know better than eat spicy food after ten."

"Sounds like a sign of getting older." She smirked.

Duncan rolled his eyes and balled up the biscuit wrapper. "Okay, here's what I found. I sent you the list of contacts on the doll people. I thought I'd call the businesses to see if they were having issues like Chaz, but not all of them are linked to a store." He yawned and stretched before he continued. "And I did a quick check on the Cheeky Monkey employees. I'll need to do more, but everyone looked clean except a busboy named J. J. and a former dancer named Pete."

"What did you find?" Delanie opened her spreadsheet, ready to take notes.

"Let's see. James 'J. J.' Jensen was arrested several times for drunk and disorderly. He also had several minor drug charges, and it looked like he had some sealed juvie offenses before he turned eighteen. Pete Fontaine, one of the rowdy cowboys, was arrested several times for political protests at rallies in different states. He got hauled out of the opposition's event once for causing a disturbance. It seems he mooned the VIPs and the camera crews. Most of the other charges were for trespassing, unlawful assembly, and disorderly conduct charges. He was terminated about a month ago, and he lambasted Violet on social media for ruining his life even though the choreographer fired him. He made a lot of comments about that on Facebook, too."

"Interesting. Anybody else?"

"I'm still digging. Lots of possibilities. I'll work on the list more today."

Delanie nodded. "Chaz's club has had a string of pranks lately that have amped up as time passed. He thinks someone's trying to sabotage his club."

After several clicks on his laptop, Duncan made a harrumphing noise. "Most of these sound like childish pranks, but the mixed-up liquor order could have been costly. And it's disturbing that someone keeps messing with his computers and cameras."

"Think the creepy doll is related?" she asked.

"I'm not sure about coincidences. The timing seems to fit with the pranks. I say we don't rule it out yet."

"I'm going to drive by some of the other locations this afternoon to see if they're still there. Maybe an idea will jump out at me if I see the other dolls. The one at Chaz's was about three-feet tall in cowboy gear.

I got close to it the other day, and I noticed it had no face except the black X's on the face."

"Like these?" Duncan turned his laptop around for her to see a string of images.

"Yep. They look like some kind of soft mannequin. Like you'd see in an old department store, except they're big ragdolls."

"Here's a fun fact. It says here that they were originally used in some auto crash tests and that clothing designers also used them as models. Hmmm. The article also says they're collectible in some circles. So, we're looking for someone who has a bunch of old dummies?"

"You never know what bit of information is going to be the missing piece. If you have time today, could you dig into Chaz's folks? I'm guessing it's probably someone who had or has some kind of access to the club. It seems too random for a complete stranger. Can you see if you can find out where J. J. and that dancer are these days? Maybe revenge is the motive."

"Sure. You never know what's hiding out there."

"I'll check in at the club later this afternoon. I'll let you know if I find anything interesting." Delanie printed out the locations where the dolls were found and packed her gear.

After a quick ride, she pulled into the parking lot of an empty bowling alley. The little white figure in a bowling shirt hugged the sign near the edge of the road. Delanie snapped a few pictures and headed to her next destination.

Ten miles away, the nursery still had the little girl doll standing by the stop sign at the curb. Her flowery hat resembled an Easter bonnet. Delanie took more pictures from the driver's seat of her car before heading to the next stop near Forest Hill Avenue.

She drove up and down the intersection but didn't spot the doll. After one more pass with no doll sighting, she headed toward Granite and Libbie to see if the boy with the balloon was still there.

At the stoplight before the intersection, she spotted the doll in the median next to a light pole. She merged and ducked into a parking lot to get a few photos. The little guy had a cap on and overalls, but the balloon was gone. *The dolls are kinda cute. Someone took a lot of time with the themed costumes.*

She sent her photos to Duncan and had enough time to grab a sandwich at the Corner Bakery Cafe before heading to the Cheeky Monkey.

The club's parking lot looked lonely with only the little costumed cowboy and monkey standing sentry near the road. Pocketing her keys and phone, Delanie left her jacket and purse in the car and jogged to the glass door. Locked. She rapped on the door, but no one responded.

After a quick hike around the building, she headed for the back door, propped open with a wine crate. Nobody in sight. She stepped into the dimly lit hallway and followed the sound of muted voices.

"From the top, one more time." A buff man in jeans and a white dress shirt with rolled up sleeves jumped on the stage and stood at the end of a line of three dancers. "Friends in Low Places" blasted through the speakers positioned on every wall.

The four men stepped through a routine with a lot of gyrating and pretend lassoing of imaginary audience members. A bald dancer stepped forward as the song melted into "Ring of Fire." He took the lead in a lip synch, and the others backed him up.

After the last few closing notes, all the dancers took a bow.

The man in jeans said, "Take five, and we'll pick up with 'Rhinestone Cowboy' and 'Mountain Music.'" The three other dancers exited the stage and rummaged through bags for towels and water bottles.

"Diego, your guys have it down." Easton Marsh clapped several times. Delanie gave his designer jeans, burgundy turtleneck, and a tweed blazer a second look. *Almost too model perfect.* She hoped she didn't roll her eyes.

Diego said, "Thanks. We want to mix it up to keep the guests coming back." He picked up his cell phone and scrolled while the other guys stretched and chatted.

Easton straightened up and strode toward her like he was walking on a fashion runway. "Hey, Delanie. Enjoying the rehearsal?"

Delanie smiled and tucked a loose curl behind her ear. "It's a fun place."

"It's our job to keep our guests happy."

A scream and string of profanities echoed from the back.

Easton turned and dashed to the kitchen with Delanie close behind him. "What's up?" he said to the two guys in black.

A scowling Violet stood nearby with her arms crossed. "When Hector went to put appetizers in the fridge, he noticed the temperature wasn't cold. Someone unplugged this, and now we have to throw out everything."

"Who's been back here?" Delanie asked.

Hector and the other man stared at her.

"This is Delanie Fitzgerald. Chaz hired her to get to the bottom of all these dirty tricks," Easton said.

The taller of the two men in black replied, "Just me and Hector. The wait staff doesn't come in until later."

"This is Howard 'Duck' Carlson. He does lots of stuff around here," Easton added. "And Hector is the sous chef for the club."

"What did we lose?" Violet glared at the group huddled around the giant fridge. A puddle oozed out from underneath.

Hector held open the other massive door. "All the appetizers we'd prepped. All the cheese and other condiments. The Jell-O shooters are the only thing I can save."

"Luckily, the meat is in the other unit and the walk-in freezer. I'm guessing we lost close to a thousand dollars' worth of stuff," Duck said.

Violet let out a heavy sigh. "What do we do tonight? It's too late to get a replacement order here."

Duck and Hector opened the large silver doors across from the mess. Delanie felt a frosty blast of air.

"We can feature mini-pizza and specialty drinks. I'll get a replacement order in ASAP. We'll be okay for tonight and tomorrow. I'll update the chalkboards with our new specials," Hector said.

The scowl never left Violet's face. "Let me know if you need help cleaning this up."

"Nah, Duck and I can handle it. We'll be ready to go when the doors open. I got this. Duck, start the pizza prep, and I'll work on this mess."

Hector and Duck flew into recovery mode. Easton put his hand on

Delanie's back and guided her toward the dining room. She felt a surge from the warmth of his hand.

He's too touchy feely. Delanie quickened her pace and stepped away from him. She paused by the bar, turning to face Easton. "So, this is the latest. It sounds like the pranks are getting costlier. You have any theories or suspicions about who's behind this?"

He shook his head. "I've been in my office all day except to pop in here to check out rehearsal. The door's always open. Anybody could have wandered in. Maybe some random person."

"I'm going to talk to Gwen. Maybe she captured something on camera," Delanie said.

"Doubtful. We've been having issues with the equipment all week. But we can try. I'll walk you over to her office." Easton darted down the back hallway and led the way.

I don't really need an escort. She tried not to resent all his helpful overtures. Delanie followed him down the long hallway to the security office.

"Hi, Gwen. Delanie wanted to stop by to see you."

Gwen looked up from her laptop and stared at Easton.

Delanie leaned on the doorjamb. "We were in the kitchen with Hector and Duck, and someone unplugged one of the refrigerators and made a huge mess. Any chance you have a camera feed of that area?"

A pained look crossed the young woman's face. "The cameras are down again," she said quietly. "Marco said that Steve is working on it. No, no cameras last night or today. They went down about three yesterday afternoon."

Easton muttered something and covered it with a cough. Both women looked at him. "Sorry, I got choked. It's a shame about the cameras. We need to get that resolved. It would probably help us figure out who's doing this."

"Marco said that Steve thinks he may have a solution," Gwen added.

Easton raised his eyebrows. "We'll see. They haven't been able to fix it yet." After a long pause with no response from the women, he continued, "Hey, Delanie. I need to get back to my office but stop by before you leave. I have something to tell you."

Delanie nodded and sank into Gwen's folding metal guest chair.

When they heard Easton's footsteps fade, Gwen leaned forward. "I don't know what's going on. Every time we verify that the computers and cameras are working, they go down again. It's like someone's watching our every move. But Steve from the Treasure Chest has a plan this time," she whispered and leaned closer. "We'll see if it works. I hate having to keep calling Marco with all the bad news."

"The culprit is getting braver, and the pranks are getting more expensive and damaging. Any hunches about anyone here?"

Gwen looked at the open door. "Not really. Diego fired a dancer a couple of weeks ago. He was pretty hot about losing his job. He's the first name that popped in my head, and the first one on the list I sent you. With the regular staff, we have a few grumpies and big mouths, but I don't get the sense that they're trying to make trouble. It's tiring to be constantly on high alert with nothing to show for it. Uh..."

"What?" Delanie stared at the thirty-something across from her.

"I was going to say that the dancers are paid well. We all are, so it's probably not a money thing. I guess if anyone has a gripe, it would be Violet. She's been super loyal to Chaz, and now he's brought his cousin in to be groomed to take over the business," Gwen said in a hushed tone.

"If you think of anything else, call me. I'll let you know if I spot anything. Have you tried the old-fashioned way?" Delanie asked.

A puzzled look crossed Gwen's face, and Delanie continued, "Do one of those 'see something, say something' campaigns with the staff. Let them know that you're all in this together, and they need to be on high alert too for anything out of the ordinary."

"You may be on to something." Gwen jotted a note on her desk calendar.

"And it will put some pressure on the bad guy if he knows everyone is watching." Delanie tapped her lips with her index finger.

Gwen raised one eyebrow. "It's worth a shot. I do random rounds. I try to mix up my routine by popping in and out of rooms. Nothing seems to help. It's like someone is watching me."

Easton stuck his head in the doorway. "Delanie, you about finished here? Come see me before you leave, please."

Delanie nodded. "Call or text me if I can help."

"Of course." Gwen flipped open her laptop.

Delanie followed Easton to his office, and he leaned against the desk. "Come in and sit down."

"What can I do for you?" She remained standing in the doorway.

"It's getting late. I thought I'd check to see if you wanted to grab some dinner," Easton said.

"I appreciate the offer, but I have some things I have to wrap up at the office. I'll take a raincheck." *A dinner invitation is that important?*

"Sure. Sure. If you're back this week, we'll do lunch or dinner."

"Thanks again for the offer." She waved over her shoulder and made a beeline for the front door.

Chaz's cousin could probably show a girl a good time, but he had a creeper vibe. Delanie wasn't ready to cross the line on an assignment, especially when she hadn't cleared anyone of being the serial saboteur, and Eric was still her phantom boyfriend. A flutter of excitement sparked a smile as she thought of the handsome FBI agent.

Chapter Four

Delanie drained the last few drops of her hot cocoa and changed lanes to exit the downtown Expressway. After zipping through a series of narrow streets, she pulled into the almost empty lot of the Treasure Chest.

She glanced at the statue of Edgar Allan Poe near the road and smiled at the memory of last fall's adventure. She and Duncan had solved the mystery of why someone kept digging around the statue's base. The Treasure Chest, Richmond's Finest Gentleman's Club, according to Chaz, stood on the former site of the *Southern Literary Messenger*, where Poe worked when he lived in Richmond.

Shaking off thoughts of the Father of the American mystery and his spooky stories, she spotted Marco, head of security, leaning against the large metal door next to the side of the club.

"Hey, Marco. How are you?" Delanie asked as she approached.

The mountain of a man, who looked like he played linebacker in a former life, held the door for her. "The boss said you were on your way over. I didn't want you waiting out in the cold."

"You're the best. It's good to see you again." Delanie followed him down several narrow hallways to Chaz's office. Marco knocked with one knuckle. He turned the knob and held the door for her after he heard a faint "come in" from inside. Marco backed out into the hallway and closed the door.

Chaz sat in his overstuffed chair behind the black lacquered desk covered in file folders, papers, and Diet Pepsi cans. "Hey, how are things going?"

"Good. Not sure I'm making enough progress to give you an update. Duncan's looking into the list of current and former employees. Your cowboy doll is definitely like the others left around the city, but I'm not sure if it's related to the other stunts." Delanie sunk in the guest chair in front of him and pulled out her notebook.

"Speaking of that, give Noreen a call. We had dinner the other night, and she mentioned the doll story. She and her team are covering it for her network. I'll text you her personal cell." Chaz tapped on his phone, and Delanie heard hers ding. "Of all the things going on at the Cheeky Monkey, the doll is probably the least of my worries."

Delanie scribbled "Noreen Nurelli, Intrepid Reporter" in the margin next to "creepy dolls." "I stopped by to see if I could see Marco and Steve about the issues they're having at the other place with the computers and cameras."

"Reach out to anyone you need. I want to find this idiot. His stupid pranks are making me nuts. The latest freezer thing made me lose my mind and a lot of food that spoiled. This stuff has to stop."

Delanie rose. "I'll send you an update as soon as I can."

"I know you'll get to the bottom of this," Chaz said as she stepped into the hallway.

Marco materialized behind Chaz.

"Oh, good," she said to the head of security. "I was coming to find you."

"Let's take a walk." Marco led her to the big metal door that he held for her. He trotted down the stairs two at a time.

Delanie had to quicken her pace to keep up with him.

"What's on your mind?" He slowed down, so she didn't have to take three steps for every one of his.

"I talked to Gwen. The cameras have been down every time one of these incidents happens."

Marco grunted. "She liked your suggestion to crowdsource the effort to watch for weirdness. Steve and I are working on something with additional surveillance. We've got some cameras we're going to install on the sly that aren't on that network. They should be in place in a couple of days. Steve called in sick today, so that may delay it a little. Keep it on the down low."

Delanie nodded. "Of course." She watched traffic zoom by Chaz's club. "I have no suspects yet."

"Only a small group, Steve, Gwen, me, and you know about the new plan," Marco said.

"My lips are sealed." She mimicked locking her lips. "It would be nice to catch this person red-handed. My gut tells me it's an inside job. Duncan's looking at former employees, but my guess is that it's someone with access and who's aware of what's going on."

Marco nodded. "I'll let you know when Steve gets the new stuff in place. He's going to do it under the guise of troubleshooting the problems over there."

"Clever. Hopefully, no one will be the wiser."

"You need to talk to anyone else?" Marco asked as they approached her Mustang.

Delanie shook her head. "Steve, but you said he wasn't here. I'm going to head over to the other club." She opened the door and slid in.

He tapped on the roof of her car as she started the engine.

She waved. "See ya soon." Delanie retraced her route through the old warehouse district that had been converted to trendy restaurants and clubs and found the ramp to the interstate for a quick trip to the West End.

Delanie made a detour for a drive-thru coffee before heading to the Cheeky Monkey. Thirty minutes later, she pulled into the lot where the creepy doll still kept the monkey company. A huge white and purple tractor trailer blocked the front of the building and the road to the back parking lot. She found a spot in the lot next door and hiked over to where Violet stood, feet planted and one hand on her hip. She waved the other arm at a man with a clipboard. Gwen, Diego, and several of the waitstaff stood at the club's door watching the action.

"I am going to tell you this one more time. We did not place this order, and we are not taking receipt of any of the items. Do not take any more off that truck. You can give me your office's number, and I'll get it straight through them. This is not ours, and I'm refusing it." Violet clenched her jaw.

"You can't. We're supposed to get payment and drop off this order. We have another load after this."

"Not my problem. There was a mix-up somewhere. This is a bar. Why would we order so many mattresses?"

The guy in the back of the truck snickered.

Violet gave him a look that could wilt flowers. "Give me the number," she snapped. "And get those off our sidewalk. You're in the way."

"I gotta call my supervisor," the driver said, waving his clipboard.

"Call anyone you want. My next call will be to the police. We've got a food order coming in late this afternoon, and you're blocking the entrance." Violet stormed toward the club's glass doors.

The driver shrugged. "Help me load these back."

"But we're supposed..." the other guy said, jumping out of the back of the truck.

"I know. We'll get it straight on the ride back to the warehouse."

The crowd around the truck disbursed as the men reloaded the mattresses and then started the truck. Delanie followed Gwen and Diego inside.

"Okay, who placed the mattress order?" Diego grinned.

"I have no idea, and I don't think it's funny," Violet barked, heading to her office.

Looking over his shoulder at the empty doorway, he mimicked Violet's gait and finger waggle.

Gwen stifled a laugh. "Hopefully, she'll get this straightened out. We would have had a mess with all those mattresses in the dining room."

Diego looked like he was going to make a wisecrack, but hesitated. "I'll be in the prop room if you need me. I need to check inventory for next week's routine."

Before Delanie could talk to Gwen, Easton appeared beside her. "Hi there. It's good to see you. Doing more investigating for Chaz?"

"Getting ready to head out in a little while. I missed lunch."

"Hey, why don't we grab something to eat, and we can catch up on all that you've been doing."

Delanie could have kicked herself for bringing up eating. This visit was to check on things, but the mattress delivery shook up her original plans. "I've got some calls to return back at the office."

"But you have to eat. If you don't have time to go out, how about if I get Javi and his guys whip up two plates from tonight's menu? You can help me taste test." He looked at her with the most soulful eyes, and she caved.

Maybe she could learn something from him that would help, and her stomach rumbled, reminding her that it was close to lunch time. "Sure. That will be fun." She smiled faintly.

"Grab one of those tables by the bar, and I'll be back before you miss me." Easton turned on his designer loafers and disappeared in the kitchen.

Delanie sat in a chair, facing the stage. The flashing lights and booming sound system created a party image, but without them, the place looked like a bar in a ghost town. She pulled out her phone and checked email while she waited.

About twenty minutes later, Easton returned with Javi in tow and a cart full of plates. "Javi and his team have outdone themselves. Here are samplers of all the appetizers and our specialty tacos. What can I get you to drink?" Easton asked, stepping behind the bar.

"Just a Coke," she said, looking at the mounds and mounds of food that could have fed a party of six. "Thanks, Javi. This looks wonderful. I heard the food was excellent here. Did you all get the refrigerator issue fixed?"

The man pursed his lips as he set the table. "It was unplugged. All fixed, but there was a lot of clean up. I don't like people messing around in my kitchen." He set the silverware down on the table enough force to shake the glassware. "Enjoy. I'll be back with dessert soon." Javi guided the cart back to the kitchen, and his black chef's hat bobbled in time with his gait.

"Wow. This looks great." Easton put Delanie's drink down and settled in the wooden chair across from her. He set two bottles with labels from a nearby brewery on his side of the table and immediately started scooping food onto his plate.

Delanie sampled the loaded mushrooms, potato skins, and crab dip. She decided to grab a chicken taco before they all disappeared. Easton munched on fish tacos and downed them with a local craft beer.

"How bad was the damage from the unplugged fridge?" Delanie asked.

He chewed slowly and swallowed. "A couple of thousand dollars' worth maybe. We had to throw out all the food and restock. Can't take chances that anything spoiled."

"Any ideas why anyone would do this?"

He shook his head and took an oversized bite of his taco.

After a long silence, broken only by his chewing, Delanie asked, "So, tell me about Chaz. The early years."

"How long have you known him?' Easton wiped his chin with the cloth napkin.

"A couple of years. He hired me when the mayor was murdered and left outside of the Treasure Chest."

"He sings your praises constantly." Easton adjusted the right sleeve of his tailored gray suit. His crisp white oxford peeked out near his wrists. "He's your biggest fan."

Delanie tried her best coy look. "So, what's the scoop on the real Chaz? Not the one we see at the clubs." She batted her eyelashes for good measure. Sizing up her tablemate, she noticed his starched shirt, open at the collar. No tie today.

Easton turned on his best impish grin. "We're cousins. His dad and my mom were sibs. He's a few years older than me, so I always thought he was one of the cool kids. He probably hated that I followed him around a lot."

She leaned forward. "Come on. There's got to be something fun that no one else at work knows."

Easton popped a stuffed mushroom in his mouth and shook his head. After a moment, he continued, "When we were kids, he was always the tough guy. We lost track of each other in my teen years. I didn't see him much. After college, I worked long hours, and I lost touch with family."

"What made you rekindle the relationships?" Delanie asked, disappointed that he didn't have any anecdotes to share.

"I woke up one day in southern California alone. My parents were gone. My sister didn't talk to me, and I hadn't seen family in way too long. I reached out to Chaz, and now I'm in Virginia. Not much to tell."

"Well, thank you so much for the food. I am going to need another trip to the gym this week." She pushed her plate forward.

Before she could excuse herself, Javi reappeared with two plates loaded with sample desserts. "I hope you saved room for these."

"They look great. But I'll need a take-out box." Delanie winked at the chef.

"Have at it. I'll drop one by in a few minutes." Javi headed toward the kitchen.

Easton didn't waste a second before diving into the key lime cheesecake.

Delanie tried part of the killer chocolate shot glass dessert. Stuffed, she pushed the plate away. "I'll take him up on the offer for the box."

"Not staying for tonight's show?" A look of concern crossed Easton's face.

"I've got some sleuthing to do. I'll be back tomorrow." *Hopefully tomorrow I might accomplish something. The mattress delivery messed up my plan for today.*

By the time Delanie picked up her purse, Hector approached the table with to-go boxes. "Boss said that you all needed these."

Delanie smiled and took the container he offered. She filled hers with the remaining desserts. Duncan would finish these off for her. "Thanks, y'all. Please tell everyone in the kitchen how wonderful this was. I enjoyed it."

She picked up her container and purse and made her way through the nightclub. Dancers and waitstaff had started to arrive, and the noise level increased. She waved to Diego who made a beeline for the sound booth.

She barely had the door to her Mustang closed against the wintry blast of cold air when her phone alerted.

"Hey, there. This is Noreen Nurelli returning your call."

"Chaz asked me to give you call about the doll that was left in his parking lot. He said you were covering the story."

"Yeah, it's a puff piece that's gone viral on social media. That's always good. Businesses are kinda glad when they get one. Free news coverage. I don't think it bothered Chaz too much. I think he kinda likes it. He's all about the publicity. What did you want to know?" Noreen asked.

"I've been to several of the sites and read the coverage online. Any idea where they're coming from?"

"Nah. There some conspiracy types out there who are offering rewards for videos. So far, the culprits have been pretty stealthy. They seem to appear in the early mornings, so our guess is that they're dropped off before the sun came up. Someone had to do some setup with a ladder on the light post ones. Those weren't a drop and dash. So far, no video evidence or witnesses."

"I can't believe no one admits to seeing anything," Delanie said.

"Nope. And some are on really busy roads. You'd think somebody would have noticed."

"When you talked to the other business owners, did any of them indicate they were having other problems or pranks?" Delanie asked.

"Uh, no. Like I said most of them are pleased to get one of the creepy dolls. Nobody hinted at any problems. Gotta run. Getting another call."

"Thanks for all of your help," Delanie replied to dead air.

Delanie headed home to comb though her notes. Who was the mysterious joker? And was it even related to the Cheeky Monkey and Chaz?

Chapter Five

The next day, Delanie picked up subs, along with her container of Cheeky Monkey desserts and headed to the office. Juggling the items in her hands, she relocked the door and made her way down the darkened hallway to the conference room.

"Whatcha bring?" Duncan asked, taking his feet off the conference table. Margaret, his sidekick, looked up and scanned the room.

"A mega-Italian sub for you and Miss Margaret. And I brought dessert samples from the Cheeky Monkey that Javi and his team made."

"Yum. Thanks. We missed breakfast because someone rolled in something stinky in the backyard and needed a bath." He stared at the English bulldog.

Margaret avoided eye contact and slinked under the table.

"Need anything from the kitchen?" Delanie asked.

Duncan shook his head and stuffed his mouth with bites of the loaded sandwich.

Delanie returned with a drink in time to see Duncan slip pieces of ham and pepperoni to Margaret. She smiled at the way her partner took care of his fuzzy sidekick.

Delanie nibbled on the end of her turkey sub. "Find anything new?"

"I did a deeper dive last night on Chaz's employees. There are some interesting characters, but you probably knew that. Let's see. Easton Marsh is Chaz's cousin. Not much on him. I'll do some more digging later. Gwen Richards did six years in the army. She's been working private security since she got out. She grew up here in Richmond, so she came back after her last deployment. She's divorced with two kids. Her mom lives with them." Duncan paused and took another bite of his sandwich. After some chewing, he continued, "What else? Oh, Violet Martin has had a string of managerial jobs over the years. She worked in operations for Circuit City before it went defunct. Then she managed a couple of bars and restaurants and a fitness club. She's twice divorced and lives in a condo. She has one grown son from her first marriage. He lives in Colorado. Let's see what else." Duncan flipped through files on his laptop. "Not much more on Violet. She lives modestly, no parking tickets, and no major debt. She has two cats."

Delanie raised her eyebrows. "What about the kitchen crew and entertainers?"

"Diego Diaz was a dance and music major in college. He worked at several theme parks, managed shows at entertainment venues in Orlando and Myrtle Beach and returned home to Virginia to be near his elderly parents. He's not married. No kids. Javi Gonzales made a good name for himself as a sous chef and later chef at a variety of restaurants in the area. He's been a contestant on several Food Network shows."

"And he made all the desserts in that box," she said. "With that kind of resume, why is he here working for Chaz? You'd think he'd be in a bigger city."

"Hey, Richmond's a foodie town. But he's had a couple of arrests for assault in the past, and I'm sure that tarnished his record." Duncan's eyes widened as he reached for the take-out container. "Want any?"

"Nope. I brought those for you."

After a few minutes of munching and lip smacking from Duncan and drooling from Margaret, he continued. "Where was I? Sorry, I got distracted by the gourmet desserts. That key-lime cheesecake was awesome. Oh, the kitchen crew. Hector Nunez is the sous chef and

Javi's backup. They've worked together for about ten years. Even before the Cheeky Monkey. The other guy is Duck Martin. He's an assistant who does all the prep and cleanup. They hired him after they let the last guy go. I already told you about Javi. Hector did some jail time in the early two thousands, but his record's been clean since then."

"What did he do time for?"

"Embezzlement from a bar he worked at in Hampton."

Delanie's eyebrows shot up. She jotted a note to watch Hector. "And they hired him knowing that?"

Duncan shrugged. "He hasn't had so much as a parking ticket since then. He's divorced with four grown kids. Duck is a twenty-something that has been in and out of trouble as a young man. He hung out with some bad apples, and he got arrested for possession, theft, and some other petty crimes. He did some time in a juvie facility. Nothing on his record lately."

"Hmmm." Delanie balled up her sandwich wrapper and drained the last of her iced tea. "What about the entertainers or former employees?"

"The entertainers are Diego, Mark Isley, C. J. Roth, Jayden Hayes, Sebastian Jones, Stone Howell, Bruce Emerson, and Eliot Simons. Sven Dahl is the head bartender. He's worked for Chaz for years at the Treasure Chest. The dancers are the backup bartenders and waiters when they're not performing. No one from that group had anything that stood out. Clean records. Most had been models or dancers over the years." Duncan paused to finish off the last of the brownie bites.

"Violet and Diego seem to be murder on the hired help," Duncan remarked after wiping his mouth. "For a club that's been in business for not quite two years, there are thirty former employees."

Delanie's brow furrowed. "That does seem excessive. Even for the restaurant industry." She scribbled more notes of things to check on. "Thanks. Keep digging in your dark places to see if any have any deep, hidden secrets. Why would someone want to ruin Chaz's business?"

Duncan shook his head. "I'm sure he still has an enemies list." Duncan leaned back in his chair and stretched. "I'm probably going to need a nap now after that sandwich and all that sugar. What are you planning?"

"I'm headed back to the Cheeky Monkey tonight. Marco said that he and Steve from the Treasure Chest are cooking up something to counteract the camera issues. In the meantime, I'm going to keep my hidden camera on when I'm there to see if I capture anything."

"You spend a lot of time there lately." Duncan raised one eyebrow.

"The show's pretty much the same each time, but the food is good. I'd take Paisley with me, but I'm afraid she'd be distracting while I was trying to snoop." Paisley Ford, with her big and unpredictable personality, had been Delanie's best friend since middle school.

Duncan smiled and tapped on his laptop. "I'm stumped on this one."

Delanie listed all the pranks and disturbances on the whiteboard behind her. She capped the marker and stepped back to look at her list.

"The mattress one was pretty funny." Duncan cracked a smile. "Lots of players at this place."

"But so far, no one jumps out as super suspicious. Thanks for all your research. You gave me a couple of ideas to focus on tonight."

"Let me know if you need anything. Tonight's date night with Evie. I need to clean up my place and pick up dinner. Text me if you need me." Duncan packed up his gear.

Delanie threw away the lunch trash. "Have fun."

Margaret rose and followed her guy down the hall. A few minutes later, Delanie heard the back door slam. She gathered her things and headed to her office. She rummaged through her credenza for her purse with the hidden camera. After checking the battery, she transferred items from her every-day purse and checked to make sure all the lights were out in the suite. Picking up her things, she slipped out the front door, double checking that the doors locked behind her.

After a ride on 288 N that gave Delanie time to formulate a plan of who to watch tonight, she pulled into the front lot and glanced over at the creepy doll hugging the sign. Several people stood nearby, snapping photos of it.

Delanie picked up her magic purse. She hoped the tiny hidden camera might capture things she didn't notice. *I need a break on this case fast.*

She walked briskly to the front of the club. The temperature had dropped since this morning. Draping her purse strap over her shoulder, she made sure the secret lens faced in front of her. *Come on, let's uncover something we can use. I seem to get thwarted at every turn.*

Delanie stepped through the empty lobby to the main room. "Back again," Easton said, causing her to jump. "Wow, you're jittery this evening. Need a drink to calm your nerves?"

His boyish grin and piercing blue eyes sent a spark through Delanie. "Maybe a ginger ale," she said. Remembering his over-attentive habits and no respect for personal space, Delanie quickly quashed any excitement about Easton.

"My pleasure." He pointed ahead of him toward the bar and a slight sneer crossed his lips.

Ignoring him, she hopped on a barstool and placed her purse on the counter next to her.

"Here you go. Bottoms up." Easton grasped an icy bottle of beer and stepped around the bar to sit next to her.

Delanie pretended to rummage through her purse as she pointed the lens in his direction.

"So, what's the plan for tonight?" he asked.

Delanie shrugged. "I'm here to watch the show and maybe get lucky."

A dark look crossed his face. He paused and then smiled. "Let me know if I can help with anything."

"Get lucky with the investigation," she said, her lips forming a straight line. *Geesh, more fourth-grade humor.*

Delanie took a sip of her drink and tried not to say something sassy about his overly aggressive willingness to help. "Any odd goings on?"

"Nope. All's quiet on the western front." He turned his head as a group of entertainers in jeans and casual clothes entered the bar. "Hey, guys." Easton saluted the men carrying gym bags. "That's Mark, C. J., Stone, Bruce, and Elliot. Your cowboys for tonight." He mimicked a gun with his finger and pointed at the dancers. "Guys, this is Delanie. She's a friend of Chaz's."

The entertainers paused to nod and smile.

Delanie gave a quick finger wave. "It's nice to meet you all."

The entertainers drifted toward the dressing room, and the dining area grew quiet enough to hear air blowing through the heating ducts.

As Delanie drained the last bit of her ginger ale from the glass, yelling emanated from the back of the building. She froze as the volume increased. Easton jogged down the hall. She followed with her camera-purse.

The fussing got louder outside of the prop room. Easton blocked the door, but Delanie wiggled around him to get a better view of what was going on inside. Bruce and Stone stood in the middle of a pile of props. Hats, whips, chaps, and other items lay scattered in a pile.

"I'd like to know who did this," Stone said. "Diego had us spend all last week organizing this room. And now we're back to chaos. What is going on around here?"

Someone tapped Delanie on the shoulder. She turned to see Violet behind them. "Excuse me," she said, barging inside the room. "What's going on?"

"Someone trashed the props," Bruce said.

"Go get some of the other guys. We need to get this cleaned up, so you can find what you need for tonight. Now!" Violet ordered.

Stone pushed his way out in the hall and disappeared around the corner. A few minutes later, he returned with C. J. and Elliot. Easton and Delanie stepped out in the hall with Violet as the men sorted through the pile of props.

"I walked by before Delanie got here, and nothing was amiss," Easton said. "It's got to be someone who was already in the building." He shook his head. "I'd hate to think it's one of the guys," he whispered.

"There's a crowd of entertainers, waitstaff, and the guys in the kitchen," Delanie added.

"On the other hand, it could be a coincidence, and someone wandered in from outside. The door is always propped open." Easton tapped the toe of his shoe as he spoke.

"I don't believe in coincidences," Violet interrupted. "There have been too many things that wouldn't make sense if it were an outsider.

A stranger would have to be here almost every day. I've had enough of this. I'm watching and waiting. And when I find out who keeps doing these things...." Violet turned and stormed down the hall.

Easton rolled his eyes and pretended to shudder. "We all need to be afraid. Sounds like she's ready to pounce." He laughed like it was the funniest thing he had ever heard. When she didn't respond, he continued, "Make yourself at home and let me know if you need anything. I have a few phone calls I need to make before show time."

After Easton retreated to his office, she returned to her seat facing the stage to mull over what Violet had said. It made sense that it wouldn't be a stranger. Too random. But it could be someone who has connections to the bar, someone who had a reason to cause problems. She needed to look into Chaz's enemy list, too. *Why would someone try to ruin this business when it isn't as controversial as his strip club, the one that always sparked protests and calls for closure?*

Chapter Six

Delanie stood behind her office desk, stretched, and did several yoga poses. She had spent most of the morning pouring over footage from her hidden camera. It hadn't revealed anything out of the ordinary at the Cheeky Monkey. *Am I just spinning my wheels by spending so much time there? I need a new lead. The camera always catches the same people.*

In the middle of downward dog, Margaret waddled in and sniffed Delanie's hair. Delanie stopped and patted the brown and white log with legs. "Hey, girl. How's it going? Where's Duncan?"

"Right here. I'm going to work on a website for a local car dealer. Whatcha doing on the floor?"

"Got tired of sifting through my camera feed. The purse camera works great, but I haven't had any gotcha moments. I'm going to head home in a little bit. I'll try the club again this evening."

"I got the text you sent me last night. I've looked through Chaz's nemesis list. They all want to see him go out of business, but they've been lobbing criticisms and complaints at him for years. Why start now with sabotaging his new business that's not as controversial as his old one?"

Delanie stood and shrugged. "I know it doesn't make sense. Unless it's something personal."

"I've got a list of folks he's had public battles with. None seem to care that much about the Cheeky Monkey. They want to shut down the Treasure Chest."

"His cousin Easton keeps hinting that it's an outsider. I know he doesn't want to suspect any of his coworkers, but a total stranger doesn't seem plausible," Delanie said.

"I'll dig some more into his enemy list, but I think I'm going to focus on the employees to see what I can find." Duncan retreated to his office, and his fuzzy co-worker followed him.

"Thanks. Let me know if you have an ah-ha moment. So far, I'm not having much luck," Delanie yelled through the wall. When there was no answer, she stood and started packing her computer gear in her messenger bag.

After slogging through some household chores, Delanie showered and changed outfits several times. Lately, she'd tried not to stand out. She liked hanging out in the shadows. Tonight, she decided to mix it up with a purple tunic, black leggings, and black stiletto boots. She styled her hair with long corkscrew curls and put on more makeup that she usually wore. *Tonight, I mean business.*

She made a quick stop for a salad and iced tea. On her way out, a twenty-something cashier at the counter flirted with her. A coy smile played across her face. The outfit worked. Once back in her car, she polished off her salad, touched up her lipstick, and zoomed out of the parking lot for the West End.

When she signaled to turn into the Cheeky Monkey lot, she was surprised to see cars everywhere. She scored one of the few empty spaces near the monkey sign and the weird doll. Lifting her purse off the passenger seat, she looked around and spotted a grand opening sign at the mega craft store next door. *That explains the crowd.* She walked as fast as she could in her heels to the front door. The winter chill felt like snow was in the air.

Sizzling fajita smells greeted her when she opened the club door and made her stomach rumble, even though she had already had an early dinner. She threw her surveillance purse over her shoulder and sauntered into the club.

Sven stacked plastic trays of clean glasses behind the bar. He stood when he saw her and wiped his hands on his black jeans. "Nice to see you again."

"It's nice to see you, too." Delanie set her purse at an angle to catch Sven and the bar area. "Do you like working here better than the Treasure Chest?"

"The ladies tip better than the clientele downtown. They're freer with the bigger bills. Strip club guys tend to stick to the one-dollar bills. You want anything? I make a mean daquiri."

Delanie smiled. "I'm working tonight. How about a Coke?"

He nodded and pulled out a frosty glass.

"Any ideas on all the weirdness going on around here? Any scuttlebutt?" Delanie asked, lowering her voice.

"Not really. The waitstaff and dancers aren't here much except for rehearsals and their shifts. The guys in the kitchen area always busy. Gwen, Violet, and Easton are here a lot. Maybe, they'd have a better idea." He wiped his hands on a black dishrag with a monkey embroidered on it.

"You're out here all the time. Anybody unusually angry or vocal about the club or management?"

"No. It's mostly friendly banter at the bar. The ladies come in with friends for a girls' night out. They don't sit at the bar and drown their sorrows and complain like at other clubs. It's a nice place to work. I rarely have to cut anyone off or call security."

"Anybody you suspect as the prankster?"

He shook his head. "Nah. Like I said. It's usually calmer here than other places I've worked. But the jokes are getting out of hand. It started as funny pranks, but it's gotten worse over time. The guys said someone wrecked the prop room after they had organized it. It took them several hours yesterday to clean it up."

"If you hear anything, let me know." Delanie set one of her business cards next to her empty glass.

Sven glanced at her card, pocketed it, and wiped down the bar. "Can I get you a refill?"

"I'm good for now. Thanks. I'm going to wander around and see what I can see."

As she turned the corner to the back hallway, she almost tripped over feet sticking out of the computer closet.

Delanie stepped back as the legs moved. Steve, from the Treasure Chest, stood and slid a screwdriver in his back pocket. "Hey, Delanie. Long time no see."

"How's it going?" she asked, trying to will her heart rate back to a normal beat.

He winked and replied, "Just troubleshooting some of the internet problems that Violet and Gwen seem to be having. Not quite sure what's going on. Hopefully, I can figure it out. Might have to call in the big guns." He dusted off his hands, grabbed his backpack, and shut the closet door.

"Good luck." Delanie continued down the hall. Skipping Gwen's dark office, she moved on to the next one. Violet's gaunt face looked more tired than usual. She flipped through the mail while jazz played from a radio on her credenza. As Delanie stepped into the doorway, the older woman looked up and stared at Delanie.

"Hi. Any word on who caused the trouble in the prop room yesterday?" Delanie asked as a saxophone filled the tiny space.

Violet shook her head and pressed a button to stop the music. "Probably one of the guys who didn't like his schedule this week. I'm getting tired of this stupidity. And didn't Chaz hire you to get to the bottom of this?"

"He did. And we're doing background checks on all the employees." Delanie tried not to react to the woman's brusqueness.

"Check, check, check, one, two, three check," blared through the speakers from the dining room.

"Well, it will be nice to see a report soon on your findings. If you don't mind, I have work to do. And could you close that on your way out?" Violet returned to whatever was on her laptop screen.

Delanie stifled a sassy comment as she stepped out in the hall, pulling the wooden door behind her.

Finding a seat off to the side of the stage, she strategically placed her purse facing the action. Diego and a sound guy stood in the back as Bruce, C. J., Stone, and Jayden found their marks on the stage.

Diego yelled from across the room, "All right guys. Take it from the top of 'It's Raining Men,'" The music blared and drowned out his remaining directions.

The four cowboys stepped through their routine, full of umbrellas, cowboy hats, and lasso props.

The last few beats blasted, and the music stopped suddenly. The quiet echoed in Delanie's ears.

Diego leapt up on stage with a clipboard. "We have three bachelorette parties here tonight and two big birthdays. Turn on the charm, guys." He pointed at the reserved tables in front of Delanie. "Any issues? Everybody ready?"

The men nodded and gathered their abandoned props and made their way backstage. Diego nodded at the sound man and disappeared.

"Can I get you anything?" Sebastian asked, leaning over the bar in a white cotton shirt unbuttoned to the navel. He looked like a bartender from Key West or somewhere in the Caribbean.

"I'm good for now. Thanks," Delanie said.

"Just call me." He winked and returned to rearranging the cut fruit and other garnishes.

Taking advantage of the moment, Delanie sidled up to the bar and positioned her purse to capture the conversation. "You're backstage a lot. Any idea who keeps pulling these pranks here?"

"I have my suspicions." Sebastian lowered his voice and leaned forward.

Delanie moved in closer, too.

He continued, "Stone and Bruce have made it perfectly clear that they think they should have been picked for Diego's job. He gets choreographer money in addition to salary and tips. They have it out for him. It wouldn't surprise me if one or both were trying to get him fired."

"Why Diego?"

Sebastian raised one eye. "He's not the easiest manager. He's constantly picking, and he calls rehearsals all the time. He wants everything to be perfect."

"Do you know who hired Diego?" she asked.

"Violet. She worked with him at some other club. He's hard on the guys, and some of them don't like all the rules. Plus, he and Violet are buddy buddy, so she naturally sides with him whenever the guys complain."

"What about some of the folks they let go like J. J. and that busboy Pete?" she asked to see if she got any reaction from him.

He shook his head. "Why would they start this stuff now. Wouldn't it have made more sense right after they were canned? Don't tell anyone I told you all this. I don't want to get on anyone's bad side. And Diego makes the schedule." He stopped abruptly and picked up a crate of glasses. "Let me know if you need anything." He strode off toward the kitchen.

"Well, hello there," Easton said, sliding on the barstool to her left.

Delanie pointed the purse toward him. "Hello." She turned on her best smile.

Chaz's cousin smiled his megawatt version in return and moved closer to her. "You look very nice tonight. Are you here for work or play?"

Delanie batted her eyelashes. "It's always work."

"That's not good," he said in a soft tone. "How about you have brunch with me this weekend. I can squeeze in some off time if you don't tell Chaz, and I'd love to show you my favorite spots to hang out on the weekend. Come on. Everyone needs a break once in a while." Easton winked.

Thoughts of Eric popped in her head. She hadn't heard from him in a while. He was doing another out-of-state investigation. And brunch would be work, not a date. Maybe she could pry some information out of Easton if he was away from the club. "Okay. How about Sunday morning? Where should I meet you?" she asked.

"Let's do tomorrow. Sunday's can get hectic around here Let's have a relaxing meal that I can look forward to before work. I'll text you the address of the place." Easton's smile looked like the one worn by the cat who ate the canary.

"When?" she asked, trying to ignore her dislike for his smarminess.

"Eleven too early?" Easton leaned closer to her.

"Not for me." Delanie added the appointment to her phone's calendar, hoping that she wouldn't regret it later. Her relationship with Special Agent, Eric Ellington, was complicated. She met him during a counterfeiting case, and the prickly agent surprised her afterward when he asked her out. Eric softened as she got to know him as a "go on a fun date" kind of guy. But he was always working. Delanie liked the company, but the relationship wasn't going anywhere. She pushed thoughts of the handsome FBI agent out of her head and tried to focus on her assignment here.

Easton slid even closer to her.

She motioned for Sebastian, who swooped in. "What can I get for the lady in purple? A ginger ale?"

She nodded.

Easton leaned back and stared at the door.

Sebastian filled her glass using the bar gun. Then he topped it off with a plastic sword full of pineapple chunks and cherries.

"Thank you," she said, picking up the tiny sword and swinging it around in the air.

Sebastian waved off her offer to pay for the drink, so she dropped a five in the tip jar.

About half-way through her soft drink, the doors opened. Groups of women of all shapes, sizes, and varying degree of dress spilled in through the lobby. The tables filled quickly, and the noise level tripled.

"I gotta go." Easton winked at her. "I'm emceeing tonight. I'll catch you before you leave." He slid off his barstool and hurried down the hall.

About fifteen minutes later, Diego dodged waiters and patrons as he made his way to the sound room. He disappeared inside. A few seconds later, the lights started flashing. A strobe zigzagged across the stage curtains as "It's Raining Men" blared from the speakers.

Then as quickly as it started, all the stage lights darkened as a drumbeat echoed through the dining room. The curtains flew open, and Easton stepped on stage. The spotlight circled him like an aura, and his model looks made him perfect for the job. The audience erupted into cheers and catcalls.

"Hello, everyone. Who's here for a good time?" The whoops and whistles drowned out all other conversation.

Eventually, the crowd noise waned. "Well, let's get this party started. I'm Easton, and I'll be your host for the evening. If you need anything, let me know. I'll be around to check on you lovely ladies. Remember to tip your bartenders and servers, and let's go to the rodeo."

Music blared from the speakers as he exited backstage. The backdrop changed, and the cowboys came out to a medley of country tunes. Delanie turned her stool around and put her purse in her lap to capture anyone approaching the bar, hallway, and stage area.

The crowd was raucous with lots of audience participation. It would have been a fun evening if she had been a patron. She would definitely have to arrange a girls' night out after she solved this case. Her gal pals, Paisley and Robin, would love it.

About ninety minutes into the show, Delanie needed to stand and stretch. She'd been sitting too long, watching Easton and the waiters mingle with the audience. Everyone seemed to be too busy for pranks. Even the four dancers were always on stage. Gwen and her other guard edged around the perimeter, trying to blend in. Violet was the only one Delanie hadn't seen all evening. Could Violet be hiding something?

Delanie walked through the crowds and stood near the kitchen to change angles. From that vantage point, she could see the dancers exiting and entering the stage. Still no Violet.

When her feet started to ache from the heels, she wormed her way through the crowd to the lobby where Gwen leaned on the host stand.

"Quiet evening," Gwen said. "But I'll take it."

Delanie nodded. "Except for the music. My ears are still ringing. How are you?"

"All's well. We'll hang out here and make sure everyone gets home safely. Be careful out there."

"See you soon," Delanie waved over her shoulder and stepped out on the sidewalk. The icy breeze made her shiver and speed up her pace.

She moved through the rows and rows of cars watching for traffic when she stepped out in the travel lanes. Mid-way across the lot, the lights flickered and dimmed. Then all the parking lot lights went out. She glanced over her shoulder. The club was in darkness too. Headlights from the main road provided enough light to get to her car. She moved forward, slowly picking her way across the asphalt.

Stepping between two minivans, she heard a noise and paused. It sounded like something scratching noise.

Someone grabbed her around the neck and mouth. A thick arm in some kind of soft material. The arm squeezed hard on her neck. Then he whispered in her ear. "Mind your own business. There's nothing to see here. Quit nosing around before you get hurt." Then he shoved her. She put both hands out to break her fall against a dark-colored minivan.

By the time, she recovered from the shock, he had disappeared between two SUVs. Delanie stepped out and tried to see where he went. She heard faint footsteps, but it was too dark near the club to see anything clearly.

Delanie stood in the darkness for a few minutes, listening for any footsteps. Should she try to find the guy? Then she heard a pop and a buzz, and all the club and lot lights returned. She took a deep breath to calm the bats in her stomach. *Not much I can do in an empty parking lot.*

She walked to the front door, looking for any movement. Her heart pounded like a bass drum in a marching band. Delanie took another deep breath and opened the front door. Gwen looked up. "Back so soon?"

"Everything okay with lights?" Delanie asked peeking inside the club.

"Just a brown out. The guards are patrolling inside. Most of the patrons thought it was part of the show."

"Someone came up behind me in the parking lot and told me to stop nosing around," Delanie said.

"Did you get a look at him?"

She shook her head. "It was dark. He had on a sweatshirt. And he whispered, so I couldn't identify the voice."

"Do you want to call the police?" Gwen asked with a look of concern in her brown eyes.

Delanie shook her head. "Just let me know if you hear any chatter about it. I'll be on high alert from now on. See you tomorrow."

"Do you want one of my guys to walk you out?"

"No, I'm fine. I think he's long gone." Delanie blew out a sigh.

This time, Delanie didn't dillydally. Not pausing to relax until she had the doors locked, she stared the engine and blasted the heat. What had she stirred up that would make someone threaten her?

Chapter Seven

At nine forty-five, Delanie found street parking on Grace, a few blocks from Perly's deli. Easton had changed the location twice late last night. So much for this being his favorite place in town. Her phone binged as she climbed out of the car. Expecting it to be another last-minute change, she glanced at the screen before she hiked down the block to meet him. Sure enough. More changes.

Sorry about the short notice. Need a raincheck. Maybe next week?

She blew out a puff of air that fluttered her bangs.

Not a problem. We'll find another time, Delanie replied, annoyed that Easton had bailed on her at the last minute. *If there is a next time.*

Thanks. Problem at the club. *What's going on at the Cheeky Monkey now?*

Delanie started the Mustang and clicked the button on the steering wheel. "Call Marco." She glanced at the clock on her dashboard.

"Hey D. What's up?"

"I hope I didn't wake you."

"Nah. I'm at the gym. Whatcha need?"

"The lights at the Cheeky Monkey went out last night as I was heading to my car. Some guy came up behind me in the dark and told me to stop nosing around."

"Gwen called me. Sorry about the creep. We're going to add extra security there for the next few weeks. Too much weirdness. We thought the power thing was a brown out, but it only affected us. I guess it's something else to add to the joker's list. I think someone fiddled with the fuse box." Marco let out a heavy sigh. "You okay?"

"I'm fine. It makes me more determined to find out who this guy is. It wasn't random. He followed me after somehow managing to kill the lights."

"Stick close to Gwen or one of her guys. I trust her. She and Sven are the only two over there that I can vouch for. Steve got the cameras fixed, but Gwen is the only one who knows right now. Let's keep it that way."

"Can you have Steve see if he caught anything about the power outage on his new feed. The guy who attacked me was wearing a dark sweatshirt. There couldn't have been that many guys there besides the staff."

"I'll get him on it as soon as he comes in this afternoon," Marco said.

"You're the best."

"I'll let you know what we find. Let me know if you need me. Be vigilant. May the force be with you."

"I appreciate it. See ya." Delanie disconnected and pointed the car toward I-64 west.

About twenty minutes later, she parked in front of the glass doors with the twin Cheeky Monkeys grinning at her. She tried the doors. Locked. Changing her mind about hiking around back, she drove around the building and parked next to a black Audi Q5 and a blue plumbing van. Someone had propped the door next to the dumpster open.

Box fans in the hallways whirred and hummed, despite the cold temperatures. Delanie picked her way over cords and headed toward the kitchen. Easton stood in the doorway watching Violet and Hector mop water in the men's restroom while two plumbers worked in a nearby stall.

"Oh, hi," Easton said, as Delanie approached. "We had a little accident after we closed last night."

Violet looked up and glared at the pair. "It wasn't an accident. Someone put a cherry bomb in one of the toilets. Thankfully, the club was empty, and no one got hurt. Just a huge mess. We're almost done here."

Easton looked like he had been scolded by his fourth-grade teacher.

"Are you able to open on time?" Delanie asked. The majority of the clientele were women. Loss of part of that bathroom could have caused issues when they reopened. Only the entertainers and staff used the men's room. *I wonder if a guy planted the cherry bomb here. It would be habit for him to go directly to the men's room, but the mess would have caused more havoc in the ladies' room.*

Violet pushed water toward the drain in the cement floor. "Probably. If they can't get it fixed in time, we'll close that stall. Everything else is working. We've got to catch this idiot soon before he does something that causes someone to get hurt."

Delanie turned and walked down the hall to find Gwen. Easton followed closely behind her. Glancing over her shoulder, she quickened her pace.

The security officer sat at her desk, clicking away on her laptop. A navy hoodie lay draped over one of the guest chairs.

"Hey, everything okay?" Delanie asked. Easton lurked in the hallway. She turned slightly, so she could watch him as she talked with Gwen.

"Fine. I haven't pulled an all-nighter in a long time." Gwen stifled a yawn.

Easton cleared his throat.

The women turned to stare at Easton. He shifted his weight from foot to foot, dressed in his gray suit with a fresh maroon shirt. *Fancy for the early morning. Maybe it was his brunch outfit?*

He returned Gwen's stare. "I need to take care of some things in the office. Delanie, stop by before you leave."

"Sure," she said, moving the hoodie. "Who's is this?"

"It was left in the lobby last night. I haven't had a chance to move it to the lost and found."

"Interesting. The guy who confronted me in the parking lot had one on like that. Anything identifiable in the pockets?"

"Nope. No tag either. I'll see if anyone comes to claim it." Gwen rubbed her temples.

"I talked to Marco earlier. He said he was adding extra security here for the time being."

Gwen nodded and stared at Delanie like she was trying to telepathically send her a message.

"I know," Delanie whispered, putting her finger in front of her mouth. "Mum's the word."

Gwen let out a sigh. "I'm sick of these stupid pranks. He's making us look like clowns."

"We'll find him or her. The person can't keep tempting fate and thinking that he's going to get away with it. A cherry bomb in the bathroom? That seems so high school."

"The incidents run the gamut. Thankfully, most are juvenile pranks. It's almost like he's creating a distraction. It takes a lot of energy to stay on high alert all the time."

Delanie looked over her shoulder. "We'll figure this out. Steve's changes will definitely help. We have an edge now that nobody knows about," she whispered.

Gwen managed a half-smile. "I'm going to head out soon. I'll be back in time for tonight. Anything else you need?"

Delanie shook her head and fingered the sweatshirt. "I'm going to go check on Easton."

She tiptoed over the extension cords and poked her head in his office. No Easton. Delanie retraced her steps. Violet, Hector, and Duck huddled in a group, watching the plumbers pack their gear.

Delanie slipped out back and climbed in the Mustang. As she headed toward the interstate, she clicked the button on her steering wheel. "Call Duncan."

"Hey, there. Happy weekend," he replied after one ring.

"What are you up to today?" she asked.

"Margaret and I are wrapping up that website for a client. What's new with you?"

"The Cheeky Monkey had another prank last night. Well, two if you count my incident. I was hoping you had some time to brainstorm."

"Works for me. Have you had lunch?" he asked.

"I haven't had breakfast. How about if I swing by Arby's and meet you at the office?"

"We'll be here. Margaret wants a beef and cheese slider, and I'll have my usual."

Delanie smiled. "Can't forget my favorite guard dog. See you all in a bit."

Thirty minutes later, she pulled into the lot beside Duncan's Tweety-bird yellow Camaro. Delanie juggled her messenger bag, purse, lunch, and drink carrier and followed the "We're back here" to the conference room. Margaret had taken up residence under the oak table, but she was suddenly interested in the smells that circled Delanie.

"I remembered you, girl," Delanie said, setting down her armload of stuff.

As they dug into their roast beef sandwiches, Duncan tapped on his laptop. "I didn't find anything new on Violet. She's the proverbial goody-goody."

"Crabby, but she follows the rules. She works hard, too." Delanie dunked her French fry in ketchup.

"Easton went to college in the nineties and moved out west," he said.

"TV weatherman? Gameshow host? He has that perfect TV smile."

"Nope. Car salesman. Actually, used cars," Duncan said.

Delanie chuckled. "That matches his personality."

"There's not much on him. He just showed up one day." Duncan continued to tap on his keyboard.

"That fits with what Chaz said. He needed a job after he sold his business. The timing was right to move back East."

Duncan handed Margaret a curly fry. "Gwen's background is

squeaky clean, too. She has lots of medals and commendations from the army, not to mention a boatload of security clearances."

"Marco said he can vouch for her." Delanie balled up her sandwich wrapper. "Sebastian, one of the dancers, told me that Bruce and Stone felt they were passed over for Diego's job. Diego is tight with Violet. Maybe there's some hard feelings or bad blood with the entertainment? Plus, Diego and Violet are the ones who fire people."

"I poked around the dark web and found a couple of things. Not sure if they'll be helpful. Bruce had some possession charges that were eventually reduced. He also had an assault charge that was later dropped after his divorce. He got in a fight with his current wife's new squeeze."

Delanie raised her eyebrows. "Interesting."

"What else? Stone's real name is Charles Higgins. He changed it to Stone Howell when he did some male modeling and porn films."

Delanie's eyebrows shot up again. "Hmmm. You're a wealth of all kinds of information." She jotted the random facts in her notes. Maybe it would be important later.

"He also had a domestic dispute under another name. It was when he went by Rock Howell."

"Assault?"

Duncan nodded. "When he was going by Rock, he held his partner hostage at knifepoint when the guy told Rock he was going to leave him. I guess it didn't show up on any background checks since it was under another name in California."

Delanie continued to scribble notes. "Lots of people to keep an eye on. The pranks are odd and annoying. Some on their own are not that serious. But together, there's definitely a pattern. So, are they juvenile pranks, or is it a distraction from something else? I'm slightly baffled."

"It's like death by a thousand papercuts." Duncan stood and stretched. He picked up the trash and headed toward the kitchen.

A few minutes later, he returned with a box of chocolate chip cookies. "For later," he said. "These pranks are like being bombarded constantly with a swarm of gnats. They aren't going to kill you, but you'll be annoyed and tired from dealing with them all constantly."

"I still have the feeling that something's afoot," she said.

Duncan snickered.

"What are we missing?" she asked.

Duncan shrugged and reached for a cookie. "Can you talk to Chaz and find out if the books are good? No skimming? No weird charges or unexplained withdrawals?"

"Sure. The creepy doll thing has been tickling at the back of my brain. It doesn't seem to fit with the other stuff. After talking to Noreen and Ami, I'm not sure if the dolls are part of this. I think it was a happy accident."

"It's definitely weird, but I think the incidents are like some hacking attempts. They try it to see if they can do it. And since they didn't get caught, the fun continues. They get braver."

"I can't believe with all the cell phones around and all the doorbell cameras on peoples' homes that no one's caught a glimpse of the doll masters." Delanie pursed her lips and pulled out her cellphone and tapped Chaz's contact.

"Hey, tell me something good," Chaz said.

"Duncan and I are still investigating. We think that the creepy doll was a coincidence and not part of the things that keep happening. We might have a working theory that we want to bounce off you. Have you noticed any abnormalities in the expenses, deliveries, or profits in the last few months?"

Duncan waved his arms and pointed to the side of her phone. "Put him on speaker," he mouthed.

Before Chaz could answer, she added, "I'm going to put you on speaker, so Duncan can hear."

"Sure. Hey, Dunc. And I'm sure Margaret's there, too. Hey, Margaret, baby. Lemme think. No, not really. We've had those weird or mixed-up orders. The money is about the same. Some weekends are better than others."

Duncan bobbed up and down in his seat. He looked like he was going to bust. "Hey, Chaz. Can you get someone you trust to look your accounts and credit cards to see if there are small withdrawals or charges? Sometimes the bad actors do that for a few months to see if anyone is paying attention. If not, they get braver. You may want to change passwords on everything important, too."

"Okay. If you say so." Chaz paused.

"We think the pranks may be a diversion, and that something bigger or worse is going to happen. It's like you're really busy fighting a battle on multiple fronts, and you don't have the energy to keep up with what's coming next."

"Possible. Or it's some dodo who gets his jollies from asinine behavior."

"That's a possibility, too," she said. "We want to cover all angles."

"Okay. I'll pull up with my guys and make sure we're on top of this. And we'll change all the passwords."

"Good. I'll have another update for you early next week," Delanie said.

"See ya," Chaz said, as he disconnected.

"I think I'm going to take the night off from the club and pour over my notes. There has got to be something that I'm missing," she said.

"Let's map it all out with a list all the players. It may make it easier later. Then Margaret and I need to head out. It's movie night, and we're in charge of snacks. Tonight's hotdog night with the classic, *Top Gun*. Get it?"

Delanie furrowed her brow, not following him.

"Hot dogging pilots. Evie and I always theme our food for movie nights."

Delanie and Duncan spent almost two hours talking through all the people and incidents in the timeline she had created previously. Right before four, he packed up. Margaret stirred and followed her guy to his office.

Deciding that it was probably too late to see what Paisley had planned for the evening, Delanie packed her gear and headed home. It was too bad that Eric wasn't in town. She missed him. Thoughts of her last boyfriend, John Bailey, popped into her mind. A tell-all author had hired her to find out if he was really eighties rocker Johnny Velvet who may have faked his death. Delanie solved the case and got her heart bruised in the process when he hightailed it out of town instead of confronting what he did. Then out of the blue, last November, he showed up on her porch with flowers while she was hosting a

Friendsgiving. Sometimes, she wondered what it would be like to be dating Johnny Velvet.

In a moment of weakness, she almost called his number, but she wasn't sure she wanted to reopen old wounds. Instead, she'd order pizza and settle in to stare at what she and Duncan had mapped out. Maybe a glass of wine and some chocolate would help her find some of the missing pieces.

Chapter Eight

Delanie ordered a double espresso from the drive-thru and headed to the office. She slept in after staring at the Cheeky Monkey timeline until the wee hours of the morning. Lots of disparate facts and no red arrows pointing to a viable suspect. Right now, it could be anyone. The sugar and caffeine charge should help get her out of the lethargic funk. After a quick stop at the office, she planned to check out Chaz's Sunday brunch and male revue.

Pulling into the strip mall in front of her office, she noticed activity across the parking lot. A new store. No sign up yet. She wasn't sure who the new tenant was, but she was glad that the space would be filled. It had been empty since she and Duncan solved the case of the previous owner's sudden death at the reptile store. She shuddered when she thought of the missing, giant snake that had been slinking around for days right above her head in her office ceiling. Margaret would always be her hero for cornering the snake in the kitchen.

Picking up the mail from the box that she hadn't checked in a while, she flipped through the advertisements and bills. She stopped at a soft package addressed to her in capital block letters and postmarked from Richmond. Ripping it open as she walked, a tuft of red curly doll's hair poked out of the top. She ripped the envelope to find a voodoo doll in purple with long, curly hair. Six silver hat pins stuck out in all directions. A note, also in black, block print, read, "I'm still watching you." She didn't know whether to laugh or to be worried. Wait, that warning sounded like something she'd heard recently. Delanie combed through her recollection of recent conversations. *Who said that? Violet? And what's with all the dolls lately?*

Delanie snapped pictures of the envelope, note, and doll and texted them to Duncan. She looked at the handmade figure again and laughed. Opening her bottom desk drawer, she dropped it inside. A new addition to her Falcon Investigations souvenir collection.

After checking her voicemail and paying the bills, she retraced her steps to the black Mustang. Was the voodoo doll supposed to spook her or was it someone's weird sense of humor?

Her phone chimed. She glanced down at Easton's text. **Another incident. Can you come by the club?**

On my way, she responded.

Delanie shook off the feeling of foreboding and cranked up the classic rock station to keep her company on the ride. Thanks to the Mustang and light traffic, she made it to the Cheeky Monkey in record time.

Pausing for a moment in the car, she transferred the essentials from her normal purse to the one with the camera. A few minutes later, she entered the quiet lobby.

No one was in the dining area or near the bar. She ventured down the hallway. Her heels clicked on the tile floor. No more electric fans in the hallway. Hopefully they repaired the destruction from the cherry bomb. Delanie clicked on the hidden camera and carried her purse in front of her.

A loud, "No. You are not going to do that," echoed down the hall.

Delanie picked up her pace and poked her head in Easton's office. It looked like a standoff at high noon in Dodge. All that was missing were the pistols. Violet stood with her feet firmly planted and both hands on her hips. Her scowl looked like she had sucked on a lemon. Easton's handsome features were scrunched up into a sneer. He stood with one hand on his hip. He waved his other arm in the air and then banged his fist on the desk.

"You will not call the police. You're the operations person. You know logistics and management. I know marketing. You do not want to make a big stink out of this." His fierce glare and contorted face made Delanie pause. It was like the charm had oozed out of him.

"It's a credible threat. I can't put our staff or patrons in danger," Violet insisted.

"They're not in any danger. We have security. And Marco added a few extra sets of eyes with the new rent-a-cops. It's another prank. If you make it more than it is, it's going to hurt business. Our guests won't feel safe here. And if they don't feel safe, they'll shy away. And there goes the money."

Violet paused, and the stare down was on. *I wonder who will blink first. Both look like they've dug in their heels, determined to fight for their positions.*

Easton blinked first. "You're going to have to trust me on this one."

Delanie's glance darted from Easton to Violet.

"If anything happens, I'm holding you responsible, and I will call the police and Chaz." Violet stomped out. Her door slammed a few seconds later.

Easton's face relaxed, and his smarmy smile returned. "Thanks for coming down here so quickly."

"What happened?"

"Somebody posted on our Facebook page a warning that our club wasn't safe and that there would be a danger this weekend. I saw it when I was doing some promos."

Delanie whipped out her phone and started scrolling. "I don't see anything."

"I deleted it. Usually, Chaz doesn't shy away from any kind of buzz, but we have an all-female clientele here, and we don't want anyone to feel like they are unsafe."

Delanie frowned. "We can't trace it now. What did it say? And was there anything similar on any of your other platforms for the club?"

"Uh-unn." Easton shook his head. "I saved a picture of it. Here," he said, showing her his phone.

Rick Jones posted, "This place needs to be shut down. It's a den of iniquity, and rumor on the street is that something's going down this week. I wouldn't be there when it happens."

"Send that to me, please." She searched for Rick's account with a bloody dagger as his photo. No matches popped up.

Delanie stared at the photo he texted and then forwarded it to Duncan with a plea to do a quick search.

He responded with a thumbs up and a knife emoji.

"I know about the marketing angle and reputational risk, but don't you think Violet has a point?" Delanie dropped her phone in her purse.

Easton's brows furrowed. "I don't think it's a credible threat. We get stupid comments all the time that we have to monitor. I took care of it. We delete a lot of comments that are contrary to our brand. We don't need idiots stirring up stuff."

Maybe Duncan can work his dark web magic and figure out where this came from.

Easton's expression softened. "Have you eaten? Since we missed brunch yesterday, we could have it here if you have time. Javi makes a killer brunch, and we have several potent potables at the bar that pair well with anything. Come on. You know you like brunch."

Too tired to argue, Delanie followed him down the hall to a high-top table near the bar.

Before she could say anything, Easton darted to the kitchen. While he was gone, Delanie scanned the empty dining room and lobby. Gwen waved to her from the next room. When she opened the front door, groups of women flocked inside and filled tables around the stage.

After Delanie had enough time to scan a few emails, Easton sauntered back to the table. More than one patron's head turned to check him out as he passed. "Javi's going to take care of us. Can I get you a drink?" he asked.

"Iced tea is fine."

"Sweet?"

"No, I'm sweet enough."

"I bet you are," he said. She smiled as he disappeared toward the bar.

Javi swooped in with steaming platters of home fries, biscuits and gravy, bacon, and bananas foster French toast.

"You outdid yourself. That's enough food for four people." Delanie smiled.

"I can always bring you a to-go box." Javi winked. "Need anything else?"

"Ketchup and tabasco," Easton yelled as he approached with an iced tea and bloody Mary. "Wow, that smells good." Easton slid in his seat and handed her the tea.

"Mmm. The French toast tastes like dessert." Delanie wiped the syrup that dribbled on her hand. "You're not worried at all about the threat that person posted?"

"Are you kidding? We get bad reviews, negative posts, and protests all the time. Chaz has a publicist to take care of the big stuff."

Thoughts of Petra, the statuesque fashion plate, who helped Chaz with his mayoral campaign last fall crossed Delanie's mind. "I don't want you to dismiss a credible threat."

"Trust me. It was some crackpot. We'll be fine." His charming smile shifted slightly. "Do you like the biscuits and gravy? I missed them when I left the south." He raised his glass in a mock toast.

She nodded and moved the food around her plate with her fork. "So where has your career taken you?"

He took another swig of his drink. "All over. I left for college and haven't looked back until now. I did some time in New York, Boston, Chicago, New Mexico, and Arizona. But I love to travel. I've been to all kinds of places. Did I tell you that I'm a photographer, too? It's a natural fit visiting all these cool places."

"You on Instagram?" she asked.

He shook his head. "No, most of the framed ones are in my house or storage. I need to bring some in for the office here. I'm not much for social media."

Before he could continue, Violet stormed over to the table with Gwen on her heels.

Violet balled her hands into tight fists and planted them on her hips. "You didn't tell Gwen what happened?"

"Keep your voice down. We have guests," Easton said, with his teeth clenched.

"Gwen had no idea. She needs to be informed if there's an issue with the club. How is she supposed to do her job if she's not aware it?"

Gwen opened her mouth to reply, and Violet continued in a harsh whisper. "She should have been involved in the conversation. She's responsible for the safety of everyone in this building." Violet's face turned as red as a beet. She made a harrumphing sound and stomped toward the kitchen.

"I don't mean to interrupt, but what exactly happened? Violet's on a tear about some imminent danger," Gwen said.

Easton waved his hand for her to lower her voice. "It's nothing really. We had a bad comment on our Facebook page about something going down soon. We get lots of negative comments. You know how it is. There are way too many unhappy people out there, and they use social media to vent."

Gwen nodded. "I know the world is full of crazies, but I need to know when this happens. Understood?"

"Of course. I got busy and didn't loop you in. It won't happen again." His Cheshire Cat smile crept across his face. "Can I get you something to eat or drink?"

"I'm good. Thanks. Any names I should be aware of?" Gwen asked.

"It was from a Rick Jones," he said. "No photo on the account."

Gwen rose. "Just keep me posted. You have my cell if I'm not in my office. I need to be your first call or text."

"Got it," Easton said as Gwen walked through the crowd toward the stage. "Oh, it's time. Be back in a little bit. I need to do introductions." He disappeared backstage.

The lights flashed and the music pulsated as the curtains swooshed open. Easton stepped out into a double spotlight. "Hello, ladies. How's everybody doing? Enjoying brunch?"

Whoops and hollers drowned him out. When it faded, he smiled and waved. "Chef Javi always does a fantastic job on the brunch. Make sure to tip your waiters and bartenders generously. And without further ado, welcome to the Cheeky Monkey. Give it up for your cowboys. Today, we have Sebastian, Stone, C. J., Jayden, and Diego."

The crowd went wild, and Easton disappeared.

Delanie pushed her plate away and drained her iced tea.

"You want a refill?" Easton asked, approaching the table.

She shook her head, and he turned on the heels of his fancy shoes.

When he returned to the bar, a woman in her late forties with a platinum blond helmet cut followed him. Delanie watched her lean close to Easton as he ordered refills. She laughed, hugged him, and pointed to her table.

Delanie busied herself with her phone. When Easton set her drink down, Delanie said, "Made a new friend?"

"Hazards of the job. It's good for the ego. I have quite a collection of hotel keys and phone numbers. Not my style. But it's always in my best interest to be attentive. Repeat customers are always better tippers." He winked.

Delanie hoped she didn't wrinkle her nose. *Slimy like a used car salesman.*

"You wanna talk in my office. It's quieter back there," Easton said.

"I think I'm going to watch the rest of this show and head home. Thank you for brunch. I enjoyed it."

"See you around and don't be a stranger. And if you figure out who the Facebook guy is, let me know. Probably some bot or fake account." Easton rose and disappeared down the hallway.

Delanie watched the show and the audience. Nothing seemed amiss. After the finale, she slipped down the hallway and through the swinging doors to the kitchen. Hector washed pans as Duck prepped fruit.

"The food was wonderful. Thanks so much," Delanie said.

Javi walked in with a pan full of cookies. He smiled. "Come back anytime. We love to hear good things."

"Anything else going on here since the cherry bomb?" she asked.

"That was enough," Javi said. "Hector and I hit the dirt when it went off. We thought we were under attack."

"I've never seen so much water," Hector said, wiping his brow with his sleeve. "I'm glad it didn't cause any other issues."

"Hopefully, the idiot got bored and moved on." Javi cut bread into thick slices.

"If you hear or see anything, let me know." Delanie left several business cards on the aluminum counter.

Next was a stop at the gym and then home to see what she captured on her hidden camera. *Can it really be an annoying prankster? Something doesn't feel right.*

Chapter Nine

Delanie's phone buzzed, and she rolled over and glanced at the time, seven-thirty. The late hours at the Cheeky Monkey were taking a toll on her.

The buzzing stopped for a few seconds, but then it continued again. She groaned when Easton's number popped up.

"Delanie, this is Easton. I'm at the club. Someone has trashed the kitchen. Can you come by?"

"Sure. Be there in a few." She disconnected and hopped in the shower. Time to rise and shine. *I wonder if he called Gwen this time.*

A few minutes later, she pulled on a T-shirt and cardigan with a pair of skinny jeans. The casual look would have to do this morning. She made time for a quick run through the drive-thru for coffee before heading to the Cheeky Monkey. The caffeine and sugar boost were necessary to ward off the nagging headache behind her eyes.

Delanie rolled into the empty parking lot, still guarded by the creepy doll and the monkey sign. She pocketed her phone and keys and headed to where Easton stood sentry with his arms crossed at the front door.

"Thanks for coming so quickly. I came in to work on some

marketing ideas and check on the cleaning crew. I found this in the kitchen." Delanie followed him to the back.

Flour, sugar, and pans littered the floor and every flat surface.

"It doesn't look like they damaged the food. Which is good. But they made a horrific mess. Javi is going to have a stroke." Easton checked the bottoms of his fancy loafers.

Delanie noticed footprints in the flour. Most of the prints look like someone slid in the mess. The one almost full print looked like a man's shoe or a sneaker. She snapped a couple of pictures. "Did you get anything on your shoes?"

He stepped into the mess and out again like he was playing the hokey pokey. "Uuh, I guess I did."

That was kinda dumb. And you smeared the only good footprint that was there. Hoping her face didn't give away her thoughts about his stupid actions, she asked, "Did you call Violet or Gwen?"

"I called you first." His glance darted around the room that resembled an exploded snow globe.

Delanie tapped a text to Marco about the security cameras. "Where's the cleaning crew? I thought you said they'd be in this morning. Maybe they saw something," she said to Easton.

"They'll be in later."

"Should we start cleaning this up after you call Gwen? What about Violet and Javi, too?" Delanie asked.

"I guess so. Let me go get my phone. I'll be back with the vacuum."

This room is going to need more than a vacuum.

Delanie's phone chimed with Marco's response, **Checking cameras. Gwen's on her way.**

"Hey, Delanie. Delanie!" Easton called from somewhere in the dark club.

Delanie's eyes adjusted to dim light from the exit sign above one of the doors in the hallway. She turned the corner and walked toward where she thought she had heard Easton.

She felt a rush of air, and a hand covered her mouth. Delanie tried to bite the hand as she struggled to free herself. The grasp tightened around her nose and mouth. Raising her foot, she mule-kicked the guy behind her.

"Ouch. Delanie, it's me," Easton whispered and nudged her into the nearest room. "Shh. Someone else is creeping around the club. It might be the guy." Easton shut the door except for a crack.

Delanie took a few breaths to calm down. Then she scooted closer and tried to peek out the door, too.

She thought she heard a noise, but she couldn't be sure. It could have been the hum of a freezer or the heating duct. Delanie's heartbeat raced again. She was sure it was loud enough for Chaz's cousin to hear it.

Footsteps tapped on the tile floor at a distance. The noise approached and stopped. A few more steps. Then quiet.

Delanie held her breath.

Easton leaned over and whispered in her ear. "We're sitting ducks here. I'm going in." He jerked the door open and yelled like a banshee.

"Stop! What in tarnation are you doing?" Gwen yelled. She held a Maglite flashlight like a bat.

Easton stopped suddenly in the hall with both hands in the air before she could take a swing at him with her long-handled flashlight.

Gwen slowly lowered her Maglite. "What is going on here? Why are you in the closet? I was on my way in when I got Marco's text."

"I showed Delanie what I found in the kitchen, and then I heard a noise in the club. We hid in here."

Delanie glared at him. She thought she saw a slight smile cross Gwen's face.

"You probably heard me. Too bad the cameras aren't working." Gwen stared at Delanie like she was trying to send her a secret message.

"Yep, too bad," Easton said. "Maybe if we can get them fixed, we can figure out who this clown is. Here, let me show you what he did in the kitchen. Javi's on his way, and so are the cleaners. I left Violet a voicemail. We need to get this straightened up before they need to prep."

Easton and Delanie followed Gwen to the kitchen where they found Javi and Hector with rolled up sleeves. The walk-in freezer door was the only thing not covered in flour.

"What can we help with?" Delanie asked.

Easton looked around. "I've got to go return some calls. Let me know if you need me." He zipped out before anyone could respond.

"I can help, too," Gwen said.

"Hector and I have it covered." The chef had a pained look on his face. "We'll be done in a flash. It's a couple of bags of flour."

Hector ran steaming water into a deep sink. "I checked what we prepped last night, and it's all good to go."

"We'll be a little behind schedule, but we'll make it work." Javi plugged in the vacuum Easton had left behind.

"Let us know if you need anything." Gwen motioned for Delanie to follow her to the lobby. She held the front door open, and they walked across the parking lot.

"Did you see anyone else in the club when you came in?" Delanie asked.

Gwen shook her head. "You and Easton. Steve and Marco are checking the special cameras. We'll see what they find."

"Easton traipsed through the footprints, but I got a photo of the man's shoe print before it was destroyed."

Gwen rolled her eyes. "Send me a copy, but it's probably futile now to do a shoe check." The pair walked to the edge of the lot.

Gwen stopped when her phone buzzed. She stared at the screen. "The camera only picked up Easton and you until I arrived. There's no clear shot of the kitchen, but it was only you and he walking around. No sign of any intruder. Just you two in the closet."

It was Delanie's turn to roll her eyes. "He snuck up behind me and shoved me in the closet when he said he heard a noise. Before I realized it was him, I got in a couple of good kicks." Gwen chuckled, and Delaine continued, "I heard footsteps and then you arrived. The rest of the building was quiet."

"If there was another person, he or she managed to dodge the cameras. I'll talk to Steve and Marco about the coverage. They were able to get a couple of cameras up. They're battery powered and use some special connection. We have to watch them without drawing too much attention to them. Hopefully, we'll be able to catch some action."

"I'm going to head back and see what my partner has been able to turn up. Call me if anything else weird happens," Delanie said.

"Will do. I need to be getting back, too. Let me know what you find." The taller woman jogged across the lot and disappeared in the front door.

Delanie fired up the Mustang and blasted the heat. "Call Duncan," she said.

"What's up?" Duncan sounded like he was shuffling papers.

"Hey, there. They had another incident at the Cheeky Monkey. Someone decided to cover the kitchen in flour."

"Sounds like a bunch of kids. I found some more tidbits. You coming in?"

"I'll be there in about a half hour," she said.

"Lunch at the Golden Panda? I always work better on a full stomach. Plus I skipped breakfast."

"Sure. Get a table and order spring rolls. I'll be there as soon as I can." Delanie disconnected and hightailed it to the southside of town.

Delanie found Duncan in a leatherette booth in the corner under a huge wooden carving of the Great Wall of China. A lone spring roll sat on a white square plate.

She pointed to the plate.

"Breakfast," he replied. "I was hungry. I'll get a second order when the waiter comes back."

On cue, the waiter approached the table. "What can I get you to drink?"

"I'll have a Dr. Pepper, and I think we're ready to order. I'll have the honey sesame chicken with hot and sour soup."

"And I'll have the beef and broccoli, and can I get another order of spring rolls?" Duncan asked.

The waiter nodded and zipped through the double black lacquered doors that swung back and forth long after he disappeared in the kitchen.

"What did you find?" she asked.

Duncan pulled out his phone and scrolled. "Let's see. I already told you about Gwen's commendations and security clearances. Impressive credentials. And then there's Easton. He's had a lot of jobs, and he moved around about every two years."

Delanie reached for the last spring roll. "He said he moved back here after a divorce."

"He divorced Missie Carlton Marsh back in 2005. No record of another, more recent wife." Duncan raised his eyebrows. "He did some modeling, a cable-access show, and marketing for a TV station. Then he moved to Arizona where he was car salesman. He came into some money when his dad died and bought into the dealership with a guy named Dare Davidson."

"It fits with his personality. Overly attentive, but sometimes, he has a smarminess about him like he's going to try to talk me into something." The waiter sidled up to the table and dropped off drinks and their lunches.

After chomping several bites, Duncan continued, "He left the TV station after three years. I found a site with lots of gossipy type information. He'd had an affair with one of the blond talking heads, and there were rumors that he was let go because of some accounting irregularities."

Delanie's eyebrows formed a "V." "Think there's any truth in it?"

"I'm trying to corroborate it with other sites, but so far, it's a single source of information. There was also a bad car crash that he was involved in in Arizona. He and Dare were driving in the desert, and there was an accident. The car caught fire, and Dare couldn't get out. Easton hiked miles until he got to a main road and help, but Dare didn't survive. After his partner's death, Easton sold the dealership and split the profits with Dare's kids. Then he came back to RVA and reconnected with Chaz."

"Anything on their family?" Delanie took a bite of chicken and her fried rice.

"I knew you were going to ask that. Okay, you know all about Chaz being an only child. Both his parents are dead. His mother was an only child, too, so no living relatives that I could find on that side. His dad had an older brother and a younger sister. The brother and his wife are deceased with no children. The sister has also passed, but she and her husband had Carlton, Easton, and Llewellen. Carlton lives in London with his third wife. Llewellen is divorced, has two French poodles, and lives in Honolulu."

"Not a close family."

Duncan shook his head and snuck a bite of his lunch. After a pause, he continued, "They all have money, though Easton's net worth isn't as much as his siblings or Chaz. He had a falling out years ago with his parents."

"Gwen and Marco have a few cameras up and running at the Cheeky Monkey that no one else knows about except Steve, the security guy, and us. After the kitchen disaster, Gwen checked, and Easton and I were the only two who showed up in any of the shots. Easton said he had heard a noise. I'm guessing the guy ran out after making the mess."

"You gonna eat those?" Duncan pointed to the two remaining spring rolls.

She shook her head, and he did his best boarding house reach to snag both of them. "What?" he said. "Margaret and I went for a walk this morning. She gave up halfway, and I had to carry her home. The ordeal made me miss breakfast. And I'm a growing boy."

"Help yourself. I'm stuffed. I've got a couple of errands to run and then I'm going home to update my notes. We've got to be missing something. Call me if you find anything else."

The waiter returned to refill the water glasses. "Can I get you any dessert?"

"No, thanks. Everything was good. Just the check and a box," Delanie said. He set a plastic folder on the corner of the table and cleared the plates.

Returning a few minutes later, the waiter picked up her credit card.

"I'll keep poking. There's got to be stuff in their pasts. We'll find it. And I'll see if I can find out anything on the Cheeky Monkey's weird Facebook guy, the harbinger of doom. Nothing so far," Duncan said.

When the waiter returned with her card and to-go box, she signed the receipt and pocketed the copy for her expense report. "Send my love to Margaret." She picked up her things and waved over her shoulder.

Delanie set up shop at her kitchen table about twenty minutes later. She added all the random things they'd uncovered to her timeline and fact sheet. Then she created a file with all the people involved and where they were during the events.

She stared at her files and rubbed her temples. *Nothing stands out as a clear lead that points to a suspect. Can it be more than one person? And no one but staff show up on the cameras.*

Her phone vibrated across the table and interrupted her inner dialogue with herself. "Hey, Easton. What's going on?"

"It's never a dull moment here. Stone and Diego had a fight, and now Stone has locked himself in the dressing room with all the props for tonight's show. Violet and Diego aren't having any luck talking to him, and I've lost my patience. I was wondering if maybe you could help."

She hoped he didn't hear her sigh. "I'll be there in a little bit." They'd probably have it settled before she got there.

Delanie clicked off and rummaged under the table for her shoes. She fluffed her hair and put on lip gloss.

About twenty minutes later, Delanie opened the glass door of the Cheeky Monkey and followed the sound of loud voices down the hall.

When she turned the corner, a crowd blocked the closed door to the dressing room. Delanie inched closer to see what was going on.

Diego pounded on the door with his fist. "Don't make me take this door down."

"Here, let me try again," Violet said, pushing the choreographer aside. "Stone, it's me, Violet. I know you're upset, but I need you to come out. If we don't do the show tonight, it's going to affect our bottom line, and I may have to layoff people if we have to cancel shows. You don't want that, do you? We can't shoot ourselves in the foot."

A mumbled response came from inside, but Delanie couldn't hear what he said.

"Yes, if we lose money because of cancelled shows, I am going to have to cut staff. It sounds harsh, but this is a business. You don't want to be fired, do you? Open this door. The guys need to get ready for this evening." Violet pounded on the door again.

"Go away," came from inside.

Delanie moved next to the door. "Let me try. Stone, this is Delanie.

I'm a friend of Chaz's. We really need to get in the dressing room. Time is running out, and you have a show to do."

"Diego doesn't understand me. He doesn't get that my art is my core. He's always yelling at me. Rehearsal was the last straw. He picks, picks, picks."

"I know you care very deeply about your art. We can work this out, and the show can start on time," Delanie said.

Gwen pushed her way through the gawkers. She held up the key and mouthed, "I found it." Then she said, "Stone, this is Gwen. We have a ton of reservations for tonight, and they will be so disappointed if we have to cancel. There are some birthday parties and a retirement party coming tonight. You don't want to ruin someone's celebration. You are too caring for that." She stepped closer to the door and inserted the key. The lock clicked, and she pushed gently on the door. Stone sat on the counter wearing only his boots and chaps. He ran his hand through his long locks and stood. His bare chest glistened under the fluorescent lights. It looked like he had bathed in baby oil.

"Y'all go back to work and make sure we're ready when the doors open," Violet said to the staff behind her.

"Come on, Stone," Gwen said. "You, me, and Diego will talk in my office. We can straighten this out."

Stone nodded and followed her down the hall. Violet looked like she was about to say something as Gwen stared at her. Then Violet turned and stormed off toward her own office.

"Diego, please join us," Gwen said. The three disappeared into the security office as the other dancers filed into the dressing room.

Delanie felt a hand on her shoulder. She turned and got a whiff of Easton's strong cologne.

"Well, that was easier than I thought. I guess it always helps to have a key. Thanks for coming down here. Our new normal is waiting for the next shoe to drop. Everyone's on edge, and Violet threatening to fire people didn't help deescalate any tensions. I thought he'd barricaded himself in. Nobody seemed to have the key handy."

"Sometimes the simplest approach is the best. I'll loop back with Gwen after she's done with her talk," Delanie said. She made a mental note to check with Gwen on the keys.

"Can I get you a drink? We all probably need one after this." Easton looked comfortable in a tan jacket with a white dress shirt, open at the collar and his relaxed fit jeans. Today, he sported loafers with no socks. *He must have an amazing closet.* Delanie hadn't seen any repeat outfits yet, and he always looked like he had stepped off the pages of a magazine.

Delanie followed Easton back to the bar. She claimed a stool at the corner that offered a good view of the stage.

"What'll ya have, little lady," Easton drawled.

"A sarsaparilla. But if you're all out, I'll take a glass of water."

"That I can manage. Anything in your water?"

She shook her head, and he slid a glass toward her.

"So, what do you do for fun?" he asked, leaning forward.

"I own my own business, so I work a lot. I like to read, watch old movies, and travel. What about you?"

Easton's eyes softened as he smiled. "I love all those things, too. We should get together and enjoy each other's company. I need a break from work. And there are a bunch of places I want to visit around town."

Delanie tried to dodge the offer. "That sounds like fun. We'll have to find some time." She really hoped she had plastered on a poker face. It was difficult to find ways to wheedle information without making it seem like she wanted to date him.

"What about dinner soon? I'd like to try some new place. I heard some of the rooftop bars in Scott's Addition are neat."

"They are," she replied. "The sunsets are magnificent, but we may want to wait for spring and better temperatures."

"It doesn't have to be that. We could go bowling or to the movies. How about that indoor shooting range? That would be fun."

"How about if we celebrate when we figure out who's causing all the trouble here. I'd feel better, and I'd enjoy myself more when my work was finished." Delanie paused. Trying to change the subject, she added, "Plus, I owe Chaz an update on what's been going on."

"Deal. Now get busy and go solve this case, Nancy Drew. I'd like to still see you after you solve this for dear old Chaz."

She took a sip of her drink to stall. "I'm going to go check on

Gwen. Thanks for the water."

She hurried past the kitchen. Sven and Javi waved as she rounded the corner toward Gwen's office. The door was open. *Hopefully, that's a good sign.*

Gwen glanced at her phone and set it down.

Delanie leaned on the doorjamb. "How did it go?"

"Good. We had a chat. Diego calmed down and apologized for offending Stone. And Stone promised to be more focused and pay attention during rehearsals. We'll see how that goes. But at least for now, we dismantled the bomb, and the show goes on."

"You have a calming effect on people. Good job. And no one thought to unlock the door."

Gwen smiled a weak smile. "I'll take my wins where I can get them. Lately, it's been one problem after another. I couldn't find my keys, and the office spares weren't where they were supposed to be. So, it took longer than it should have. Will you be around this evening?"

"Yep. I'm going to talk to some more folks. Something's got to break in this case soon." *If not, I'm going to have to think of something to stir things up.*

Delanie wandered by the prop room to the dressing room. C. J. and Sebastian were doing last-minute touch ups before the show. A thick cloud of hair spray and a musky cologne hung in the hair.

"Hey," Sebastian said. "You here for the backstage tour?" He grinned and whipped out his lasso.

"Just checking to see if everything's okay."

"We had a late start, but all's fine now." C. J. took a swig from a water bottle.

"Any idea who's pulling all the pranks and causing all the chaos?" she asked.

"Besides Stone?" Sebastian raised his eyebrows.

"Any hunches?" Delanie shifted the weight from one leg to another and tried not to fidget.

"Somebody's trying to sabotage the show." Sebastian picked up his hat and gun belt. "I don't think it's any of the performers. I can't speak for the other guys, but I like the tips and the hours. It's a good gig. I wouldn't do anything to rock the boat."

"Yep. Many months, I make more here than I do at my day job," C. J. added.

"Which is?" She probed.

"I'm a personal trainer," C. J. said.

"And a cowboy by night. What about you? Do you have another gig?" Delanie asked Sebastian.

"I teach eighth grade algebra," Sebastian added.

Delanie tried to suppress a smile. She would have paid more attention in math class if her teachers had looked like him.

"So, no theories on who the culprit is?" she asked.

"Theories on what?" Diego stepped out of the back room.

"On who would want to damage the club."

Sebastian moved toward the door. "Nope. Stuff happens, and nobody seems to see anything or be around to catch him."

"Or her," Diego added. "Don't rule out the ladies. I have no hypothesis either, but I wish it would stop. We have enough on our plates with keeping the show fresh each night without having to clean up a bunch of messes. Ready guys?"

The other two nodded and followed Diego backstage.

As Delanie turned, she heard rustling in the back room. Stone stepped out and dropped a towel on the counter.

"Did they leave?" he asked in low tone.

Delanie nodded. "They went backstage."

"I heard what you asked them. I think you need to look at Diego and Violet. They're thick as thieves, and nothing goes on here without them approving it. They're both micromanagers." Stone picked up his gear and hurried out the door. "I better get a move on."

Diego and Violet. Why would either one want to damage the club?

Delanie wandered around behind the scenes and found a spot to the left of the stage. She leaned against the wall near a fire exit to watch part of the show. The routines and songs were the same, and like the drag show that she investigated last fall, there were lots of opportunities for the entertainers to interact with the guests. Delanie stayed longer than she had planned.

She stifled a yawn and glanced at her watch. Ten-thirty. Time to head out. Enough excitement for one evening.

Chapter Ten

"I should buy a lottery ticket," Delanie mumbled as she pulled into what looked like the only empty spot on Cary Street during the lunch hour. Spotting an opportunity to jump out of her car when there was a break in traffic, she jogged around the Mustang and strolled down the sidewalk, window shopping at the eclectic stores. Her favorites were the novelty toy store and the vintage clothing shop on the corner.

Checking her fitness band, she pulled open the door of the Jumping Bean Cantina. Smells of sizzling fajitas tickled her nose and made her stomach growl as she approached the hostess station.

"Hi, I'm meeting a friend for lunch," Delanie said to the gal in the aqua and orange dress. "He's a tall guy with sandy blond hair, and a tattoo right here." Delanie pointed to the corner of her eye.

"I don't think he's here, but do you want to take a peek in the dining room? If he's not here, we can find you a table and get you a drink while you wait."

"Sounds good." Delanie scanned the room crowded with folks enjoying their lunches. "I don't see him."

"Follow me." The hostess stopped in front of a table near the bar. "What can I get you to drink?" She set two menus in front of Delanie.

"I'll have unsweetened iced tea. Thank you." Delanie had time to check her email and return several texts before Chaz dropped into the chair across from her.

"Sorry, to keep you waiting. I got stuck in traffic."

The waiter set Delanie's drink and a basket of chips and salsa on the table. "What can I get you, sir?"

"Uh, do you have any of the local craft beers?" Chaz asked.

"We have Ardent and Hardywood," the waiter replied.

"Bring me your most popular Hardywood, but nothing too frou-frou. I want the shrimp fajitas."

"Ma'am?" The waiter looked at Delanie.

"I'll have the shrimp tacos no tomatoes."

"Very good. Be back shortly." He picked up the two menus.

"It's good to see you." Chaz leaned forward. "Gwen and Easton have nothing but good things to say about you. Easton, especially. I hope I'm not dropping any bombshells, but he seems to be smitten with you."

"That's flattering. Tell me more about your cousin."

"You interested?" Chaz snickered and continued, "I dunno all that much. I was older. I saw him at some family gatherings once in a while. He followed me around when he was a little kid. Then I went off to college, and I didn't see him anymore. My dad's family wasn't really that close. I got a call from Easton out of the blue last summer. He said he was divorced and out of a job, and he was heading back east. When he got into town, we had dinner. It was when I was getting ready to open the Cheeky Monkey. He had skills, so I said I would give him a try. We'll see how he does." Chaz reached in the chip basket and snagged a handful. He licked his fingers as he ate.

Delanie tried not cringe and pushed the chip basket toward him. "What kinds of skills?"

"He's got a degree and a background in marketing. And he's family. He does a good job of chatting up the clientele. He's not much of a manager. He's been here for three months, and he hasn't shown me the least bit of initiative. I want him to step up as a leader. I think he likes to stick with marketing." Chaz shrugged. "Violet can keep the trains running on time. She's just, uh...a little prickly. I'm watching how they work with the staff and clientele. She's not too thrilled with me for hiring him."

Was that enough of a motive for Violet to cause problems at the club?

Delanie wasn't sure whether he knew about the new cameras, so she didn't mention them. She stifled her question about Marco and Steve. Before she could continue, the waiter appeared with Chaz's sizzling platter of fajitas and Delanie's tacos. "Be careful. The plates are hot. Let me know if I can get you anything else."

"More chips and salsa. And another beer," Chaz said, reaching for the hot sauce.

Delanie shook her head, and the waiter moved on to check on another table.

"I do remember one thing from when we were kids at my grandparents' lake house. I took the boat out after my grandfather specifically said not to. I got back late and missed dinner, and I found out Easton had covered for me. It really surprised me that a kid of nine or ten would go to all that trouble to cover for an older cousin who was clearly in trouble. He was always kinda shy as a kid."

"He said he idolized you." Delanie took a bite of her shrimp taco.

"I guess. Like I said, we're not that close. That's the one memory I have of him. A quiet kid who flew under the radar."

"Somehow he blossomed over the years. He doesn't seem to shy away from the limelight these days," Delanie said.

"He said he went to Los Angeles to be an actor after he didn't have much success in New York. I think he did a handful of local TV commercials." Chaz reached for the beer and chips the waiter dropped off.

"He definitely gets as much attention as your dancers do." Delanie wiped her hands on her napkin and pushed her plate forward.

"If you're interested, I can put in a good word for you." Chaz winked and stuffed another forkful in his mouth.

Delanie pasted on her sweetest smile. "Right now, I'm seeing someone. And I have my hands full with work."

"Seeing someone, huh? He better treat you right. If not, you let me and Marco know."

She smiled again. "Eric's a good guy. Anybody at the Cheeky Monkey who gives you pause?"

"Hmmm. Not really. The dancers and waitstaff come and go, but that's standard in this industry. Violet is an awesome logistics person, but." He dragged out the last word, and Delanie leaned closer. "She's not a people person. She butts heads with everybody. Gwen's good though. I trust her. Diego's a dance guy. He keeps the entertainers organized and on point. Uh, no. Nobody jumps out as suspicious. I don't have any concrete reasons not to trust them. What are your thoughts?"

"Whoever is doing this is slippery. Nobody has caught him in action. I do think it's someone affiliated with the club, someone with access and who knows what's going on. I thought it might be a disgruntled employee, but Duncan and I haven't had much luck with that list. They all have alibis. We're focusing on the current staff now, and I carry a hidden camera every time I'm in the club, but it hasn't done much good to date."

"You're doing fine. I know you'll figure this out. I did have my accountant start looking at the books closely. He noticed a few little charges we can't account for, but nothing serious. It may not be anything, but we're keeping an eye on them."

"Good. I still think the prank stuff is a distraction for something else. I also think that all that's happened may not be related, or at least planned. The perpetrator may be taking advantage of opportunities at random times."

"Like what?" Chaz asked, reaching for a handful of chips.

"First, I think the creepy doll is someone else. So that's off the table. As is the other day when Stone locked himself in the dressing room. These don't seem like they're on the same level as the cameras winking out, the guy who snuck up on me in the parking lot, the unplugged freezer, the cherry bomb in the bathroom, and the messed up kitchen. That's what Duncan and I are focusing on."

Chaz raised one eyebrow. "Makes sense. I'm tired of all the dirty tricks" He let out a heavy sign and signaled the waiter. "I appreciate the info. Hey, you want dessert?" Chaz asked.

Delanie shook her head as the waiter approached the table. "I didn't finish my tacos."

"You all doing okay here?" The waiter asked, picking up the used plates and silverware.

"Nah. Just the check," Chaz said, reaching for the chip basket again.

"I'll send you an update later this week with anything else we uncover," Delanie said.

"I have faith in you and your partner. I'm not worried about it. You'll solve it for me." Chaz handed the waiter a credit card when he approached with the check.

"Thank you for lunch. It was good to see you," Delanie said.

"Good to see you too. Steve, Marco, and the guys said to tell you hey. And if you change your mind about Easton, let me know." Chaz winked as Delanie rose.

Outside, the temperature had dropped, and it felt like snow. Delanie didn't dawdle this time on her way back to the Mustang.

The sleet started when Delanie exited onto the Powhite Parkway. Nixing the plan to work at the office, she made an emergency stop at the grocery store for necessities like wine and chocolate cupcakes in case the ice and snow got worse as the day progressed.

After lugging in several bags with lots of snacks, Delanie made a work area out of her kitchen table and found a rock station to stream for company.

Pulling out her notes, she scanned the pages and stared at the stack of papers. Nothing new popped out at her, so she drew another timeline and listed everyone who was around for the pranks. It took hours to pull work schedules. She taped five sheets of paper together and color coded the players with their involvement. Violet, Hector, Diego, Gwen, Stone, and Easton were present at a majority of the events. A good list to focus on, but this person was cagey or lucky that no one had caught him on video so far.

Her stomach growled, and she looked at the clock. Seven-thirty. She stretched and packed up her notes.

Not finding anything she wanted for dinner, she microwaved a bag of popcorn and decided to catch up on her binge-watching of a Harlan Coben TV series.

A tick, tick, tick distracted her. She sprang up and peered out at the darkness from the front window. Ice pellets hit the glass and side of the house. She flipped on the porch light and opened the front door. A sheet of glistening ice covered her steps and walkway. A few houses on the streets had soft lights glowing from their family rooms. Delanie soaked in the peaceful moment before returning to the murders on TV.

Chapter Eleven

Delanie woke to bright sunlight streaming in her bedroom window. She pulled the curtains back. Slick puddles covered the sidewalk and the street. The ice had already started to melt. Reaching for her phone, she glanced at the weather app. Today's temperatures would hit almost fifty. Welcome to the south, where the weather could change hourly.

After a quick breakfast and another look at her Cheeky Monkey timeline, Delanie headed to the office. Her phone rang, and she clicked the button on her steering wheel. "Hi, Easton. What's up this morning?"

"Hey. We got another weird Facebook post, and when I pulled in the parking lot this morning, there was a crowd outside protesting."

"Protesting what?"

"I'm not sure. I'm going to go out in a few minutes and talk to them. Can you come over?"

"Be there as soon as I can." Delanie switched lanes on Hull Street for the exit to Route 288. She let out a heavy sigh when she disconnected and made a quick detour through the coffee shop's drive-thru for another wave of caffeine to fortify her against whatever was waiting in the club's parking lot. *I hope he called Violet and Gwen. I seem to be his go-to girl.*

When Delanie approached the front of the Cheeky Monkey, it was packed with minivans and pickup trucks. She found a parking spot on the outer edges. Not seeing anyone from Chaz's staff, she sent a flurry of texts to Duncan and Gwen.

She clicked on the hidden camera in her purse, locked the Mustang, and jogged across the parking lot. About forty men and women, mostly over thirty held signs and shouted. The signs referenced human trafficking, kidnapping, and the exploitation of women.

Delanie made her way through the crowds that had surrounded the front door. A chubby woman with a megaphone climbed in the bed of a nearby truck and started yelling chants to the group. The noise level gave Delanie a headache as she roamed through the crowd.

Easton was nowhere to be seen. she dashed off a text, **Where are you?**

Not waiting for his response, she moved to the edge of the gathering for a better viewing spot. When she typed "Cheeky Monkey protest" into Google, she found a link to an open invitation for those who were against human trafficking to make themselves heard. She texted the link to Duncan. **Can you trace this?**

She panned the crowd and the parking lot with her hidden camera to capture as many faces and license plates as she could.

The noise dropped to a dull roar as two other women climbed in the back of the truck. The taller of the two took the megaphone from the original chant leader. She waved her arms around and yelled at the crowd about the cause and the need for stopping human trafficking at establishments like this. The crowd was working itself into a frenzy.

At about the time Delanie wondered whether to call the police, she spotted Gwen near the edge of the building. She made a beeline for the club's head of security.

"Hey, it seems to be getting bigger and louder," Delanie said when she was close enough for Gwen to hear her. "Do you think we need to call Chaz or the police?"

The Channel 12 van pulled into the lot, and the chanting increased in ferocity and volume.

"It's private property," Gwen said. "We can make them leave. I was waiting to see what Easton wanted to do. When I talked to him earlier, he said to wait until he tried something, and then he disappeared somewhere over there." Gwen pointed toward the pickup that served as a makeshift stage.

The svelte Noreen Nurelli from Channel 12 and her cameraman set up a live shot with the Cheeky Monkey sign and the crowd in the background. The protestors yelled louder for the camera.

The noise changed to a string of boos. Delanie and Gwen craned their necks for a better view of the cause. Easton, in a tailored suit and dress shoes, jumped in the back of the truck with the three women. He talked to the tall woman who waved her arms around. He waved his arms around, too. Gwen edged closer to the truck, and Delanie followed.

Then the tall woman in the truck handed Easton the megaphone. More booing. The woman took it back and yelled, "Give him a chance. He wants to say something."

The booing stopped, and the crowd noise became a dull roar. "Hi, everyone. I'm Easton Marsh. And I could come out here and yell about you all trespassing on private property and call the cops." Loud boos echoed through the crowd. When they subsided, Easton continued, "But I'm not. I know you are caring people and you're trying to make a difference. Human trafficking and exploitation need to be rooted out wherever they are. But it's not here though. I'm not sure how this rally got started, but our clubs do not employ anyone ineligible to work and no illegal activities go on here. We have a strict code of conduct for our employees. This club has a male revue. All are paid well and respected. This club is not a cover for any illicit activity. It's a place where guests come to enjoy bachelorette and birthday parties. There is no exploitation of anyone here."

A rumble rolled through the crowd as Noreen and her cameraman approached. Easton ignored the noises and cat calls from the protestors.

"So, I'm going to ask that you continue your peaceful protest but know that the Cheeky Monkey should not be the target. No human trafficking goes on here. I invite you to come back any evening and check out the show." Easton handed the megaphone back to the woman and descended to the parking lot.

Noreen zeroed in on him for an interview. Easton waved over the women from the truck to talk to the reporter as the crowds started to dissipate. Delanie videoed more license plates.

Then as quickly as it started, the protest was over as the minivans and pickups left.

Gwen and Delanie joined Easton in the grassy area next to Noreen and her cameraman.

"So how do you think it all started?" Noreen asked, with her heavy northern accent. "You'd think they'd be downtown protesting the Treasure Chest and not this place."

"I came in to do some work this morning, and I heard the shouting outside. I'm not sure who organized it, but the turn out was from groups in the area who answered the call on social media," Easton said. "It spread like wildfire."

"I'm going to run this on the noon broadcast, and then there will be another segment this evening. I want to highlight the cause, but also that not everything you see is what you think it is on social media. And what you read may not always be accurate. Thanks so much, Easton, for the interview." She patted him on the shoulder and then followed her cameraman to the truck.

"You diffused that well," Delanie said.

"I've got a degree in marketing and a minor in psychology. I call on them both frequently in this job." Easton smiled. "Anybody want a drink? I need one." Gwen and Delanie followed him inside and shed coats and gloves.

"What'll ya have?" Easton stepped behind the bar and pulled out a metal shaker.

"Coffee, black," Gwen said.

"I'll have coffee, too," Delanie added.

The espresso machine chugged and spewed out steam. Easton prepared three clear cups.

"Well, I didn't expect to start my day this way," Gwen said, sinking into a chair at a nearby table.

Before anyone could respond a crash and glass breaking came from the lobby area.

Gwen rushed out with Delanie on her heels. Gwen tore out the door like a shot and across the parking lot after a guy in an olive-green ski jacket and hat. The pudgy guy didn't stand a chance. He tripped over one of the parking space stops, and Gwen leapt on his back as he face-planted on the asphalt in a puddle of icy water. "Call the police," Gwen yelled.

"Got it," Easton responded.

The guy on the pavement wiggled and tried to shake Gwen off him. Delanie rushed over. He reared up and flipped over. The tussle was on. He tried to bite Gwen. She grabbed his arm and bent it backward, and Delanie kneeled on his legs.

"Ow," he whined. "You're hurting me."

Gwen put one of her boots in the middle of his stomach. "Stop fighting me. I know you did it. Calm down, and the police will get this all sorted out."

"I don't know what you're talking about," he whined.

The man relaxed for a second, and Gwen pulled him to his feet. "Get up." She turned him around and marched him to the club while holding his arm at an uncomfortable angle behind his back. Delanie followed in case he tried to escape.

"Sit down," Gwen ordered when they got to the curb. "Why'd you break the window after the protest was over. Didn't you hear our guy say that you all had the wrong location?"

"I have nothing to say," the man growled. He glared at the women and Easton, who stood near the broken window taking pictures.

The man fidgeted until a Goochland Sheriff department's cruiser pulled into the lot. A few minutes later, an officer approached. "I'm Deputy Hudson. What's going on here?"

"I'm Gwen Richards. I'm in charge of security. This is Easton Marsh and Delanie Fitzgerald." She pointed toward the club. "We had a peaceful protest here this morning until this guy decided to break the front window."

"What do you have to say?" Deputy Hudson asked.

"Nothing. They're corrupt, and they traffic humans here. And they exploit women! We have to let the world know by any means possible."

"Didn't you hear me at the protest. I explained to the crowd that the cause is valid, but they were mistaken about this club. This is a male revue. The only women here are Gwen and our office manager," Easton said.

The deputy almost cracked a smile. "Did you break the window?"

The man nodded. "In peaceful protest."

"How is that peaceful?" Deputy Hudson asked. "You destroyed property. And now this man has to replace the window and clean up his business. Stand up. You're under arrest."

The deputy cuffed the man and continued to talk to him before he put them in the back seat of his cruiser. After locking the door, he returned and handed Easton his card. "I'm taking him to our holding cells."

Easton shook his hand and handed him his business card. "I've got to get this cleaned up and fixed before we open tonight."

"I'll send you a copy of the report when it's filed." Deputy Hudson returned to his car.

Delanie fidgeted on the sidelines. She managed to snap a photo of the guy before the deputy took him away. She'd get the name off of the report later. Could he be responsible for all the things going on around here? *Her gut told her that it was an inside job.* It seemed like this guy just appeared out of the blue with the protesters.

When the deputy's cruiser made a slow loop in the parking lot and headed for the main road, Easton said, "I need to call Violet, and get her on these repairs." He tapped into his phone and paused.

"I've got some things I need to take care of, too." Gwen disappeared inside.

Delanie waved over her shoulder to Easton who talked in low tones on his phone. Climbing into her car, she clicked the button to call Duncan. "Whatcha doing today?"

"I was looking into the protest post you sent. Found some stuff," he said.

"I missed breakfast," she said. "How about if I meet you at the office, and I'll bring lunch."

"Sounds good. Don't forget Margaret the Wonder Dog."

"Gotcha" Delanie disconnected. Before pulling out, she texted Gwen and Easton, **Please send me a copy of today's police report when you get it**.

After swinging through Taco Bell's drive-thru, Delanie parked in front of the office and gathered her things. She picked up a shadow as she walked to her office. Margaret followed Delanie and the spicy-smelling paper bags down the hall.

"Find anything good?" Delanie asked, sinking into one of the conference room chairs.

"Tacos. Our favorite. Right, Margaret?" The bulldog woofed on cue. "I did some digging. A Doug Carlson made the post that caused the protest. He fancies himself an activist. He has a blog and lots of pictures of rallies all over the country. He doesn't seem to be affiliated with any one cause or organization. His human trafficking posts are often conspiracy-theory related. Just like the one he did for the Cheeky Monkey."

"I'm guessing the content doesn't have to be true or vetted by the way he's able to draw crowds with his posts." Delanie unwrapped a taco and added mild sauce. "He attracted about fifty people to Chaz's place."

"Some are activists and regular protestors. Others are folks who found it online and joined in. My next task is to go through our video and trace as many license plates as possible," Duncan said.

"Do you know anything else about Doug Carlson?"

"Let's see. He works at a restaurant in Scott's Addition when he's not protesting." He jotted the name on a sticky note and handed it to her.

She looked at the name of the restaurant, Thai One On, and laughed. "I'm going to pay him a visit later. Do you want me to go through the video feed and write down license plates?"

"That'll help. I'll see if I can find anything else on Mr. Carlson." Duncan stuffed the rest of his second soft taco in his mouth while Margaret waited patiently for her cut.

They worked in silence for about an hour. The only sounds were typing, and Margaret trying to get every last speck off her taco wrapper.

Delanie needed a stretch. "There. I emailed you the list of all the license plates I spotted. Hopefully, this will help. I'm going to see if Mr. Carlson is working today." She fished through her purse for her burner phone and tapped in the number.

"Thai One On. How can I help you?"

"Hi. This is Jen. Is Doug Carlson working today?" Delanie asked.

After some shuffling, he replied. "Yup. He's in the back. Want me to go get him?"

"Nah," she said in her best southern drawl. "I'll stop in and surprise him." She disconnected the call and then gathered the trash on the table. "I'm headed out soon. Let me know if you need anything."

"Thanks for lunch. I'll send you what I find on these plates and your friend Doug Carlson. It may be tomorrow. Tonight is date night."

"Enjoy. I'll let you know what Doug's like." *Date night would be fun. I have to find out when Eric will be back in town.*

Delanie zipped onto the Powhite Parkway and headed for the downtown expressway. She navigated through the narrow streets in Scott's Addition, formerly an industrial area revitalized with a resurgence of wine bars, craft breweries, and cool eateries.

She found street parking about a block away from the restaurant that boasted Asian fusion cuisine. When she pushed open the door, Delanie turned on her hidden purse camera.

It took a few minutes for her eyes to adjust to the interior of the restaurant. The walls and bar were a smoky gray, and all of the flat surfaces were shiny metal. Metal mobiles dangled from the ceiling.

"What can I get you," the short guy at the bar asked. "Late lunch?"

"A ginger ale, please." Delanie sat on a barstool in the corner. She could see the kitchen and the front door from her perch. "I'm new around here. What's interesting to do in town?"

"Me." He laughed, setting her drink in front of her. He coughed when she didn't react. "Richmond's a cool town. Whatcha into?"

"I'm Liz. I like hiking and kayaking, and cooking. And I love hanging out with friends."

"Hi, Liz. I'm Doug, and you're in the right place. This area has lots of cool places, and we've got one of the best Asian fusion menus in the city."

Delanie looked around. "It's a nice place. How long have you worked here?"

"About three months. I do the day shift here. You look familiar." He stared at her and squinted.

"Nope. I'm new here. So, what do you do for fun?" She batted her eyes and pasted on her best flirty smile.

"You sure I haven't seen you in the West End?" She shook her head, and he continued, "I do a lot of social media promotions and attend a lot of rallies and events. Most of it for community activism. It's my calling."

"For a specific cause?"

"Social injustices. You know, looking out for the underdog. Truth, justice, that kind of stuff."

"So not for any particular organization?" Delanie asked.

"Nah. It's a lot of free form these days. We find out about events and protests, and we join forces. It's pretty cool."

"It sounds really remarkable." Delanie leaned forward. "How do you know they are, uh, legit. I mean not everything is what it seems." Her voice trailed off.

"It's on the Internet." He laughed. "We're here to help each other. When we find an issue, we share the information."

"That is fascinating." Delanie nodded her head and leaned forward. "Have you been to any around here lately that I would have heard of?"

Doug puffed up his chest and stood taller behind the bar. "In fact, I was at one this morning before work."

"Really? How did you find out about it? I mean, was it planned a while back?" Delanie leaned closer.

"Nah. I saw a post for it last night. I blasted it out and emailed my peeps and voila. We had a good crowd today. Easy peasy."

"How much notice do you get on these? Or are they things you have to drop everything and go?"

He wiped the counter. "It depends. Most are planned in advance and publicized. This was an emergency. There was some human trafficking going on at a business. And we had to round up people pretty quickly. And if I do say so myself, I have quite a following. We have dedicated folks around here."

Delanie nodded. "So, you're an influencer? Where do you get your information from?"

"Lots of sources. We have a network on Facebook and Twitter. I'm plugged into some special chatrooms." He used air quotes to highlight "special."

"How did you find out about the protests here in Virginia?"

"The deep web. It came from a guy names Jeeves," he whispered. "Our network is vast. The internet is a beautiful thing." He grinned and stood up straighter.

"What happens if you go to the wrong site or if what you're protesting isn't true?" Delanie asked.

He paused and stared at her. "That doesn't happen."

She hesitated. "Never, ever?"

"Never. There is so much out there that needs to be righted."

Opting to not burn any bridges, she nodded again and took another sip of her drink. "How much do I owe you?"

"The first one's on the house. My treat. Come back for lunch and dinner. You know where to find me if you want to get active in the protest community. They're some great people. You'll love it."

"Will do. I appreciate it." She drained the rest of her drink and slid off the stool. "See you around." She waved over her shoulder and headed for her car. *Wonder if Duncan can find this Jeeves?*

Chapter Twelve

The next day, Delanie's phone rang as she changed lanes on Hull Street Road near a sushi restaurant in front of a strip mall. "What's up, partner?"

"I took most of the night, but I found out who your Jeeves is."

"The Butler?"

"Yep. I'm at Gotham Pizza. Wanna meet me here?" Duncan asked.

"See you in about twenty minutes." She disconnected, and the phone rang again. "Falcon Investigations."

"Hey, lady. This is Kathy Meyers at Lion Insurance. How are you?"

"It's good to hear from you. What can I do for you?"

"I have another workman's comp case if you're interested. This one is out on a long-term medical disability from a big box retailer. We have reason to believe he's not as injured as he claims to be. I'd like for you to see what you can find out. He's getting close to retirement age, and they suspect that he's trying to stay out on leave as long as possible."

"Be glad to. Thanks for calling us."

"I'll send over the file and all his contact information," Kathy said.

"Duncan and I will get right on it and have a report to you in a few days."

"Sounds great. You're the best." The insurance adjuster clicked off.

Delanie pointed the car toward the restaurant. *It's nice to have more than one client at a time.*

A few minutes later, she parked in front of the pizza parlor and its bright red and white awning. Inside, Duncan scrolled through screens on his phone and nibbled on pepperoni pizza. She ordered an iced tea and joined him in a vinyl booth near the window. "So, what's this about the butler? Are we playing Clue?"

He cracked a smile. "It's Jeeves Butler. Pretty sure that's not his real name, but it is kinda funny. I did some crowdsourcing of this last night with a few of my buddies who were up for a challenge. I put a fifty-dollar Starbucks card up for whoever could help me find this guy. I had ten guys jump in for the challenge, and all they wanted was bragging rights. So, I wasn't out the gift card, and they dug around in the dark corners for hours."

"Pretty clever, so what did you uncover?"

"His real name is Phillip Butler. He lives in Washington, D. C., and he's a software developer at the Department of Agriculture. He runs about twenty Facebook sites for a variety of causes and claims to be a clearing house for protests and marches. Some of his pages specialize in conspiracy theories. Someone going by the screenname of Darrel Lick posted about the Cheeky Monkey." Duncan laughed. "Ha! Derelict. Good pun. But his posts are way more serious. He's asserting that the Cheeky Monkey is a front for all kinds of human exploitation. Still trying to chase down the mysterious Darrel Lick. There was a lot of chatter on the site ahead of the protest you attended." He took a bite of his pizza and twirled the stringy mozzarella around his finger.

She took a sip of her tea. "It shows how quickly misinformation can spread these days. A bunch of people showed up in the parking lot of Chaz's club. It's pretty amazing that they can rally folks that quickly. Anything else?"

"Butler makes his money to fund these sites and his activities by selling data on the dark web. I found a site where he's offering account information." Duncan shook his head.

Delanie felt a wry smile cross her face. "People who think they're doing something good are getting taken advantage of. I don't think

Phillip is who we're looking for though. I'm more interested in Darrel Lick. Can you keep digging?"

"I'm on it. Everybody leaves an electronic trail. I'm gonna start a new quest for the guys on this Darrel Lick." Duncan tapped on this phone. "Let's see how quickly they can work their magic. What did you find on the guy at Thai One On?" Duncan chuckled.

"Doug, the local guy, thinks highly of himself. He's proud of his social media contacts and how he's tapped into a network of socially conscious folks. He's chatty. I'm guessing that he saw Darrel Lick's post and spread it around to his connections." Delanie took another sip of her drink.

"So, if we trace this like a virus spread, Darrel Lick is patient zero. He posted it first. A bunch of other people shared it, including Doug. And since most normal people aren't poking around the dark web, it's pretty likely that the people who showed up at the Cheeky Monkey saw it on Doug's site or through someone who shared it from there. I'm hoping I can find out more about this Darrel Lick and why he's so interested in a club in Goochland, Virginia." Duncan popped the last bite of pizza in his mouth. "What's next?" he asked as he slurped what was left in his cup.

"I got a call from my contact at Lion Insurance this morning. She has a workman's comp case for us. I'm going to try to find him this afternoon and then head over to the Cheeky Monkey."

"Let me know if you need anything. I've got a website to finish for a piano teacher, and I'm going to keep poking to see what we uncover on the mysterious Darrel Lick. And who knows. If by chance the Jeeves sites go down suddenly, I have no knowledge of why that would happen." Duncan winked at her.

Delanie gathered their trash. "Hmmmm. Interesting. I'm curious to see what the connection is with Chaz's place. This could be the break we've been waiting for. You're always able to get to places on the internet that mere mortals don't have access to. I'm glad you're on my side."

Duncan pocketed his phone and rose. "See ya. I'm off to check on Miss Margaret."

Delanie retreated to her Mustang and turned on the heated seats.

She scrolled through the files and pictures that Kathy Meyers sent. Peter Sanders, her mark this time, was a sixty-something warehouse supervisor, who injured his back and had been out of work for the last six weeks. She typed his address in the GPS and followed Route 288 toward the courthouse area of Chesterfield County. The bossy lady on the GPS guided her into a subdivision of cottages that according to the sign was designed for "adults fifty-five or better."

She cruised through the little village of colorful homes with lots of gingerbread work, wide sidewalks, and amenities everywhere. She parked next to the mailbox with a house number that matched her file. The mailboxes looked like replicas of the houses. Pocketing her phone, she rummaged through her spy bag in the trunk. Pulling out a clipboard and a lanyard, she moseyed down the driveway. Her knocks and the doorbell didn't get a response.

"Hey, you looking for Pete?" A round man in a ski jacket wandered through the shared side yard.

"Hi, I'm Emma, and I was checking on an order he placed last week. I wanted to make sure everything was okay with the delivery and service."

"Wow. That's good service. I rarely get any kind of follow up except those dumb surveys. I can't believe they sent someone out. Cool. I'm Mac Branch, Pete's neighbor. He plays pickleball most mornings up at the big park across from the airport on Iron Bridge Road. He won't be back for hours. I'm not sure where his wife is. I haven't seen her today."

"Thanks for the information. I'll try to get in touch with him later this afternoon. Lovely neighborhood."

"Yup. My wife fell in love with it because it looks like the villages in those British TV shows she watches all the time. I like it cause it's quiet," Mac said.

Delanie waved and jogged back to her car.

A few minutes, later, she drove into the park and followed the wooden signs to the tennis and pickleball area. A crowd of players surrounded the court, awaiting the next game on this crisp winter day. Delanie turned on her hidden purse camera and checked her phone for Peter Sanders's photo.

It didn't take long to find a match to the photograph. The meatball of a man huffed and puffed on the far court as he chased the whiffle ball around. Delanie adjusted her purse to make sure she captured Pete in action. He made wide, exaggerated serves and swung his paddle the length of his arm span on almost every shot. *What form. Pete is more drama than skill. But he moves swiftly for someone who's on medical leave.*

She walked around the court to his side and stood behind the fence to get a better view.

When the game ended and the players decided to break for lunch, she shut off her camera and wandered back to her car. Time to work on her report. Workman's comp cases usually didn't require much sleuthing.

🐾

DELANIE FOUND parking near her office door. Inside the lobby, Margaret barreled through the dark, open space and greeted her with woofs and slobbery kisses.

She petted the bulldog's boxy head. "Where's Duncan?" Margaret turned her head and loped down the hallway. "Hey, Dunc. I didn't know you were still here."

"Got stumped with the dark web postings. I decided to come in here and map stuff out. I needed the whiteboard. Maybe it'll help if we talk through it." Duncan stared at his drawing on the conference room board.

"What have you got here?" Delanie set her purse and messenger bag on the table and stared at the board. His sketch looked like a wheel with hundreds of spokes.

"Okay, Phillip 'Jeeves' Butler is the owner of lots of sites for protestors. Some guy name Darrel Lick posted about the Cheeky Monkey and probably caused the protest. Then there's the local guy Doug who posted it on his site and ginned up interest in the cause. But wait, there's more. There are hundreds of comments on the Facebook posts. So far, I have the list of license plates that you videoed. I'm not having much luck matching them to the comments. Most of the people are using nicknames or screen handles."

"It's like a spider web that keeps growing." Delanie stood behind Duncan, starting at the board. "I think we should focus on Darrel Lick. He seems to be the central figure in Richmond for the post we're concerned about. Any way to trace him?"

"No luck so far, but my team is on it. If he's out there, we'll find out who he is," Duncan said.

"He might be the one who'll lead us to who's causing all the problems at the club. If he's not the one, at least we can find out who contacted him. It's one step closer. And it's progress. It feels better than all the other dead ends. Talk about frustrating."

"I know, but it's part of the process. You're not confirming who did it, but you're eliminating or clearing a lot of suspects."

Delanie raised both eyebrows. "That's not what Chaz wants to hear. He wants to figure out who's messing with his business. Speaking of that, I wanted to see if Marco had any luck with the new cameras." She pulled out her phone and tapped his contact, hoping it wasn't too early in the day for the Security Director.

"Hey, Marco. Can you talk?"

"I'm in the car heading to the Treasure Chest. What's up?"

"I wanted to see if you and Steve found anything on the new cameras related to the kitchen vandalism or the intruder Easton thought he heard?"

"There's no camera near the kitchen yet. The only person walking around that morning was Easton. Steve saw him walking up and down the hallway to the dining room. Then you arrived. We caught the two of you on camera and later Gwen. So, no. Nobody unusual except who we expected to see."

"Thanks. I was hoping you caught a glimpse of our mysterious phantom."

Marco laughed. "Isn't it vampires who don't show up on film?"

"Maybe. Or maybe it's in mirrors. Anyway, I hope we're not getting into the woo woo stuff. Duncan's digging in dark places on the web to help us narrow down who some of those protesters were. I hope to have an update for you all soon."

"Sounds good. See ya." Marco disconnected.

"So, nothing on camera?" Duncan asked.

Delanie shook her head and made a wry face. "Speaking of cameras. I need to download my footage of the not-so-injured pickleball player for his workman's comp case. It was a nice break from the Cheeky Monkey stuff. At least in that one, I knew who the culprit was." She pulled out her laptop and started her report for the insurance company. Duncan wandered back to his seat.

Steady keyboard tapping and Margaret's soft snores from underneath the table filled the conference room as the pair worked. Could an anonymous person on the internet be a linchpin in all of this?

Chapter Thirteen

A buzzing that wouldn't quit woke Delanie. *Two in the morning. Phone calls at this hour are never good.*

"What's up, Duncan?"

"Sorry to wake you. My guys found something, and I had to let you know. You sound funny."

"It's after two." She sat up and turned on the light next to her bed.

"Uh, sorry. But this is too good to wait for daylight. We had a hit on Darrel Lick. One of my guys did some amazing work. His real name is Darrel Davidson."

"Okay." Delanie rubbed her eyes. "It may be because it's really early, but I'm not making the exciting connection."

She could almost see the overly caffeinated Duncan rolling his eyes.

"Darrel Davidson is the guy behind the Darrel Lick posts," Duncan said.

Okay, but can't that wait until the sun comes up?

"Let me break it down for you. Chaz's cousin Easton had a partner when he owned an auto dealership in Mesa, Arizona. He went by Dare, but his real name was Darrel Davidson."

"Okay. I'm sorry. I still need caffeine." Delanie sat up and rubbed both of her eyes with the heels of her hands.

"Darrel Davidson was the guy who was killed in the bad car accident that Easton walked away from."

A bolt of realization shot through Delanie. "When was…"

"Exactly. Either he didn't die like your Johnny Velvet or someone's using his name. Or there's two of them, but I don't think so. And I already checked. He didn't have a kid who is a junior."

Delanie's thoughts flashed back to John Bailey, living incognito in Amelia County, who was rumored to be Johnny Velvet in the eighties. Falcon Investigations' research helped solve the mystery. *Can this Darrel guy be alive? And if so, what's his connection to the Cheeky Monkey?*

"You still there," he asked.

"Sorry. I was trying to figure out what a dead guy has to do with Chaz and the Cheeky Monkey."

"My friends and I are redoubling our efforts today to see if this is the same guy. Or just someone with a warped sense of humor. Hopefully, I'll know more later, but I wanted to give you an update."

"Thanks." Delanie disconnected and rolled back over, but her dreams of blissful sleep were marred by thoughts related to this case. She tossed and turned until the sun streamed in. Dragging herself out of bed, she hoped a hot shower and caffeine would clear away the fog.

She slathered peanut butter on a bagel and plotted her day. With nothing pressing from other clients, Delanie decided to spend more time at Chaz's club. Her phone's ringtone jarred her from her thoughts. "Hey there. What's shaking, Duncan?"

"We're still like Margaret with a bone on the Darrel Lick lead, but I had an idea. How 'bout you see if you can get some DNA from some of the key players at the club. I have some resources that can do some testing for us," Duncan said.

"Don't blow the budget." Delanie sighed. *Will this even pan out or will it be another dead end on this case?*

"No worries. I did a favor for a friend. He's happy to assist with his resources."

"Do I want to know?" she asked, taking a sip of her espresso.

"Probably not. But DNA verification couldn't hurt since this case has way too many question marks and blanks that need to be filled in. Science doesn't lie."

"I'll see what I can do. I plan to head over to the club this evening. I'll take a big purse."

"I'll let you know what else Margaret and I uncover."

"Get some sleep." Delanie disconnected, and her phone buzzed again. "Hello?"

"Hey, Delanie, this is Easton. How are you?"

"Fine. This wasn't the number you used last time," Delanie said.

"This is my other phone. Add me to your contacts. I don't want you to miss a call because you don't recognize it. Hey, I was wondering, would you like to grab dinner tonight? I've eaten way too much bar food lately. I wanted to try this place down the road. Whatdaya say?"

Delanie hesitated and then reasoned that she could use it as an opportunity to get the sample that Duncan wanted. "Sure. What time?"

"How about if you meet me at the club at five? We can go have an early dinner and still get back in time for the show."

"Sounds like a plan," she said.

"I'm looking forward to it." Easton disconnected.

This guy is model-gorgeous, but something makes my antennae tingle, and not in a good way.

After vacuuming her bungalow and catching up on mounds of laundry and unread emails, Delanie changed outfits three times and settled on a teal sweater dress and a pair of black leggings. She pulled on her thigh-high boots and headed to the bathroom for hair and makeup.

Her phone vibrated across the counter as her curling iron heated up.

"What's up?" she asked Duncan as she cradled the phone between her chin and shoulder.

"Someone is definitely using Darrel Davidson's identity. We found online purchases, some wire transfers, and some social media posts," Duncan said.

"You think it's him?" Delanie swiped on mascara.

"Not sure yet. It could be a stolen identity. Or maybe somebody he knows is using the account. He had an ex-wife at the time and a girlfriend. Still working on who it might be."

"I'm headed to the club soon. I'll see what kinds of samples I can get for you."

"Margaret and I are worn out. I can't do all-nighters like I used to. We're going to take a nap."

"Sleep well." She disconnected and created a blush storm with her makeup brush.

Doubling back to the kitchen, Delanie stuffed a few plastic baggies and discarded shopping bags in her hidden camera-purse. *I don't want things to get contaminated or clink around in my purse.*

Light traffic and good driving music made the trip to Goochland go by fast. She parked in the lot and glanced at the sign. *The creepy cowboy doll still greeted visitors at the entrance. The kid-sized doll is almost a fixture in the club's lot.*

As she approached the glass doors, Easton rushed out and clasped her elbow. "Delanie, it's great to see you. I'm parked over there." He rushed her to the black Audi under the lamppost.

"It's nice to see you to. How have you been?"

"Good. It's been quiet for a change. I've been able to get some work done instead of putting out fires." He unlocked the door and held it for her. "I was thinking about trying something new. You up for an adventure?"

"Sure," she said as he revved the engine. He looped around the parking lot and cut across empty spaces. He floored it and headed east toward Richmond. He drove like he was playing Frogger, dodging cars and changing lanes way too many times. Delanie felt like using the imaginary brake on her side. She liked fast cars, but this felt too much like a Formula One race.

He cut off a U-Haul truck and tore into the left lane for a turn that made her grab the dash. "You okay over there?" he asked.

"Fine," she said, righting herself and adjusting her seatbelt that had locked in place.

"I thought we'd try this place I spotted in Scott's Addition." Easton whipped into a space down the street from Thai One On.

Delanie could feel the heat rising in her cheeks. She took a deep breath to calm the jitters. *Hopefully Doug doesn't cover the evening shift, too.*

They hiked down the street, and Easton held the door for her. He made a peace sign at the hostess, and she seated them in a booth across from the bar.

Doug filled pint glasses at the other end near the cash register. She shifted in her seat to face the inside of the booth. Maybe he wouldn't notice her.

The noise level from the packed restaurant made it difficult to carry on a conversation. When a young waiter appeared at their table, she ordered chicken in brown sauce, and Easton selected a sushi platter.

He leaned closer toward her, grabbing her hand and holding it in both of his. "I'm watching the entertainers closely. I think it's one of them."

The waiter interrupted with their drinks, and Delanie used the moment to withdraw her hand and cradle the glass. "What led you to that conclusion?" she asked Easton when the waiter returned to the bar.

"Just a hunch. I think they'd benefit the most. I'm even watching Diego. He's been shifty lately."

Delanie raised both eyebrows. "How?"

"He acts weird around me. I get the sense he's hiding something. I haven't figured out the motive behind the pranks if he's the culprit. The next time you're at the club, I'd like for you to watch him closely and report back to me."

Before she could comment, Doug appeared at their table with a large black tray. He handed out orders and condiments like he was dealing cards. "Anything else I can get you?"

Easton dug into his food like he hadn't eaten all day.

Doug paused and said, turning back to the table, "Hey, it's Liz, right? How are you? Are you still on your tour of Richmond?"

She turned her head and smiled. "I'm Delanie."

He paused and looked like he was going to say something. "My mistake. You look so much like someone I met the other day. They say everyone has a twin. Let me know if you need anything else." Doug returned to the bar.

Easton side-eyed Doug before he disappeared in the kitchen. "Wow. This is really good. I'm going to have to come back here. I'm staying at a temporary place off of Staples Mill. I'm trying to figure out the lay of the land and where I want to settle. I like this part of town. There's a lot of night life in this area. I looked at some condos near here. The ones in the old cookie factory. And there's a new apartment complex going up on the next block. It would be good to be within walking distance of all this action. Though, I never seem to get any time off. I'm going to have to have a talk with Cousin Chaz about the schedule. He thinks his representative has to be there any time the doors are open." Easton wiped his chin.

"Chaz is very dedicated to his businesses."

"He needs to get a life," Easton muttered. The pair dug into their meals and the conversation faded away.

Doug stopped next to their table. "Can I get anyone any refills?"

Delanie shook her head.

"Did you all save room for dessert?"

"I'm good," Easton said. "What about you?" Delanie waved her hand and put her napkin in her plate. "Just the check, please."

Doug placed the tab face down on the table. "I'll take it when you're ready." Doug stared at Delanie.

"I'll be back in a sec." Easton handed Doug his credit card.

Doug backed away. *His staring is starting to get creepy.*

While he ran the credit card, Delanie rummaged through her purse for one of the plastic bags. She leaned across the table, covered the edge of the glass carefully with the bag, and dumped the remaining beer in Easton's plate. Stuffing the glass in her purse, she tried to look nonchalant.

Doug returned and set the receipt on Easton's side. "You can pretend to be Delanie in front of your boyfriend. I get it. You can be anybody you want. But admit it. You're Liz. I never forget a face."

She pulled out her driver's license. "See."

Doug tried to snatch it from her, but she snapped it back and dropped it in her wallet. "Sorry. It's Delanie."

"Are you still bothering her?" Easton's voice boomed from behind the waiter, who jumped a foot. "Not good when you're working for tips, man." He picked up his card and receipt. "Come on, let's get out of here."

"What'd ya do with the glass?" Doug yelled to Easton's back.

Delanie guided him toward the door. *She'd have to wear a wig or better disguise the next time she snooped.*

Once they were outside, Easton continued, "Some people. I'd say let's go dancing or watch the sun go down over the river, but Chaz wants me to live at the club. Sorry to cut this short. I had fun."

"That's fine. Thank you for dinner. I need to pop in at the club, too."

He held the door for her, and she settled in the front seat. *Hopefully, the return ride will be calmer.*

"You and your partner find anything?" Easton signaled and pulled out on Broad Street. This time, he found the expressway for the short ride west.

"We're tracking down people at the rally. I'm also working on a timeline of events and who was present at each of the incidents."

"I wish this guy would slip up, and we'd nail him. He's really good at evading detection this long. What happens if we never find out who it is?"

"He'll trip up sooner or later," Delanie said. Her phone dinged and distracted her from his questions and his driving.

I'm back in town late tonight. Wanna grab dinner tomorrow?

Delanie smiled. Eric Ellington, her favorite FBI agent, was back in Richmond. **Sounds wonderful. I'd offer to cook, but...**, she tapped in as her response.

I know you. I'll save us both the trouble. We'll go out.

Looking forward to it. The butterflies were definitely alive and awake. It would be nice to see him again.

Easton zoomed down the left lane interrupting her romantic thoughts of the handsome FBI agent. Chaz's cousin exited and zipped around cars to get to the club's parking lot. He screeched brakes and cut the engine. "Back safe and sound. And if Chaz says anything, I'm telling him I was with you." He grinned his megawatt smile and climbed out of his vehicle.

The chivalry must have ended at the Thai restaurant. Delanie climbed out and shut her door.

Inside, Violet hovered as Sven and Hector stacked trays of clean glasses.

"Hi, Violet," Delanie said, approaching the bar. "Hey, Hector and Sven."

Hector's face lit up. "It's good to see you. Sven and I were just remarking that things seem to be back to normal here."

Violet glared down her thin, pointy nose that turned up at the end.

Sven paused and filled two ginger ales. He set one in front of each of the women.

"Thanks," Delanie said.

Violet nodded. "Making any progress?"

"My partner and I are tracing the license plates and the Facebook posts of the protestors. Yes, I think we're making progress. And I hope to have something to report very soon."

Violet took a gulp of her drink. Easton stood behind the women, glancing around and fiddling with his phone.

"How are things with you all?" Delanie asked. She turned to where Easton had been, but Chaz's cousin had disappeared.

"I've been on vacation for a few days, so I'm good," Sven said. "Hector and I are playing catch up here. It seems whoever closed last night didn't restock or use the checklist."

Violet drained the rest of her drink and set it on the counter with a little more force than needed. "That would be Easton. I'll say something to him. I have to talk to him anyway about some other stuff."

The bony woman padded softly in her flats across the tile floor. When Hector and Sven returned to the kitchen, Delanie pulled out another bag from her purse and wrapped Violet's glass and laid it in the bottom of her purse. She dropped a five in the tip jar and wandered down the hallway. Gwen and Violet's offices were empty. She inched down the hall where heated voices came from Easton's office.

Delanie pressed herself against the wall and moved closer to hear better.

"Chaz is concerned that you're never here. And you always disappear when there's work to be done," Violet said.

"Well, I'm concerned that you're too busy minding my business than running the operations of this place. A lot of things have happened on your watch," Easton shot back.

"My watch!" Violet's voice went up two octaves. "You're the general manager. Don't expect me to cover for you anymore, and I will be blunt when Chaz asks for my opinion."

She huffed out of Easton's office and almost ran into Delanie. "Hi." Delanie looked as surprised as Violet did.

"And you. You need to figure this mess out and make sure you're worth what Chaz is paying you." Violet stomped to her office and slammed the door.

Delanie ducked down the hall toward the dressing room. Empty. Delanie heard something next door and moved toward the open door. Diego arranged costumes in the prop room.

"Hey there." She moved next to the long table covered with six sequined cowboy hats, lassos, and red, sparkly chaps.

"Working on tonight's look. We have five bridal parties here tonight. I thought we'd use our Valentine outfits." He stepped over to a cubby and pulled out three leather belts with giant heart-shaped buckles. The cowboy belts looked more like ones used by professional wrestlers. "Dern, that hurt." Diego dropped the belts and sucked on his thumb. "That belt has a jagged edge somewhere." He reached for a paper towel and squeezed his thumb to stop the bleeding.

"You okay?" she asked.

"Fine." He wiped his thumb again and threw paper towel on the counter as he returned to the cubby for more belts.

C. J. stuck his head in the doorway and nodded at Delanie. "Hey, Diego. Do you have a minute to look at something? The guys want to change up a couple of the steps in the third number, and they want you to look at it."

When the two men stepped out in the hall, Delanie snatched the paper towel and put it in another bag in her purse. She hoped that the glasses in her purse didn't clink together while she snooped.

Chapter Fourteen

Delanie put the finishing touches on her makeup and checked her look in the bathroom mirror. *This feels like a real date.*

Before she could decide whether to change outfits again, the doorbell rang. She unplugged the hair dryer and flatiron and did a quick check that the house was presentable before she opened the front door.

She got out a "Hi" before Eric hugged her and planted a long kiss that sent a jolt of adrenaline down her spine. When she caught her breath, she said, "Welcome back. It's good to see you."

"Good to see you, too." Special Agent Eric Ellington stepped through the doorway into her cozy living room. "It's nice to be back. Boston is too flippin' cold for me."

"Can I get you something to drink?" She hoped she had more than milk and water in the fridge. She couldn't remember the last time she had visited a grocery store for real supplies instead of snacks for the snowstorm.

"I'm good. I'm thinking Italian. You up for that?"

"Sounds good. Let me get my coat."

The tall agent in a black leather jacket and jeans helped her with her coat. She followed him out the door and made sure it was locked.

After climbing into his F-Series truck, she jiggled the seatbelt until it clicked in place. She liked the view from the behemoth truck. A truck or SUV would definitely give her a better vantage point, but she wasn't ready to give up the speed of her Mustang.

"So, anything you can talk about from your latest excursion up north?" she asked.

"The gift shop at the airport was nice. Oh wait, I got you something." He leaned over in front of her and opened the glove box. He handed her a small plastic bag with map of Massachusetts on it in red.

Delanie pulled out a handmade leather bracelet with a small "Boston Strong" charm. "Thank you. I love it."

"I saw it in the gift shop, and it reminded me of all the work we did up there after the Boston Marathon bombing."

Delanie slid it on her wrist and held it up to admire the craftsmanship.

"Plus, I knew you were a Washington fan. So, no Red Sox or Patriots stuff." She smiled, and he continued, "What have you been up to lately? Hopefully, it's not crossing any lines." He raised one eyebrow and cracked a smile.

"Duncan and I are always on the side of truth and justice."

He nodded. "Just be careful. I know you." Another smile inched across his face.

"We're working on a case for Chaz Smith. He opened a new club on the Goochland side of the West End. It's an all-male revue. Anyway, someone is pulling pranks and sabotaging things. He wants to know what's going on."

"Hanging out at a male strip club. Interesting job."

"It's not a strip club. It's a male revue. The Chippendales in cowboy hats." She paused and pursed her lips.

"What? I was teasing. Did you find the joker?"

"No, and he keeps messing with the internet and the cameras. There's never any footage when these things happen."

"You think it's an inside job?" he asked.

"That's where I'm leaning. It seems to be too coincidental for it to be an outside person. But some of the pranks are annoying and border on malicious and dangerous."

"Like what?"

"Someone ordered hundreds of mattresses, and the delivery truck blocked the club's door until they could straighten out the misunderstanding. An expensive booze order was messed up, and they delivered the wrong items. Someone unplugged a freezer and a bunch of food spoiled, and the mystery person trashed the kitchen and the supply closet. And I almost forgot about the cherry bomb in the bathroom."

"Sound like teenage pranks to get someone's goat."

"Then someone posted that the club was trafficking and exploiting women. It was all over social media, and a crowd showed up to protest. Again, it took some time to straighten it out and clear up that that wasn't happening. It was on some dark websites."

Eric was quiet for a few moments.

"And this is slightly funny and not as serious. Someone has been dressing up dolls the size of small children and leaving them around town. They're all white except their costumes. One dressed up like a cowboy ended up by the sign at the Cheeky Monkey. I don't think it's related to the other stuff. It feels like I've been on this for months with nothing to show for all the work."

"You think it's really all about the pranks?"

"No. I think it's a distraction for something that hasn't happened yet. I asked Chaz to have his accountant keep an eye on the books and the credit cards. The stunts seem too childish and annoying for someone to go to that much trouble and continue them unless they have a sick sense of humor. I think it's a cover for something else. Probably something much bigger."

"Good line of thinking. I know you'll get to the bottom of this." Eric signaled and turned into Stony Point Fashion Park and drove around the back to Bistro Incognito. "You ever eaten here?"

She shook her head. "Funny name. Perfect for your line of business. I haven't been over here in a while. Actually, since Duncan's dog Margaret won a costume contest as Sherlock Bones."

They walked across the parking lot to the giant glass doors that opened to a spacious waiting area with brightly cushioned benches. Inside, the restaurant looked like a street view in a small Italian town. Each room served as a different building with a small roof, windows, and other decorations.

"Benvenuto," said a svelte hostess with the long black hair.

"Reservation for Ellington."

"Yes, sir. Right this way." Her long skirt swished as she walked.

They followed the hostess to a room decorated like a small cottage. She seated them in a cozy booth. "Your sever will be right with you."

Delanie picked up the heavy maroon menu and flipped through pages and pages of Italian dishes. Eric slid in the booth next to her.

The waiter returned a few minutes later with water and a breadbasket. "What can we make for you tonight?"

"I'll have the pasta con ricotta with a side Caesar salad and an unsweetened iced tea. No lemon, please," Delanie said.

"And you sir?" the waiter asked, picking up Delanie's menu.

"I'll have the lasagna with meat sauce and a house salad. Tea's fine, too. But I like lemons. In fact, I'll take hers."

"Yes, sir. Be back shortly." The waiter headed toward the bar.

"It's nice here. They spent a lot on the décor." Delanie looked at the room across from theirs and gasped. She resisted the urge to duck.

"What's wrong?"

"Nothing. I didn't expect to see them here. I thought they'd be getting ready for tonight's show."

Eric looked around. "Who?"

Delanie nodded her head toward the booth where Easton and Violet sat across from each other. "They work at the Cheeky Monkey. Not sure what's going on or why they're together. Let's just say they're not that chummy."

Eric shrugged. "Maybe they're here for the food. My airport Uber driver recommended it." He looked at her more closely. "You okay?"

She nodded. "Just watching Chaz's cousin Easton and his office manager, Violet. She's a little, uh, prickly."

"Wanna go say hi?" His grin had an impish look to it.

"Not sure. Keep talking. I want to see what they do." She took a sip of water and changed the subject. "Am I going to see your work on the news? And how was Boston?"

"Hmmm. Maybe. The raid was last week. We hung around to wrap up some loose ends and make more arrests in the network. I'm glad to be back home. I've got a few days off before I jump back into investigative mode. I was busy the whole time I was there. I didn't get to see much of the city."

"Were you on loan up there?" Delanie broke a roll and swished it in olive oil. As she talked, she kept one eye on the table in the other room.

"Sorta. My partner and I were working on a case here that led to something bigger."

Easton leaned across the table and showed Violet something on his phone. The woman's face went beet red. She picked up her purse and stormed out of the restaurant. Easton threw some money on the table and ran his hand through his hair. He casually strolled out by the bar. Delanie wasn't sure if either of them noticed her.

"So much for saying howdy," Eric whispered.

The waiter interrupted with a giant tray full of steaming platters. "Here you go. Let me know if you need anything else. I'll check back on you in a few minutes."

The pair dug into their dinners.

"Mmm. This is good. My compliments to the Uber driver for his recommendation," she said.

Eric nodded and shoveled another forkful of lasagna in his mouth.

Delanie wondered why Easton and Violet were dining together and what caused her to storm out. Neither of them seemed to think too highly of the other.

About twenty minutes later, the waiter reappeared and topped off their teas. "May I get you a dessert menu? Some boxes?"

"I'm stuffed. Everything was wonderful. I'll take a box," Delanie said.

"I'm good," Eric said. She glanced at his empty plate. No box needed.

As Eric took care of the check, Delanie's phone binged with a series of texts that arrived in staccato fashion.

"What's up?" Eric returned his credit card to his wallet.

"Something's going on at the club. I hate to cut our evening short, but could I get you to take me home to get my car?"

"It'd be faster if we took the interstate and headed there from here."

"You can't resist, can you? You know what kind of club it is, right?"

"That doesn't bother me. There's nothing on TV tonight. Plus, I like hanging out with you." His green eyes sparkled when he grinned. "Don't worry about me. I visit all kinds of places, most of them seedy and dirty. How bad can this place be? If you don't mind a sidekick, the offer stands."

She smiled as he took her hand and led her out of the restaurant. "I appreciate it. And I can always use backup."

"Where to?" He slammed the truck door.

"Take the Short Pump exit near Broad Street and head west. It's near the Henrico/Goochland line."

"I know a faster route." Special Agent Ellington floored the gas pedal, and the truck lunged forward. "What's the issue?"

"Gwen, the gal in charge of security, said there was a fire in the dressing room. It's out, but the team is there surveying the damage."

"That's not a prank." He accelerated and drove with a purpose.

After about fifteen minutes on the twisty backroads, he pulled into the Cheeky Monkey's packed lot. Overflow parking filled the big box craft store's lot next door. Crowds of women stood around the front of the club in the chilly evening air. Gwen in full winter garb, stood with a clipboard outside. A security guard hovered nearby.

"I'll let you out here and find a spot." Eric idled next to a clump of women huddled together as Delanie hopped out of his truck. "See you in a few minutes."

Heaving the heavy door shut, she waved and blew him a kiss. Delanie inched her way through the crowd to Gwen and the guard.

"Hey, you doing okay?" Delanie asked, approaching the pair.

"Oh, hi. It's been quite the evening. When the alarms went off, we thought it was a kitchen fire, but it was in the prop room. Not sure how long it had been burning. Easton and Violet are with the others and the firefighters around back. We're not sure if we can reopen tonight. These ladies decided to hang around to see if there's a chance. Not sure about that. We're taking a list of names and emails, so we can do something special for them for the inconvenience."

"Do you need anything?" Delanie scanned the crowd.

"Nope. Darius and I have it all under control." The guard nodded.

"I'm going to see what's going on around back."

Gwen turned to answer a question from a busty blond with a tierra and a "birthday girl" sash.

Delanie pushed her way through the crowd to the side of the building. Eric hiked toward her, and she waved to get his attention.

When he closed the distance between them in a few steps, she said, "Gwen said there was a fire in the prop room. The investigators are still around back." She pointed around the corner.

They hustled around the building and stopped behind the firetruck, two police cruisers, and a fire car. Puddles and rivulets of water covered the tarmac next to the back door and the dumpster, and a damp, smoky odor hovered in the air.

Violet stood with her hands on her hips. She stared at the open door and chewed on her bottom lip. Easton picked his way across the wet floor and stepped outside. "It doesn't look like we can open tonight. There's still too much smoke in there, and we're still not sure what equipment is salvageable. Javi reported that the kitchen is unscathed. The dining room and front are fine. I guess that's good news. It affected the prop room, and the dressing room has water damage."

"I've called Chaz. He'll be here soon," Violet muttered.

Easton glared at her, and when he noticed Delanie, his countenance softened. "Hey, Delanie. We had a little mishap here. It's never a dull moment. But we've got it under control."

"It looks pretty big to me. Gwen and Darius are out front with quite a crowd of women," Delanie said.

"I'll go help her with that," Easton said. "Violet, get on the horn and make sure the insurance adjuster is on his way. The Fire Marshal is inside now. He'll let us know when we can reopen."

"Don't make promises to that crowd that you can't keep." Violet spat out the words like they tasked like spoiled fruit. "Do you want me to go with you?"

"I got it under control." Easton stepped gingerly over the puddles, trying not to soil his designer shoes.

"He better not give away the farm," Violet muttered under his breath. "Chaz isn't going to like this."

"Who was in the building when it happened?" Delanie asked. Eric Ellington stood close behind her.

"Sven, Hector, and Javi. Easton showed up late as usual. He always finds some excuse to miss the prep and well, work for that matter. Gwen called me when she got the building alert. I met her here."

Deciding to save the big reveal of seeing them at the restaurant, Delanie replied, "Did the first responders say anything about how the fire started?"

She shook her head. "Thankfully, this didn't happen when we had a packed house. It could have been much worse."

Javi stuck his head through the door. "Violet, the firefighters want to talk to management inside."

Delanie and Eric followed her long strides down the dark hallway. Two firefighters stood by a table with a deputy and another officer. Easton, Javi, and Gwen stood behind Violet. The smokiness in the air gave the room a closed-in feeling.

"We found an accelerant. It looked like piles of clothing and rags had been burning slowly for a while. We checked the entire building and the roof. The fire is out. There is water and smoke damage to those rooms. You may notice smoke and soot in the offices because they're close to the origin. After your insurance guy goes through the scene, you're going to need someone to put a tarp on the damaged roof and clean out the debris. Here are my initial notes and contact number. I'll have the full report for you within a few days. Do you have any questions? Also, on the back of that sheet are a list of local cleaners who specialize in this kind of damage. We're going to need to talk to everyone who was in the building."

Thoughts pinged around Delanie's head as the firefighter talked. The fire had to be there long enough to cause damage, but at a time when nobody was around to notice it. This had to be an inside job. She scanned the crowd, looking for any indication of who could have done this.

"Who was in the building?" the firefighter repeated.

"That would be this group and Hector," Easton added, looking around the room. "Except him and her." He pointed to Eric, who rested his hand on Delanie's shoulder.

"This is Eric Ellington," Delanie said. "He was with me when I got the call from Gwen and was kind enough to drive me over."

Eric nodded and squeezed her shoulder lightly. Easton's face soured, and he turned to stare at Violet.

The police deputies and fire investigator spent the next hour taking statements. Delanie and Eric were last. The club employees drifted away to other tasks after their interviews.

"And you are?" the fire investigator asked.

"I'm Delanie Fitzgerald, a private investigator. Chaz Smith, the owner, hired me to get to the bottom of all the pranks and issues happening lately at the club."

"Like what?"

Delanie listed off all the incidents, hoping to get them in the correct timeline.

The deputy nodded and scribbled on a yellow legal pad.

"And how do you fit in?" the Fire Marshal asked Eric.

"I'm Special Agent Eric Ellington, FBI Richmond."

All of the emergency responders seemed to snap to attention and sit straighter in their chairs.

The deputy opened his mouth, but closed it again when the fire investigator said, "The FBI. Who alerted you?"

"She did." He pointed at Delanie. "We were having dinner when the guard called her. It was faster for me to shuttle her over here than to go back and get her car. I'm not on duty."

All four of the men seemed to exhale at the same time.

"I think that about does it. You both arrived after the fire was out." The Fire Marshal gathered his notes and rose. He glanced at the other firefighter, who nodded and followed him to Violet's office.

Delanie paused to eavesdrop, and she caught the tail end of the wrap up and the importance of getting the roof covered before the rain. After the office cleared out, she stuck her head in Violet's office. "Do you need anything?"

"Two aspirin and a whiskey sour, but that'll have to wait. I've got a million calls to make, and I have to figure out how to get this place open as soon as possible. The insurance guy will be here in a bit. I think I interrupted his dinner."

Delanie pulled a bottle of aspirin from her purse and offered it to the woman who looked more tired than usual.

"Thanks," she said handing it back after taking a handful of the pills. "If you see Easton, tell him Chaz is on his way over to survey the damage."

"Will do." Delanie retreated from the doorway, and Eric followed her down the hallway through the dining room. He rested his hand on the small of her back.

Easton leaned against the bar like he was having a casual chat with the deputies. When he saw Eric and Delanie, he stood taller. "Uh, I didn't know you were still here."

"Violet's looking for you. Chaz should be here any minute."

A frown crossed his face, but he recovered quickly with his usual charm. "These fine gentlemen have it all under control. Now Violet and I have to figure out how and when to open up for business with a whole bunch of ruined props and a damaged roof. And then we have to come up with our official statement about what happened. We're going to be swamped for hours."

Chapter Fifteen

T he next day, Delanie's phone buzzed as she labeled the items for Duncan's DNA search. "Hey, Marco. How are you?"

"Hope I didn't catch ya at a bad time. Steve and I pulled the camera footage from yesterday."

"Anything useful?" Delanie sunk in her chair and picked up a sticky note and pen.

"About noon, Javi came in and went straight to the kitchen. Easton arrived about two. We caught him leaving and then he showed up again around six. Sven arrived about five. We caught him on camera a couple of times. Then around six-thirty, it was chaos with fire, police, Violet, Gwen. Quite the crowd."

"That's interesting." Delanie jotted notes. "I never saw Sven when I was there."

"Back it up and get a time stamp on Sven," Marco said. "Oh, Steve says hi."

"Hi, Steve. And thanks for checking on this for me."

"Let's see. Sven arrived at five-oh-eight, and he walked down the hall away from the offices. We caught a glimpse of him at five-fifteen, and that's it. No more Sven."

"I went out to dinner last night, and I saw Violet and Easton in the restaurant. I wasn't really watching the clock, but they left before we did. Maybe around five-thirty. It was definitely dark outside when we left. With the fire, I didn't get a chance to talk to either of them about it."

"Normally they can barely tolerate each other. Interesting. Maybe they made up and joined forces. We're expecting the full report from the Fire Marshal later this week. I'll make sure you get a copy. I talked to Chaz late last night. He said the insurance adjustor said the fire department was sure that the fire was set earlier, and it did a slow burn for a while. The clothes were flame retardant, so that fits with a slow burn. The prop room is a disaster. Violet's got a crew coming in today to demo it."

It was time to pay Violet a visit. And why had Sven been at the club so early? How much bar prep was needed?

"Do you have a live feed?" she asked.

"Yup."

"Anyone there now?"

"Violet walked down the hall a few minutes ago. Diego's there. He looks a wreck."

"I'm headed over there now to poke around," she said.

"I'll let you know if we notice anything unusual."

"Thanks. I'll do the same." She disconnected and sent Duncan a text. **Leaving samples on your desk. Headed back to the club.**

Hope something jumps out at you, he replied.

Not literally was the follow up.

Delanie swung through a drive-thru near the club for two cookie crumble mochas. Chocolate and caffeine might help break the ice with Violet.

After an uneventful drive to the West End, Delanie picked her way over cords crisscrossing the hallway near the open back door. Two guys in bright green suits hauled debris out of the prop room. Diego supervised from the hallway. He looked ten years older today.

"How are you doing?" she asked.

"As good as can be in this disaster area. We're going to have to start over. When they're done in here, I'm going to see what I can piece together. Not sure if we have full sets of anything left. Plus it'll take days to get that smoky smell out of here."

"Do you have reason to suspect anyone?" Delanie lowered her voice and stared at the choreographer.

"My team? No. I mean we have our creative differences, but we usually work them out. Most of us have been together since we started this. Not sure why anyone would want to cause trouble here. It's a great place to work." He blew out a long puff of air. "This could have been much worse if it hadn't been discovered before it spread to other areas."

"Can I lend a hand with anything?" Delanie asked.

He shook his head. "C. J.'s coming in a little while to help me make sense of all this. I'm hoping we can salvage enough for when we reopen. If not, we may have a mishmash of costumes."

Most of the audience won't mind. They can dance barefooted in jeans, and it will still be a hit.

"I'm going to see if I can find Violet," Delanie said.

"She's holed up in her office on the phone with the contractors."

Delanie stepped over fans, more cords, and piles of charred boxes and bins. She could hear Violet as she walked toward her office.

"I told you I need someone today. Next week won't work. There's a hole in the roof." Violet's voice went up to a screechy range. She paused and swore in a lower tone as Delanie popped her head in the doorway. Violet punched the disconnect button and curled her lip at the phone.

"Oh. I didn't know you were out there. Everyone has excuses today. I'm having trouble finding a contractor who can actually show up," Violet said, looking up at Delanie.

Delanie offered the iced coffee. "Thanks," Violet replied. "My headache's coming back with a fury. This has been a nonstop disaster. I'm afraid to ask what's next. Chaz is going to replace all of us if we don't find out who keeps doing this stupid stuff."

Delanie sank in the empty guest chair. The pressure weighed heavily on her shoulders, too. "I'm trying to get the timeline straight for yesterday. I got a text from Gwen at six-eighteen. That's when we left the restaurant and headed here. When did you hear about it?"

"About the same time from Gwen. I was on my way back from dinner."

"What about Easton, Javi, Sven, and Hector?" Delanie asked. She held off asking about Violet's rendezvous at the restaurant with Easton.

"Javi and Hector were already here to prep." Violet took a long sip of her drink. She looked chagrined when she made a slurping sound with the straw.

"What about Sven?"

She frowned. "I don't remember seeing him. Not sure if he was here."

"How was your dinner at Bistro Incognito?" Delanie asked, staring across Violet's desk.

Violet paused. Her eyes widened for a second.

"It was only a dinner meeting. Easton wanted to discuss some ideas he had for the club. It was mostly a waste of time." She moved folders on her desk and stacked some loose papers.

When Delanie didn't respond, Violet continued, "He wants to add more shows. I think that should be gradual as we watch the numbers. Shotgun marketing doesn't always work. He doesn't plan, and he didn't like my thoughts yesterday, so I left. And by the time I got back here, chaos had broken out. I was too busy to think any more about his stupid ideas. He's a smarmy salesman who's all sizzle."

Delanie cracked a smile. "Diego said he's trying to pull together costumes for his guys."

"It looks like we may be able to open tonight. The roof wasn't as bad as we thought. Chaz is beside himself about losing money." A grim look crossed Violet's face. "It took me several hours to reschedule the folks from last night."

Delanie felt a twinge of guilt. She needed to give Chaz an update. It was frustrating that none of the leads they'd been chasing had panned out. "Is Easton in?"

"Doubtful. There's work to be done." Violet returned to her laptop. "Thanks for the drink. It was a nice treat." Her mouth twitched, and Delanie almost saw a smile.

The private eye took a tour of the club. If you ignored the damage, it looked like any other night at the Cheeky Monkey. Javi and Hector buzzed around the kitchen, and Diego and C. J. sorted boxes in the hallway.

&

WHEN DELANIE PULLED in the lot in front of her office, Duncan and Margaret stood on the sidewalk, staring at the commotion across the lot. She shaded her eyes with her hand.

"The new store's opening today," Duncan said after she shut the car door. "There's been a crowd all day." He bounced and wiggled like a five-year-old.

"An ice cream shop grand opening in winter?" Delanie stared at the Utterly Ice Cream sign, displaying a giant pink and purple cow.

"I eat ice cream all year," he said.

"I'm glad to see a business in that space. It's been lonely over there since the pet shop closed." She shuddered when she thought of the missing reptiles from Snakes and Scales.

"Margaret and I are going to have to start parking around back. An ice cream shop within walking distance is too much of a temptation."

"Any news on Chaz's problems?" Delanie asked.

"Which one?" Duncan asked, following her inside the office.

"I'll take anything at this point. I owe him an update, and I haven't made much progress. Every day is about the same routine with some new prank. Rinse and repeat."

"It takes a while to track down all the details. I sent your DNA samples off to my buddy. Even with the friends' discount, it may be a month or so before we see anything."

Delanie sighed. "Not sure if they'll even help, but at least the genetics may give us some new information. Could you dig into the backgrounds of Easton, Diego, Violet, and Sven to see if there's anything we haven't found? Right now, they're the only ones on my short list of suspects who keep showing up on the hidden camera. But they're employees. We kinda expect them to be there."

"Sure." Duncan stood in the doorway of the kitchenette.

"When I was out with Eric last night, I saw Easton and Violet together at the restaurant. It looked like she left in a huff. Then a fire broke out at the club. The Fire Marshal said that the fire was set earlier, so neither of them are off my list of suspects yet."

"More junk for your timeline. It looks like a bad horror flick. If something could go wrong, it does."

Delanie rolled her eyes. "I'll be in my office if you need me. I've got to pull something together for Chaz before he loses patience and finds another PI."

Delanie woke up her laptop and let the emails download as she brewed coffee in the kitchenette. Margaret and Duncan wandered in. "Want some?"

"Nope. I'm good. I'm also going to see what else I can find on Easton's dead partner in Arizona. I'm not sure why it's bothering me, but it's tickling at something in my brain. Someone could be using his name."

When the coffee machine made its last gasping sputter, Delanie grabbed her mug and padded back to her office. She sat down to draft an update for Chaz, but there wasn't much progress to report. Hours later, she had a summary of all the major players and what had happened lately. She included all the work Duncan did on the conspiracy sites and the made-up protest. She paused and then hit send. It was a lot of work with not many answers. *Frustrating.*

Delanie copied the conspiracy information with all the Richmond contacts and tapped out an email to Noreen Norris. Maybe she could shed a little light on some of the craziness. It looked like a story that was right up her alley.

Leaning back in her chair, Delanie stared at the ceiling. *What am I missing?*

Her phone dinged with a text from the TV reporter. **Awesome stuff. Thank you. Definitely worth looking into**.

Delanie smiled to herself. Well, she didn't have all the answers, but maybe she could right a few wrongs in her own little way. The more people poking around in this mess, the better.

Her phone rang with Chaz's ringtone before she had time to bask any further about her good deed.

"Hi, Chaz."

Before she could get out anything else, he launched into a spray of words. "Hey. Thanks for the update. You guys have been chasing down a lot of stuff. I'm grateful. Mad as hell about all the stupid stuff and more determined than ever to find that creep. It really cheeses me off that it's probably someone who works for me. Sheesh. And he's getting more daring with the stuff he's pulling. I told Marco and Steve to figure out how to get more cameras over there. Nothing seems to work. So far, we've been lucky, and no one's been seriously hurt. But the costs are starting to add us. And who knows what this guy is capable of?"

"Duncan and I are going to go over everything again. There's got to be something we've missed."

"Oh, I forgot to tell you. I had my accountant do some more research into my books like you suggested. There were some anomalies with a couple of accounts that he's looking into. One had more deposits that it was supposed to, and another had less than expected. He's auditing everything. This sends me into orbit. I'm not worried about the bad publicity stuff. I can use that or counteract it. No biggie, but I'm concerned about the stuff that's affecting my bottom line."

"I've taken hours of footage over there, and nothing seems to be unexpected. I'm getting ready to go through it again."

"Let me know if you need anything." Chaz clicked off at about the same time Duncan and Margaret poked their heads through her doorway.

"Hungry yet?" he asked. "I was thinking we could get some lunch and take a break."

"Sounds good." She picked up her coat and purse and followed him out the front door.

"Margaret, you're on duty while we're gone. Keep the office safe."

The brown and white chunk turned her head and ambled down the hall toward Duncan's office.

"She's got it covered. What were you thinking about for lunch?" Delanie asked.

Duncan hesitated on the sidewalk and stared at the ice cream parlor across the street.

"Ice cream for lunch?" She squinted at him.

He nodded so vigorously she thought he was going to jar something loose. "Banana splits have fruit and nuts."

"And milk and vanilla beans. Sure. Why not. Let's support our new neighbors."

A few minutes later, they found a place in line in the new restaurant. The former reptile store had been magically transformed into a restaurant with pastel-colored cow murals and sparkles. A huge chalkboard with the flavors and menu spanned the length of the white counter. Everyone behind the counter sported cow-print T-shirts and ballcaps.

"Why don't you snag us a table. Banana split?"

"And a glass of water." Delanie found a round white table with day-glo pink and purple plastic chairs.

Before Delanie read all of her email, Duncan set Styrofoam boats full of bananas and chocolate, vanilla, and cherry ice cream on the table, along with a stack of napkins and Delanie's drink. "This place is great. There was so much up there I wanted to try. And if you bring your own banana next time, you get a dollar off. The snakes were cool, but this place is way better. Margaret will love it. Can't wait to bring Evie here, too." And Duncan didn't even get one of the complimentary, paper cow hats.

"Chaz mentioned that he had his accountant going over all the books." Delanie swiped at the mound of whipped cream with her purple spoon.

"Mmmm. Good idea." Duncan shoveled in another spoonful of ice cream. "I can't figure out a motive for all the pranks unless it's to annoy someone or to make them look bad. The sheer volume of acts is unusual. But the fire could have been deadly."

"He's getting braver, and the pranks are more dangerous as time passes," she said. "We've got to find him before someone really gets hurt. The stupid stuff is getting more and more expensive for Chaz, and he's frustrated. The tampering with the booze and the fire cross the line. The ferocity is ratcheting up."

"Ooooo. I gave myself a headache," Duncan mumbled. After swallowing a mouthful and wiping whipped cream off his upper lip, he said, "All better. Oh, I forgot to tell you. We've been monitoring the online accounts of Darrel Davidson. Not much activity, but he did change his screen name on social media to Remove the Scourge. I haven't had much luck with any of the financial transactions yet."

"Any particular reason why?"

"No. He's been posting rants on conspiracy Facebook sites about the decline of American morals and civilization. It's like he's gearing up for something."

"Do you think it's someone who knows Dare Davidson?" she asked.

Duncan shrugged. "Too early to tell, but the name choice can't be a coincidence."

"Hopefully there won't be any more flash mob protests." Delanie popped a cherry in her mouth and bit off the stem. "I'm going to go through all my pursecam footage again and then head back to the club. They plan to reopen tonight."

"It's League of Legends night. Margaret and I have to stock up on snacks for an evening of marathon gaming."

Delanie nodded and dropped her purple plastic spoon in her dish. "That's lunch and probably dinner tonight. 'Bout ready?"

"Yep, as soon as I get Margaret a pup cup to go," he said.

When Duncan returned to the table with his sidekick's snack, he cleared the trash.

Delanie followed him out the door and across the parking lot. "I've set up alerts to let me know when Darrel Davidson is active on his accounts. So far, it's a lot of posts during the workday. Not so much at night. He must have a lot of free time during the day."

"Let me know if you have any a-ha moments. I'll take any leads we can get," Delanie said.

Once inside her office, she wiggled out of her coat and draped it over the guest chair.

"Margaret and I will be in our office if you need us," Duncan yelled from down the hall.

Delanie settled in her chair and watched the videos in date order. Hours later before she moved on to the ones from last week, she stood and stretched to get the kink out of her neck. *Just a few more left.* It was like watching grass grow. People walked in and out of the shot. She looked at faces and anyone in the background.

A hand flashed on the screen. Delanie paused it and rewound the footage from the bar. Sven, in a black shirt, and another bartender darted in and out of the shot. There it was again. The hand. She saw a red shirt and a man's hand. He reached for a vodka bottle off the top shelf and left it open on the bar. The next few seconds showed the parade of people arriving and leaving from the bar. Then the hand was back. He grabbed the bottle and dropped something in it. He screwed the cap back on and shook the bottle. She played the clip over and over. *Whose hand was that? Some white guy in a red shirt. And what did he put in the bottle?*

A spark of fear surged through Delanie. She copied the clip and then zoomed in on the bottle. She made a couple of stills of the label and transferred the files to her phone. This footage was from the night before the fire. *Maybe it's not too late. If I can locate the right bottle.*

She texted the video to Gwen. **Found this. I'll be there soon. We need to find this bottle.**

Gwen's response, **Meet you there in a half hour** chimed before Delanie flew out the door.

She paused in the car to send the same text to Duncan. **Gotta stop something bad from happening.**

Again? he texted with three smiley emojis. Then a **Be safe** text followed.

Delanie floored it to the West End and hoped she wouldn't encounter any radar. She stopped abruptly in front of the club and slammed the car door. She flung open the Cheeky Monkey's front door and strode across the lobby. She skidded to a stop in front of the bar as Easton poured bottles of vodka down the drain in the small bar sink.

"Oh, hey," he said, tossing the bottle in the trash. It clinked as it hit the others at the bottom of the can. *Now there's no way of finding the exact bottle or what was in it.*

"What're you doing?" She hoped she didn't look as shocked as she felt.

"Gwen texted Violet and me with your message. I told her I'll take care of it. This idiot is costing us money. Do you know how much booze I just dumped? Chaz is going to go ballistic when he finds out."

Delanie counted at least seven empty bottles in the trashcan. *Would it be worth it to grab the trash bag?*

"This is too much. If I find out who's doing this..." His voice trailed off as Violet and Sven arrived with boxes of new bottles to replace the empty spots on the mirrored shelves behind Easton.

"Here. Let's get this cleaned up," Violet said. "We're going to lock up the bottles each night. I can't have any more tampering."

Delanie started to speak, but she hesitated. *Drinks can be easily tampered with. Marco needs to get a camera on the bar.* She pulled out her phone and tapped a quick text to him.

His response was swift. **Steve and I are on it. By tomorrow. Gwen sent me your clip.**

Delanie set her purse on the counter and angled it to capture the activity behind the bar. She pressed the button. *This will have to do for now.*

She staked out her seat and spent the next hour watching the bar setup and rehearsal. Diego and his guys, in tight jeans and cowboy hats, danced around the stage with mismatched props.

When Gwen opened the doors a few minutes before seven, the women streamed inside. Delanie sat on her perch all evening, taping the bar activity.

Before the encore, someone touched Delanie's shoulder, and she startled.

"Sorry. Didn't mean to scare you." Easton patted her on the shoulder. "You're going to know the entire show by heart if you keep hanging out here. What does your FBI guy think of you being here so much? Does hanging around all these hunks bother him? It would bother me."

Delanie felt the heat rising in her face. "His work takes him to all kinds of places, too. He knows it's my job."

Easton grinned like the Cheshire Cat. "Understanding boyfriend. Or maybe he's not paying enough attention." He turned on his stylish loafers and headed backstage before the encore.

Chapter Sixteen

T he next day, Delanie settled in at her kitchen table. The morning sun filled the room and made it feel warmer than it actually was outside. Staring at her timeline, she hoped to divine something. Watching last night's pursecam footage provided her with no new leads. *This case is proving harder than I expected.*

Her phone chimed with a text from Duncan. **Found a couple more disgruntled employees. Emailing you more details.**

She replied with a string of happy face emojis.

They might be worth talking to, Duncan replied.

Delanie opened her email and scrolled to find Duncan's latest. A very short list.

The first was Zander Phillips, an ex-bartender who was arrested for skimming from the profits. His current residence is at the Riverside Regional Jail. The second person was a former dancer, Joe "Elk" Jennings, who had relocated to Chicago.

Delanie scanned through Duncan's report on Phillips, who had a string of charges for theft and embezzlement from multiple employers. This was his second stint in jail. Chaz and Violet had pressed charges. Somehow Duncan had gotten a copy of the arrest report. *He has the uncanny ability to get his hands on all kinds of things. Scary sometimes. Did Chaz and Violet know about Zander's past before they hired him?*

There wasn't much on the dancer from Chicago. He'd spent about three months at the Cheeky Monkey as one of the original cowboys. Though, Duncan did have a contact number for him. Fumbling through her purse for the burner phone, she grabbed it and tapped in the number for Joe. Glancing at the clock on her laptop and subtracting an hour, she hoped the dancer was awake.

A gruff, "Hello" greeted her. It sounded like he was grunting.

"Hi, this is Delanie Fitzgerald, and I'm a private investigator in Richmond, Virginia. Is this Joe Jennings."

"The one and only but call me Elk."

"Do you have a few minutes to talk?"

"Yup. I'm finishing my morning workout and about ready to start the cool down. Whatcha wanna know?"

"I'm looking into a situation at the Cheeky Monkey. You were there when they opened, so I wanted to get your perspective."

He let out a heavy sigh. "It was a fun place to work. The tips were excellent. But that office manager was hell on wheels and not in a good way. Talk about a micromanager. She stuck her pointy nose into everything. I mean, she even friggin' wanted to change my stage name. I've had it for years, and she wanted something more cowboyish. Hello, lady, buffalo, elk, they all live in the west...Her smart mouth got to be too much. I could make more money elsewhere. I've got a way bigger gig here in Chicago."

"Congratulations on your new show. That's exciting," Delanie cooed. "Could you tell me if you saw anyone doing anything untoward or unethical while you were there?"

Elk hesitated. "Like illegal or just kinda bad."

"Either. I'm curious if you saw things going on that maybe weren't in the best interest of the club." Delanie tried to prod him without leading the witness.

"Uh, a couple of guys came to work loaded, but Violet or Diego eventually weeded them out. One guy was taking left-over food from the kitchen, but we all snack. I mean some of the guys collected phone numbers of the gals in the audience. Those women get crazy sometimes and throw all kinds of stuff at us or wait for us by the back door. Don't know if the guys ever followed up on any rendezvous. That's their business. It's not my thing. Are you talking that kind of stuff? Oh, wait. There was that bartender who got his hand caught in the till. What was his name? Alexander or Xander something? Anyway, Violet caught him red-handed and backed him in a corner with a knife when he tried to run. She held him until the police arrived. That was the talk of the club for a long time. Everybody walked on eggshells around Violet after that, waiting to see when she would lash out next."

"Any pranksters in the group?" she asked.

"Nah. Not that I can think of. Just the usual stuff when you get a bunch of creative folks together. RVA was a fun town, but I am lovin' Chicago. I hope this helped. I gotta go."

"Thank you for your time." She disconnected before he did.

Delanie let out a heavy sigh. *No new ideas for suspects. And again, Violet didn't get rave reviews. Would she have ticked off someone enough to make them go after her? He said she had brandished a knife.*

She decided to save the guy in jail for later. According to Duncan's finding, he was in jail when this mess started. Stuffing her papers and laptop in her messenger bag, she let of a long puff of air. *Still no progress.*

Her phone dinged with a text from Duncan. **One more. This guy's local.**

She replied with a string of smiley faces and cowboy hat emojis.

Duncan's lead was Gunner Tupuola. He was fired about four months ago, and he moved on to being a trainer at a gym called Lean Machine. She Googled the address. Not too far from her office. She clicked the link to call the gym.

"It's a great day to get fit," a squeaky voice answered. "How may I help you become a Lean Machine."

"Hi, I'm Dottie, and my friend said her trainer, Gunner, is totally awesome. Is he working today if I stop by to see him?"

"He is. He's here today until three. Would you like me to book an appointment with him?"

"I don't have a membership yet. I kinda wanted to see if I liked his, you know, style, and then I could maybe join and sign up for sessions?" Delanie added a giggle for effect.

"Of course, the introductory meeting is complimentary. How about eleven forty-five? Will that work with your schedule? And between me and you, everyone likes Gunner's, uh style. He's quite popular."

"Perfect. I'll see you then." Delanie had enough time to check her makeup and meet Gunner.

It didn't take long for her to zip over to the gym in a strip mall near Chippenham Parkway. Neon rope lights flashed in all the windows. Inside, the whirring noises, pulsating music, and the flashing lights gave the gym a carnival atmosphere and Delanie a slight headache.

She walked to the front desk where a well-endowed blond with overly stylized, black eyebrows greeted her. "Welcome to Lean Machine, how may I help you?"

"Hi, I'm Dottie. My friend recommended that I talk to one of your trainers. Is Gunner around? I made an appointment over the phone."

"Lemme check." She ran her finger down the computer screen. "He should be finishing up with a client, and he doesn't have another until three. Have a seat, and I'll let him know you're here."

Delanie sat in a white plastic chair and scanned the facility. Stationary bikes, treadmills, and ellipticals filled most of the floor space closest to her, and weight machines dominated the other half. The two areas seemed to be split by gender, too.

"Hi, Dottie. How can I help you?" a smooth voice said.

Delanie looked up. She opened her mouth and closed it again. Gunner filled the space vertically and horizontally in the lobby's small opening beside the desk. If his hair were longer, he'd look like Jason Momoa in workout clothes. "Uh, hi. My friends at work said I needed to come and see you about some personal training. I want to lose a few pounds, and I think I need someone to help me stay motivated."

"Then you're at the right place. Come on, I'll give you the tour." Delanie had to double-time it to keep with him. "This is our fabulous cardio area. We can set you up with a plan that's sustainable and fun. I find people don't stick with exercise unless they stay interested. We'll come up with a plan that includes diet, stretching, low impact and cardio. Then we'll add weights and strength toning." He pointed a beefy finger at the other side of the gym. "I'll make sure you stay captivated with the program that I design. Do you have any questions?" Without waiting for an answer, he continued, "The next step would be to take you over to our customer service reps and let them help you find the best membership plan for you. Then we can get started."

"Oh, I have lots of questions," Delanie interrupted. "Is there a place we could talk?"

"It's kind a loud in here, and all the offices are in use right now. You wanna step outside?" he asked, looking over his shoulder.

"That's fine. Is it always, uh, this busy in here?" *Stimulating was the first word that came to mind. I'm glad I didn't say that. Awkward.*

Gunner strode through the lobby and nodded to several women who turned into giggling teenagers when he passed. "This way." He held the door open for her.

"This is a nice place. Are training services included with the membership packages?"

"The gals in the back will explain it to you. It's an add-on to the membership. But I have a deal with some of my special clients. If you're interested, we could work out a direct payment and cut out the middleman. Don't mention that to the gals in the office." He put a finger to his lips and made a shushing sound. "That'll be our little secret."

Delanie raised her eyebrows. "Is that allowed?" she whispered.

"Of course. We're encouraged to bring in new clients. I haven't seen you work out yet, but you look in pretty good shape. We can come up with a plan for toning and strength building. Maybe even powerlifting. I've got a strategy that includes some really great vitamins and supplements. You'll be amazed at the quick results."

Delanie nodded. "That sounds good. I have some more questions if you have the time."

"Sure, anything for a prospective client." His smile looked sharklike.

"Could you tell me about your time at the Cheeky Monkey?"

He paused and stepped back. "How do you know about that? You a reporter or something?"

Delanie shook her head. "Just someone who's curious."

"Why does it matter?" he asked. "I love what I do now."

"Let's just say I'm a curious person, and I have a friend who has an interest there, too. And I'd like to get to know you better," she said with a wink.

"It was fun for a while." A scowl crossed his face. "Some bad memories. That woman had me fired for no reason."

"That's not right." Delanie hoped her pouty face wasn't over exaggerated.

"The pay was terrible. You'd think it would be better. I had to do side hustles to pay my bills. I'm much happier here," he said.

"I thought entertainers made big bucks. What happened?" Delanie asked.

"They're supposed to. I think something fishy was going on with the books. My pay was off more than once." He paused and looked over his shoulder. "The club manager was out to get me. She did anything she could to get me in trouble with the choreographer. She whined about everything I did. I gave up trying to please her. She didn't appreciate talent and would never stand up for her employees. She had the nerve to yell at me for having a second job when she was the one who wasn't paying me squat." He waved his muscled arms around as he talked.

"You're talking about Violet, right?"

A puzzled look crossed his face. "Yup, that's her. A nice, sweet name. Too bad it didn't match her nasty personality. Poison ivy or Mandrake would be better choices."

"Do you have check stubs or timesheets to prove your pay discrepancies?" Delanie asked.

"Nah, I got rid of all that stuff when I moved. Good riddance. It wasn't like someone was skimming. Nooooo. Violet did everything out in the open. She'd report things broken or meals eaten or missing costumes that she'd deduct from my pay."

"Were they legitimate claims?" Delanie pulled her coat closer to ward off the late morning chill.

"It felt like they owned me or wanted to. I think it wasn't called for, but I couldn't get anyone to listen. She had that new gal in security show me out. They said I was doing too much of my side business there. I was networking," he whined.

"Did you ever see anyone try to sabotage the club?"

He stared at her for a moment. "Why the twenty questions? You writing a story?"

"No. I'm trying to find out what the culture is like at the Cheeky Monkey for a friend who wants to know if he should take a job there. And I've been to the club a lot." Delanie pasted on a fake smile. She hoped her excuse didn't sound as flimsy as her smile felt.

"You remember me from there, huh. Fans are everywhere." A smile crossed his face. "Bad juju in that place. The negativity was bringing me down. Like I said, I'm much happier here. I'm appreciated, and no one cares what I do on my own time."

"So, no one pulled pranks or tried to hurt the business?" Delanie asked.

He laughed. "The guys were always teasing each other. Harmless stuff. No, I mean we all had people we didn't like, but nobody was doing anything to harm folks...Except maybe Violet who takes pleasure in ruining people's lives. It's getting cold out here, and I need to get back. Let me walk you over to our membership office."

"You gave me a lot to think about. Thanks for your time. I'll pop back in later to chat about the membership plans."

She turned as Gunner opened the glass door. Stepping off the curb, Delanie hurried to her car.

Once inside with the heated seats on, she texted Duncan, **Have anything on Gunner's background?**

Everyone's got a past. Just emailed you his.

She responded with a happy face and clicked on the attachment he included. She read the update twice. Gunner had a couple of speeding tickets through the years, but no other arrests. He had a string of jobs over the last ten years that included telemarketer, physical trainer for a soccer team, and an herbal supplements salesman. *Interesting work history.*

Delanie backed out of the parking space when her phone rang again. She clicked the button on her steering wheel. "Hey, Dunc. Thanks for the update on Gunner. I chatted with him at the gym, and he mentioned the vitamins and supplements. And he tried to sell me a gym membership with some under-the-table training fees. He and the other dancer, Elk, didn't speak too highly of Violet. But neither reported anything like the dirty tricks."

"That's sort of why I'm calling. My buddy did the DNA matching on one of glasses. It was Violet's. She had a security clearance for a previous job, so she was in the system. Her prints check out, and she's who she says she is. Her record is squeaky clean. Even if she's gruff."

Delanie snickered. "Nothing else in her background?"

"Nope. She plays by the rules. I'll let you know what I hear back on the other samples."

"I'm curious to see if anything pops up. Thanks," Delanie replied. *So many random leads, and no good suspects. This one is a struggle.*

Chapter Seventeen

After two ginger ales, Delanie slid off the barstool. She had her pursecam focused on Sven all evening. He moved like a ballet dancer in constant motion behind the bar, mixing and pouring drinks.

The show was the same as past nights except with minimal costumes and props. Delanie hoped this case wasn't going to defeat her. Lots of things kept happening, but she had no clue about the culprit's identity. *Chaz's patience can't hold out forever.*

After navigating the line for the restroom, she washed her hands and stepped out in the hall. She paused and fished through her purse for her hand sanitizer. "Open this frickin' door" floated down the back hallway. Pounding drowned out the high-pitched voice and echoed through the hall.

A busty blond in tight jeans and stilettos pummeled the wooden door to the dressing room with her palm. "Come out of there, now. I know you can hear me."

Delanie texted an SOS to Gwen. "Excuse me. Do you need some help?" she asked the woman.

The woman paused and huffed. "That jackass promised me a trip to Jamaica. We were going to go away together. And I come in tonight to see him, and he's with some floozy. I mean. I was going to move in with him," she slurred. "How could he do this to me? Open up now!" She pounded on the door with both fists.

Before Delanie could question her further, the dancers followed Diego down the hall. "Excuse me," he said, inching toward the door. He tried the knob, but it wouldn't budge. He shook it several times.

Diego pulled a key out of his skin-tight jeans and opened the door. Before he could step inside, the blond pushed him out of the way and barged in. "Where are you? I know you're in here. I saw your sorry butt duck through that door." She shoved a stool out of the way and kicked a gym bag. "I will find you."

The woman stomped into the back room, shoving anything that got in her way. The dancers snickered and stared. Sebastian recorded her outburst on his phone. The rest of the guys acted as if nothing was out of the ordinary, finding shirts and shoes and preparing to pack up.

Easton slipped out of the back room and headed for the door. The blond screamed like a gal in a horror flick and launched herself around the dancers. "There you are you two or maybe three-timing sack of scum!"

Chaz's cousin pulled Delanie in front of him like a shield. The woman lunged at the pair with her raised fist. "Get out of my way. I bet you're one of his chickiepoos." Her arm connected with the side of Delanie's head.

Stunned, she shook off the stars and looked around the room. Before she could do anything, Easton said, "Nadia, calm down. You're making a scene. And get away from Delanie."

Nadia screamed and lunged again at Delanie. The woman lashed out repeatedly.

Delanie snatched a hunk of Nadia's bleached hair and yanked her head back as the woman tried to butt her in the forehead. It was a tumbleweed of arms and legs until Delanie got a grasp on the taller woman's arm and bent it behind her. None of the men stepped in to assist.

Sebastian yelled, "Girl fight" as he continued to record the scene.

Delanie swung her purse and connected with the side of Nadia's face.

The blond stumbled backwards dazed. She shook her head and pounced on Delanie. "He's mine. And you're not going to take him from me."

"I don't know what you're talking about. You can have him. I have no interest in anyone here." Delanie turned slightly and spotted Easton slinking out the door.

"I saw the way he looked at you," she screeched and raised her fist.

"You're nuts," Delanie hissed. She twisted the woman's arm behind her back and pulled her arm upward, keeping pressure on her bent fingers. "Enough of this."

"What is going on here?" Violet demanded, glaring at the pair.

"Call the police. She's drunk, and she attacked me," Delanie said, trying to get her heart rate to return to normal.

"I only had two drinks," the woman slurred. "And she tried to seal my boyfriend."

"What? Seal? That doesn't even make sense." Violet stared daggers at Nadia.

"Steal. She tried to steal the love of my life. She can't have him. "You're hurting me. Let go of my arm," Nadia whimpered.

"I'll take her," Gwen said, stepping around Violet. "Come with me." She escorted Nadia toward the hallway.

"You okay?" Violet asked Delanie.

She nodded. "I think I need some ice."

"Sven's got plenty. Let's get you taken care of." Violet led the way to the bar.

"I've got it all on film," Sebastian yelled after them. "It was a pretty good smack down if you want a copy."

Delanie handed him her card as she passed on the way to the bar. She definitely wanted a copy for evidence.

"Sven, we need some ice for Delanie's head," Violet called to the bartender. "It seems one of our clients took a swing at her."

The blond bartender stopped his cleaning and put ice in a plastic bag.

"Do you want some water?" Violet asked.

Delanie nodded. The movement made her dizzy. She steadied herself and balanced on one of the barstools.

"You don't look so good. The police will be here in a bit. Let me go make sure the witnesses don't leave. Any idea where Easton went?" Violet asked.

"Probably hiding in his office or under a rock," Sven muttered. He paused and stared at Delanie. "You sure you're feeling all right?"

"I think so. The ice and drink help. Thanks."

"How did you get in a fight in the dressing room?" Sven wiped the bar down.

"I came out of the restroom and heard yelling. A woman banged on the door for someone to come out. It turned out to be Easton. She thought I was with him, and she attacked me."

He cracked a slight smile. "Sorry that you got hurt. But I can't see you with Easton."

A wave of nausea gripped Delanie, and she gulped in air.

"You look kinda green." The bartender leaned closer. "Do you want more water or something stronger?"

"No," Violet ordered. "She's white as ghost. Sit down. You need to get checked out."

Delanie obeyed, pulled out her phone, and punched in some numbers. After three rings, Eric answered. "Hey, what's up? It's kinda late."

"Sorry to call at this hour. I got in a little tussle at the club tonight, and I don't feel so good. Could you come and get me?"

"Do you need an ambulance?"

Delanie heard shuffling in the background.

"No, but I think I need to get checked out," she said softly.

"I'll be right there. Stay put." Eric disconnected.

"Here, drink this." Sven put a glass of rum in front of her."

She picked up the glass. The scent brought on a new wave of nausea. Pushing the glass away, she sat up straighter on the barstool and took a few deep breaths.

C. J. and Diego ambled out, carrying gym and suit bags. Their conversation stopped when they spotted the group at the bar.

"Hey, what's going on?" Diego asked. "That gal got in one good surprise hit, but you took care of her after that."

C. J. nodded. "Yep, she's going to need some extra makeup for that shiner Delanie gave her. She'll be feeling it tomorrow."

"I don't think we'll see her around again," Violet added.

About twenty minutes later, Eric strode in from the lobby in jeans and a black leather jacket and motorcycle boots. "Hey, D. Let's go get you checked out. What happened?"

"I got in the way of a scorned woman, and she got a good punch in."

"But Delanie took control of the situation," C. J. added. "I hope you're feeling better. You should have seen the other woman."

Diego nodded and followed C. J. out of the club. "Yep, be well."

"Come on," Eric said, slipping an arm around Delanie's shoulders. "Let's get you checked out. Do we want to press charges?"

"I wasn't the intended target. Not sure if it's worth the hassle." Delanie picked up her purse, hoping that the camera was still working after the pummeling the bag had taken.

In the lobby, Nadia sat on a bench with her head between her knees. She didn't move when they approached. Gwen watched from the greeter's station.

Gwen gave Delanie a once-over and furrowed her brow.

"I'm fine," Delanie said quickly, "But I'm gonna get checked out just in case. Here's my card if the police need to talk to me. Sebastian has the video of the attack."

"They're backed up tonight. Busy night for law enforcement," Gwen said. "I'll pass this along when the officer arrives."

Eric held the door for Delanie. She shivered when the blast of artic air hit her in the face.

"Which hospital?" Eric helped her inside his giant truck.

"There's an urgent care down the road. Let's do that. I want to make sure I'm not concussed."

"Any blurry vision? Nausea?" He climbed in and the truck roared to life.

"My vision's okay. I'm queasy. You a medic, too?" Delanie asked.

"Nah, but I played enough sports to get hit in the head a few times."

In what felt like a few seconds, Eric pulled up to the emergency center and jogged around to open her door.

The electric doors swooshed when they stepped on the rubber mat. Delanie approached the counter and explained what had happened.

The woman handed her a clipboard and took her in the back. Eric followed. The receptionist turned to say something to him, and he flashed his shield. "Right this way," she said.

After ten forms and enough poking and prodding to last Delanie for months, the doctor said, "You don't have a concussion, but you've got some bruising on the side of your face. Go home and get plenty of rest. Don't do anything strenuous for a couple of days. If you get dizzy, nauseated, or have blurred vision, come back in immediately. Take two acetaminophen every four hours for the next twenty-four hours. Any questions?"

Delanie shook her head tentatively and climbed off the small examination table. "Thanks."

By the time Delanie checked out, it was after three in the morning. "I'm sorry to keep you out so late. Thank you for picking me up."

"Not a problem. Do you have Tylenol, or do we need to stop at an all-night drugstore?" Eric asked.

"I'm good. I need some sleep, and maybe a day off."

Delanie startled when the truck stopped in her driveway. She must have dozed off. Eric walked around the truck to help her out. "Keys."

She handed him her keys. The floodlights popped on as they approached the porch. "Let's get you settled," he said.

"I've got to figure out a way to get my car back in case I need it tomorrow," she said, climbing the steps to the small porch.

"I can get your Mustang back here for you," Eric said.

"You don't have to do that. I can call Duncan for a ride. I'm sure he'll be around," she said. She hoped he didn't take her comment the wrong way. Her head was throbbing, and all she really wanted to do was to lie down.

"I don't mind." He held his hand out.

He pulled he fob with the silver horse on it off her keyring. "Need anything?" he asked, handing her the remaining keys.

"Nope. I'm headed to bed. See you later."

He kissed her on her forehead and touched the side of her face lightly. "You've got quite a bruise. Call me if you need anything."

Eric let himself out and jiggled the knob to ensure it was locked. Delanie made her way gingerly to her bathroom and downed two Tylenol. She cringed when she saw the teal and purple bruise on her cheek.

A few hours later, sun streamed in through her bedroom window, and Delanie rolled over. Her face throbbed when she rubbed it against the pillow, but at least her head wasn't pounding.

The pulsating, steamy shower washed off the groggies. She threw on a VCU Rams sweatshirt and jeans and used more makeup than normal to cover up her colorful bruise.

As she was hoping there was something to eat in the house, she heard a car door slam and a knock at the door. She padded through her cottage's living room and peeked out the front window.

Eric stood on her small porch with doughnuts and coffee. His truck dwarfed her black Mustang that was parked in front of it.

She opened the door and glanced over his shoulder. "Thank you so much for getting my car. You didn't have to do that. And you brought breakfast." The mental Jenga of how he had returned her car and got his truck here gave her a slight headache. Too much to think about before her first coffee.

He kissed her and followed her inside. "Feeling better?"

"Much better. Thanks."

Eric set the box of Krispy Kreme doughnuts on the table. "Those were hot off the rack. Hopefully, they're still warm after my drive across the river."

Delanie handed him a plate and napkin and settled in the kitchen chair next to him. "Yum. They're still warm."

Conversation stopped as they dove into the doughnuts. The sugar and the coffee helped, and she almost felt like her normal self.

"What have you got planned today?" she asked, licking the sticky sugar off of her fingers.

"I've got to go in this afternoon. I caught a local case, so I should be in town for a while. Let me know if you want to have dinner on Friday."

"I'd like that."

"How about I pick you up at six-thirty?" He downed the last few drops of his coffee.

"That works. Let me know if something changes," she said.

Eric nodded. "You need anything?"

"I'm good. I appreciate all you've done."

He smiled. "My pleasure. If you don't need anything, I'm going to head out." He kissed her again and sent a charge through her. "I'll check on you later today."

Delanie kissed him again. It took a few minutes to calm the butterflies that were banging around inside of her. He may not be around all the time, but he cared. Not like Easton's type who spent most of his time dodging and disappearing.

Chapter Eighteen

Delanie's phone rang as she opened her office's front door. She glanced down at the screen. "Hey, Duncan. I'm coming in the front door now. Where are you?"

"Just checking in on you. I didn't hear from you yesterday. Margaret and I are headed in too. Want me to pick up lunch?"

"Sounds good. I needed to recuperate after my last adventure at the Cheeky Monkey."

"I'll be there in a few, and you can tell me all about it. Do you like the Coney dogs at Sonic?"

"Sure. Just a hot dog with mustard on it."

"See ya in a few. Margaret went on a long walk today, and now we both need a treat."

By the time Delanie settled in her office, she heard her partner and his four-legged sidekick come in through the back. "Lunch is served. Meet me in the conference room," he yelled.

"Whoa! What happened to you?" Duncan stopped suddenly, and Margaret ran into the back of his calf.

"I got into an altercation with one of the Cheeky Monkey patrons. This woman was yelling through a door at one of the guys in the dressing room about two-timing her. And when she got in, she pounced. I happened to be in the line of fire."

"Lots of drama over there." Duncan spread out lunch on the conference room table. "You sure you're okay?"

She nodded. "It turns out she was yelling at Easton and not one of the dancers."

Duncan's eyebrows rose. "I've been poking around in his past a bit. He seems to be quite the character. I'm still digging, so I haven't sent you the details, but here's what I know so far. Besides the acting and modeling stints, he's started a variety of businesses with varying degrees of success over the years. He opened a check-cashing place with a guy in Boston. He did that for about three years, and then his partner got arrested. That's when he moved west to Las Vegas where he got involved with slot machines. The idea was to buy them and put them in local businesses. I don't think he really knew about the gaming industry, and he ended up with a warehouse of old machines that nobody wanted. After that crashed and then the warehouse burned down, he moved to Arizona and got into the car business. That seemed to do well until the accident."

"He's never mentioned his past jobs, just the cities where he lived. I may need to do some poking myself." Delanie took a bite of her hot dog and savored the taste of grilled meat.

"Just watch out for his crazy girlfriend." Duncan rolled his eyes. "Has anyone posted the video of your tussle yet?"

"More like catfight. I haven't had a chance to go looking for it. Hopefully, it's not out there," she said with a grimace.

"Hey," he said. "I found a couple of articles and videos about the accident that killed Dare Davidson. It happened somewhere in the desert on a back road, and Easton ended up walking for several miles until he found a ride." Duncan licked the last bit of chili off his fingers. "Just stay clear of his crazy women," he repeated.

"Her name was Nadia. Not sure if the angry girlfriend is important to any of this." Delanie finished her hotdog and balled up the wrapper. "Easton said he came back to Virginia after his partner's death. Let's see what you found." Duncan turned his laptop toward her, and she read several online articles and watched two clips from the news.

"The articles were old, so I had to dig through some stuff to find them. It looks like the car was completely torched," Duncan said, leaning over her shoulder.

"It's a wonder he was able to get out and walk forever to find help. I'm sorry about his partner." Delanie pushed Duncan's laptop closer to him.

"I found some more stuff in the darker corners of the big web. Easton took a hit on that business, too. That Dare guy had a lot of credit card and gambling debts. When he sold the dealership, he had to split the profits with Dare's heirs. From what I could find, the dealership was profitable, and they were living high on the hog for a few years. And then things tanked."

Delanie gathered up the trash. "I'm headed over to the club this afternoon. I feel like I'm spinning my wheels. I've got folks I'm watching, and your camera has been great. Speaking of that, I forgot to check it after my fight yesterday to see if it's still working."

Duncan reached for the purse camera and connected it to his laptop. "Seems to be downloading fine. I saved your files to the server. Let's see what the picture looks like." He pointed the side of the purse toward her and then Margaret, who opened one eye and decided she wasn't amused with the paparazzi. "It seems to be okay and ready for another night of fun at the Cheeky Monkey."

"I know all the routines by heart. I'm going to go through the footage to see if the camera caught anything." Delanie settled in the chair and tipped the laptop screen toward her. Watching hours of hidden camera footage was almost as bad as stakeouts.

After an hour and a half of forwarding and reversing footage, she closed her laptop. "Nothing. It's like the culprit is a ghost." She picked up her phone and pushed Marco's contact as she retreated to her office.

"Hey, D. What's up? How are you feeling? Gwen said you got into it with one of Easton's women."

"I'm fine. Nothing that some rest wouldn't fix. Hey, I've gone through all my hidden camera footage at the club, and I caught nothing. Just checking in to see if your new cameras have found anything?"

"Steve and I were looking at footage from last night. We've only captured the staff doing routine things. Nothing unusual."

Delanie let out a heavy sigh. "I'm watching a few people, and Duncan's still looking into backgrounds. Nothing on my end either. It's frustrating."

"Hang in there. Bad guys usually trip up, and when they do, we'll be there to catch 'em."

"Thanks. I'll let you know if I find anything."

"Same here." He disconnected.

Duncan bounded in her office with Margaret hot on his heels.

"I got the DNA results back on Diego. Nothing to raise any eyebrows. His background's pretty clean, too. Just a few parking tickets. He did have a stalking charge from the mid-nineties. From what I could piece together, his girlfriend dumped him, and he followed her around until she got creeped out and called the cops. Nothing on his record since. I'm still waiting on Easton's sample."

"I need to know the why. What would motivate someone to pull all these stunts? Money? Revenge? Attention-seeking?" She doodled on a piece a paper as she listed the names. Violet seemed to be angry all the time and jealous of Easton. Sven was mysterious. And Bruce and Stone wanted Diego's job.

Delanie packed up her things. "Thanks for all of your help with this. I'm going to the gym to take out some of this frustration on the weight machines."

"Persistence," Duncan said. "We always get our person."

"I certainly hope so. This case feels different. I hope it doesn't ruin our record," she said.

After a lighter than usual workout which included a stretching class, Delanie felt charged and ready to take on the Cheeky Monkey. She stopped for an iced tea and then made her way to Goochland for another night of fun at Chaz's male revue.

She waved to Gwen and Sven and settled in at a corner table to watch rehearsal for what felt like the millionth time. She turned on her camera and hoped it would surprise her with something tonight. *Not sure what I'll do if I don't get a break soon.*

Rehearsal blended into showtime just like twilight turned into night. Every time Delanie started to fidget, she'd walk around the bar or the stage. Easton waved to her once from a distance, but he made a point of looking busy. He hadn't spoken to her since the Nadia incident.

After the second time of his ducking to avoid her glance, she followed him down the hallway toward his office.

"Oh, hi. Where did you come from?" Easton asked.

Delanie pasted on her most charming smile. "Just checking on things around here. Anything out of the ordinary going on tonight?"

Easton shook his head and crossed into his office. "Getting some marketing ideas together for my meeting with Chaz tomorrow. He wants me to pitch him some new stuff. Ewww. You've got a shiner."

"Yes, your friend threw some wild punches."

His face darkened. "She's not my friend. Just some girl I spoke with at the bar, and she thought my politeness was more than it was. I guess she's lucky you didn't press charges. You didn't press charges, right?"

Delanie turned her head slightly and stared. "What's her name in case I change my mind?" Her hand touched the bruised side of her face, and she winced.

"Nadia Kemp," he answered abruptly. "And I think we've seen the last of her." For some gal who made a scene about broken promises and exotic trips, he was quick to dismiss her. *So much for Nadia's trip to Jamaica.*

When Delanie didn't respond, he continued, "And how's your boyfriend? I figured he would make sure you got home safely."

Double standard. Jealous, Easton?

"All's well." Delanie smiled. "Thanks for asking," she said sweetly. By the way, I was going through my notes last night, and I was curious. What brought you here to Richmond?"

He picked up several folders on his desk and slid into his chair. "I have family here."

"So, one day, you decided to come home?"

"Something like that. I was in a bad car wreck that killed my business partner. It seemed like a good time. I needed a change of scenery."

"So, tell me about Dare."

His head jerked, and then he paused. "He was my friend. And he died that awful day. The day that changed my life forever."

"I'm sorry," she said quietly.

"It was a gorgeous day, and we had gone for a ride in the desert in the Ferrari he acquired for the dealership. After stopping to take sunset pictures, he opened it up on a stretch of empty road. He lost control, and the car flipped several times and caught on fire. I got out, but I couldn't get him out. The flames engulfed the car in minutes." He paused and coughed. "What a horrible way to go. My life changed in an instant. I walked miles to get help. I guess I had a lot of time to think that day and in the weeks after the accident, and like I said, it was time for a change."

"I'm sure Chaz is glad you're back. It's nice to have family support."

He nodded. "You didn't tell me anything about your family." Easton leaned back in his chair with his hands behind his head.

"I have two older brothers. And you're right. It's good to have family." *I neglected to mention that they both work long hours, are never around, and aren't totally cool with my career choice.*

"They like what you do for a living?" He snickered like it was a private joke.

Delanie could feel the heat rising in her cheeks. "It pays the bills, and I love my job. My brothers are supportive of me."

"And protective, I'm sure."

"What about your family besides Chaz?" Delanie changed the subject.

"We're not all that close. I'm closer with Chaz and his siblings. I don't have much contact with the other side of the family."

Delanie tried not to let her face talk for her. She didn't correct him this time about Chaz's lack of siblings. *He's made this mistake a couple of times now. He's definitely lying, but I'm not ready for a confrontation yet.* Delanie swallowed her retort and said, "I have to ask. What was Chaz like as a kid?"

He turned his head slightly. "He was older, but I thought he was so sophisticated, and I wanted to do everything he did. I'm sure he thought I was a royal pain. I even started dressing like him. I'll have to see if I can find pictures. We looked like the Back Street Boys or maybe the New Kids on the Block." He laughed.

Delanie smiled, trying to picture Chaz in a boy band. Somehow that didn't seem like his kind of cool, even as a teen. "It's getting late, so I'm going to head out. See you later this week."

"Making any progress with your investigation?" he asked as she turned toward the doorway.

"It's moving along. I've collected a lot of data on folks. Hopefully, I'll have news soon." She turned and left. When she returned to the dining room, she blended in with the crowd of women of all ages who flooded out the front door. It was really classy that Easton neglected to apologize for hiding behind her during the altercation with Nadia.

It took three or four songs on the radio before she and the crowd of cars merged onto the main road. The traffic thinned out slightly near the Route 288 intersection. She let out a breath she didn't realize she was holding. Cranking up the heat and the radio, Delanie settled in for the drive across the river. Her mind wandered and lulled her into cruise mode in the nonexistent traffic back to Chesterfield County.

A few miles before the river, the high beams on the car behind her cut through her Mustang. No other cars on the straight stretch of highway. The car slowed down as it approached. She moved into the left lane to reduce the glare from his headlights. He changed lanes. She swore under her breath. Checking the other lane, she zipped back in the right lane, and the other car did the same move. It was a dark SUV or crossover. Maybe a BMW or a Mercedes. It was hard to tell with the glare. She sped up, and the car behind her adjusted its pace.

Delanie checked her mirror and cut over into the right lane. Before the car could hop behind her, she slammed on brakes, and he rocketed forward. She ducked off at the Huguenot Trail exit. She turned around in a church parking lot and hopped back on the interstate. *Crazy drivers or is it something else?*

It took several miles before her heart rate returned to normal, and her thoughts drifted to other things besides the aggressive driver. Tomorrow, she would sit down with all her Cheeky Monkey footage and notes and go through every detail again. She had to be missing something.

At the next exit, a dark sedan sat in the emergency lane. She zipped past it. A few seconds later, its lights flashed, and the car zoomed forward. *This doesn't feel like a drunk driver or an angry road-rager. Someone's playing cat and mouse with me.*

Delanie floored the accelerator, and the Mustang roared to life. Eighty-five flashed on the speedometer. She'd deal with a ticket if it came to that. The car fell back in the rearview mirror. Relaxing her right foot until she was in the seventy miles per hour range, Delanie let out a small sigh. Then the idiot sped up behind her and tailed her around the cloverleaf at the Hull Street Road exit.

"I'll fix you." Delanie jumped over into the right lane and flew past the turn. Staying in the right lane, she drove up and down the hilly route past Brandermill and Woodlake. At the top of the hill, she made a quick right into the back of the shopping center near the police substation and parked at the curb. Delanie held her breath. She silently dared the driver to get out.

The black car killed its lights and cruised slowly past the Mustang.

Delanie couldn't see anything inside the tinted windows. Her blood pressure felt like a snare drum inside her head.

The driver floored it, and the car's tires squealed out the shopping center's back exit.

Maybe she would call her cop brother to see if any of the police station cameras caught the psycho driver's license plate. It was always awkward to explain what she was doing when he got judgy about her career choice and the late hours she kept.

On second thought, she shook off the jitters and put the car in drive. She headed home, checking the rearview mirror about twenty times before the floodlights popped on in the driveway.

Once inside her bungalow, she leaned against the locked front door. *That wasn't a random encounter. But on a positive note, it meant I was getting close enough to the truth to make someone nervous.*

After a glass of milk, she climbed into bed, pulled her gun out the drawer, and set it on the nightstand. Just in case.

Chapter Nineteen

Delanie stretched and rubbed her eyes. She had been pouring over her notes and watching camera footage since seven-thirty this morning. *Absolutely nothing new. Definitely frustrating.*

She wandered over to the refrigerator and poked around to see if there was anything to snack on and settled on a piece of cheddar cheese and a glass of iced tea.

Flipping through Duncan's notes, she found what she was looking for. Dare Davidson, Easton's former partner, had two kids and an ex-wife. She plugged in the mother's name, Tamara Adkins, in her online people search website. Popping up a few hits, she said out loud, "A-ha. I found you." A Tammy Adkins who was once Tammy Davidson. She and her two kids, Chandler and Helene, still lived in Mesa, Arizona.

Tapping in the phone number, Delanie waited for the connection. "Hello."

"Ms. Adkins, this is Delanie Fitzgerald, a private investigator with Falcon Investigations. I'm working on a case in Richmond, Virginia that involves your former husband's business partner, and I wanted to know if you could answer a few questions for me."

"Sure, but he had lots of business partners. Dare dabbled in every get-rich-quick scheme that came along. Not sure if I can help, but I'll try."

"It's Easton Marsh and Mesa Motors," Delanie added.

"That was one of Dare's successful ventures, I guess. At least the kids got something out of it. He met Easton at a party somewhere, and they seemed to be birds of a feather. Smooth talkers chasing the almighty dollar and any skirt that came along. They had the car dealership and spin-off businesses for about eight years."

"Spin-offs?"

"Yep. They had a car detailing thing, a body shop, and something with classic car sales. It was going well until it didn't. We were divorced right about that time, so I didn't keep up too much with his antics except to make sure the child support payments were on time. With him, it was kind of a roller coaster. Things were great for a while, but they always tanked. There was constantly some sort of excuse of why he was late with the check. It was always someone else's fault. Even when we were married, he was busy with whatever project he was working on." Tammy lowered her voice. "We found out about the accident from a news broadcast."

"I'm sorry for your loss," Delanie said.

"It is what it is. We'd drifted apart by then. I fell for that fabulous smile and all his big dreams. It didn't take long after we were married for me to figure out that it was mostly all talk. And then came the dalliances. He always had friends like Easton who encouraged him to chase women and add notches to his conquest list. That's not how I wanted to live. That's about all I can tell you."

"Did he have any other relatives?"

"He had a sister who used to live in Michigan. When his estate was settled, she had passed away, too. So, I guess my kids are his only relatives."

"Do you know anything about Easton's background?" Delanie asked.

"Not really. I tuned him out a lot. He was from back east and quick to tell everyone that he came from money. He was proud of his Virginia roots. He liked to let it be known that his relatives could be traced to the Jamestown colonists. That's about it. He was annoying, and I avoided him any chance I could."

"Thank you again for answering my questions," Delanie said.

"No problem. I hope it helps."

Delanie jotted down what Tammy had said. *Birds of a feather. It sounds like Dare and Easton made quite the pair.*

Wondering if the accident held any clues, she opened the file on Dare's death and scanned through the photos. She Googled Mesa Motors in Arizona. A couple of stories about the accident popped up. Nothing related to the business. There was one short article that the new owners had renamed the dealership and folded it into a larger car conglomerate in the area.

On a whim, Delanie found a website with digitized high school yearbooks. She did a search for Easton and Dare. Easton had graduated from a private prep school near Philadelphia. Even as a teen, he was always in the center of the action. Most Popular, Most Likely to Succeed, soccer team, chess club, fencing team, and debate team. Easton's hair looked lighter in the grainy photos. She made copies for her file. *Interesting. Maybe he colors his hair.*

It took longer to locate Dare. Darrell Davidson attended high school in multiple cities. His last two years were in Norfolk, Virginia, where his dad had been stationed in the Navy. Delanie enlarged the pixelated photos. Dare was the tall, dark, and handsome one, always in the center of some group of kids. Tammy was right about that smile. Photography club, soccer team, rugby team, and student council. She counted over eighty pictures of him in his junior yearbook.

Delanie saved the files and all the yearbook photos. Facts were everywhere, but no strong leads. She had never had a case that she couldn't solve before. She tapped her pen on the table. *This one might ruin my record.*

Pulling out the timeline of pranks and problems that included the flour in the kitchen, fire in the prop room, and the tainted alcohol at the bar, Delanie sank deeper into her kitchen chair. It had been several days where everything was quiet at the club except for the jerk who tailgated her. Who was she making uncomfortable? Something tickled the back of her thoughts, but she couldn't quite put her finger on what it was. She picked up her timeline again. It looked like the events happened at a regular frequency with very few gaps between. *Until recently.*

She debated whether she should go to the Cheeky Monkey tonight. It felt like a waste of time but being there kept her on the scene with all the players. *Maybe I can make someone nervous if I drop a few hints that I'm onto something? It's time to shake things up some more.*

But first, a shower. The heat relaxed her muscles. After toweling off, she found a purple sweater and skinny jeans. She rounded her outfit off with her suede black boots and grabbed two aspirin to keep the aches at bay.

Glancing once more at her notes, she was determined to catch a break in this case. She flipped her purse strap over her shoulder and let herself out the side door of her bungalow.

Delanie pulled into the front parking lot of the Cheeky Monkey, pocketed her keys and phone, and pulled her camera-purse out of the backseat. "Let's see what tonight brings," she said aloud.

Stone, Diego, C.J., and Sebastian wrapped up rehearsal as she settled in at a table to the left of the stage.

Sven dropped off a ginger ale. "Let me know if you need anything stronger." He winked.

"Thanks for the great service," she said.

"And you're in for a treat. Diego's new props arrived today, so the show's got a whole new look." Sven returned to wiping down the bar. "How are things going for you?"

"Pretty well." She hoped he wasn't staring at her bruise. "I think I'm onto something and will have some news for Chaz soon."

Delanie turned on her camera and sat back to watch the goings on. The slow trickle of patrons turned into a flood a few minutes before seven. Gwen and her guards, as well as the bartenders, zipped around the club.

After Easton introduced the dancers and disappeared behind the black curtain, Delanie raised her eyebrows at the silver-sequined chaps and cowboy hats the dancers showed off. It looked like a Vegas revue, but the women packed in the dining room loved it. The noise level rivaled a rock concert. The crowd, fanning dollar bills for the dancers, flocked to the edge of the stage.

During the third set, Delanie wandered down the hall. Closed doors greeted her when she passed Gwen and Violet's offices. She heard noise coming from Easton's office, so she stuck her head in.

He was talking loudly and waving his arm around. "No. Definitely not. I'm not interested." He clicked off and slung his phone on the desk. "Oh, hi. How are you? Just dealing with my credit card company. I hate when I have to dispute something. It seems to be a monthly thing lately and a big headache. Enough of my problems. What brings you by?" He turned on his famous Easton smile.

"Just checking in. Everything going smoothly? I saw the new costumes."

"Aren't they great? I got them from a friend in Nevada. They take the show to a new level."

Delanie nodded and smiled. *Definitely Sin City costumes.* "Any trouble lately?" she asked.

"Nope. Our clown seems to have taken a break. Maybe he gave up."

Delanie hesitated. "He or she will slip up. And I have a couple of hunches. If they pan out, I'll have an update for Chaz very soon."

Easton's eyebrows shot up to his hairline. "Anything you can share? Any sneak previews?"

"Not yet. I want to make sure I'm right before I accuse anyone," she said coyly.

"No little hints?" he asked, leaning forward.

She smiled again. "Let me do a little more research. Soon. It will be soon. I promise."

"Okay, if you won't dish about our culprit. Maybe I can learn more about you."

Where is he going with the abrupt shift?

Easton looked around the room. "So, what did you want to be when you were a kid?" he asked, changing the subject.

"An astronaut and a ballerina. What about you?"

"An Indy car driver or a soldier," he said.

"How were chess club and fencing?" Delanie asked.

A puzzled look crossed his face. "I didn't do geek stuff like that.

You think I was in the AV Club or something? I played rugby and soccer."

That's not what his yearbook said. Delanie made a mental note to do some follow up. "Tough sports. My brother Robbie played soccer and baseball. He made it to the minor leagues before he got injured."

"That stinks." He paused and stared at her. "You know, about your brother's injury..."

Delanie took a deep breath, "I'm headed out soon. I'll see you tomorrow."

"Night." Easton lifted the lid of his laptop. "Drive safely. They're a lot of kooks out there on the road."

The hair on the back of her neck stood at attention. His comment caused her to pause and flashback to the crazy driver incident. She shook off the ominous feeling and made a circuit by the dressing room. She passed C. J. and Sebastian on their way out with gym and suit bags. "See ya." She waved.

Both men nodded as Diego stuck his head out of the doorway and flipped off the dressing room lights. "Night all. Good show."

"I liked the new outfits," Delanie said.

"The tips were phenomenal tonight. Maybe Easton's flashy costumes are better," Sebastian said.

The dancers filed out and left Delanie in the empty backstage area. She wandered to the kitchen where Hector buzzed in and out with his closing tasks.

"How are you?" she asked, stepping closer to the large aluminum table in the center of the room.

"Good. Wrapping up here. Everything's prepped and put away for tomorrow," Hector replied. "Be back in a sec. I need to get these glasses to Sven."

Hector hefted three trays of glassware and hustled out the door while Delanie explored the pantry and prep areas. Near the back exit, the giant silver door of the freezer stood like a sentry, guarding Javi's kitchen.

The lights flickered and went out, plunging the kitchen into almost complete darkness. She saw a red light across the room. Delanie heard a click and then a hum. She froze, listening for additional sounds.

Tap, tap, tap. She felt the air move behind her. Blood whooshed through her veins as her heart pounded.

She reached for her phone to turn on her flashlight.

Someone grabbed her around her waist and lifted her off the ground. She got a whiff of some kind of musky body spray. She smacked the intruder with her camera-purse. He slung her around and grunted.

She swung her purse again.

He snatched it and threw it across the room where it skidded across the tiles.

A blast of arctic air hit Delanie in the face. The arms around her released, and she landed on the hard floor. One last shove sent her hurtling toward the deepest corner of the sub-zero container. Stumbling, she landed on a cardboard box. Before she could scrabble to her feet, the door slammed, leaving her alone in the cold and dark.

Panic and bile welled up inside of Delanie. *Stay calm. Breathe. I am not going to die here. I can get out.*

She pulled her phone of her back pocket and turned on her flashlight. No lock on the door. Just a metal turn handle. She twisted it and pushed the door. It moved slightly and stopped. She shivered and tried again. Her teeth had started to chatter. Delanie pushed and body slammed the door several times with no success.

Something was blocking it. She took a deep breath and texted Marco, Gwen, Easton, Chaz, and Violet. Then she called Gwen.

Delanie's hands and arms shook. After two rings, an answer, "Hello."

"Gwen. This is Delanie. Are you still at the club?"

"Just getting the lights back on with Violet. What's up?"

"Someone shoved me in the walk-in freezer when the lights went out, and I can't get out. The door's blocked."

"Oh, my stars. What else is going to happen? Keep talking. I'm on my way. Are you okay?" Gwen asked.

"Just cold," Delanie said.

Delanie heard feet pounding on the kitchen tiles. Then there was shuffling. Delanie banged on the door with her fist.

The door made a sucking sound. Gwen, Easton, and Violet burst in.

"Are you okay?" Gwen asked. "Do I need to call an ambulance?"

"I'm chilled to the bone, but I'll be okay after I warm up," Delanie said, through chattering teeth.

"Come with me. We'll get you something hot," Violet clutched Delanie's elbow and guided her down the hallway to the bar. She put an empty pot on the coffee machine and flipped the orange button.

"That'll take too long." Easton pushed past Violet and poured tequila in a glass. He set the shot glass in front of her. "Bottoms up."

Delanie took a swig and made a face. The drink burned all the way down her throat. She coughed. "Thanks."

"Are you sure you're okay?" Easton leaned over and stared at her. "I should probably take you to get checked out. What if you got frostbite?" Easton leaned over and stared at her.

"I wasn't in there that long," Delanie said.

He took both of her hands and rubbed them. "I think you should let me take you to the care center to get checked out."

"She'll be fine." Violet set a mug of steamy black coffee in front of her.

Delanie pulled away from Easton and picked up the mug with both hands. "Just what I needed." Between the tequila and coffee, she could feel her toes again.

"What happened?" Violet asked.

"I was in the kitchen talking to Hector. He took some glasses to the bar, and the lights went out. Before I could move, someone attacked me from behind.

"Any idea who it was? Hector?" Easton asked.

"No. He didn't have time to put down all the glasses, cut the lights, and sneak up behind me," Delanie said. "I think someone came in through the back door." She slid off the barstool and grabbed the edge of the bar to stop the dizzy feeling. Recovering, she walked briskly to the kitchen.

"The back door is unlocked," Delanie said, opening the door. "But the freezer door was blocked by something."

"It was a door stop," Violet said. "And they leave the kitchen door unlocked when the club is open, but it's on the kitchen staff's list of things to do when closing up. Where's Hector?" Violet looked around.

"I'll find him," Easton said.

Delanie picked up her pursecam, hoping that it was still working.

"He's out here with Sven," Easton yelled from the bar.

Hector stood between Easton and Sven. His head dipped slightly.

"Hector, did you lock the back door to the kitchen tonight?" Violet glared at the bear of a man.

"Of course. As soon as we closed, I took out the trash and locked the door when I got back. That's Javi's number one rule. Follow the checklist."

"You're sure?" Easton asked. "You could have gotten distracted."

"Locking the door and verifying it is on Javi's list," Hector repeated. "I know I locked it after I took the trash out."

"Well, it isn't locked now." Violet put her hands on her hips. "Someone threw Delanie in the freezer. I'll be so glad when we get those blasted cameras fixed. Thanks, Hector. If you see anything out of sorts in the kitchen, please let me know."

"I'll go check again before I leave," he said, making a quick exit.

Delanie scooted close to him and slowed his escape. "Hector, do you know anyone who wears a lot of body spray." She sniffed to see if she could get a whiff of cologne on him.

A bewildered look crossed Hector's face. "Nah, that's for the young bucks trying to pick up girls. They bathe in the stuff. I'm an Aqua Velva man."

"Just curious. Thanks," Delanie said. "I thought I smelled heavy cologne when I was in the freezer."

Easton took a step away from the group and clapped his hands to get everyone's attention. "All right, guys, let's wrap this up and go home. It's been a long day," Easton looked at Delanie. "You sure you don't want me to drive you to get looked at?"

She shook her head. The motion made her slightly dizzy. She paused until the feeling passed.

"At least, let me walk you to your car," Easton said, moving to her side.

"Thanks, but Gwen will. I have to catch her up on a few things."

"Of course," Gwen said, motioning for Delanie to head out. "Marco needs an update."

When they were in the parking lot with enough distance from the building, Delanie said, "Thanks so much. I'm going to see if my hidden camera picked up anything. My attacker threw it against the wall, so I hope it's not broken."

"I'll check Steve and Marco's cameras and let you know what I find."

"Here I am." Delanie pointed to the lone car in the third row. "Thanks. It was definitely a guy with a strong body spray smell, and he was taller than me."

"That could be anyone around here except me and Violet." The security guard laughed. "Take care." She patted the roof of the Mustang as soon as Delanie fired the engine.

Delanie wanted a hot bath and her jammies to get that body spray smell off her clothes and hair. But that would have to wait until she checked her pursecam footage.

Chapter Twenty

After turning on all the downstairs lights in her bungalow on, Delanie started the coffee machine using with the strongest blend she could find. It was going to be a long night, or an early morning. All the hours at the Cheeky Monkey were getting old, but she was too charged to head to bed. First, someone tailgated her on the way home this week, and tonight, she had the freezer incident. *I think I spooked someone at the club.*

When the coffee was ready, she hunkered down at her kitchen table to pour over the evening's footage. She zoomed to the point right before the lights went out in the club's kitchen.

Surreally, she watched the path she'd followed into the kitchen and listened to her talk with Hector and his three trays of glasses. Then everything went black. She heard a scuffle, some grunts, and a thud when she hit him with her purse. Then more blackness. On a whim, she sped through the next few minutes. The lights came on. Delanie heard voices and feet pounding on the floor. Everything looked whitish gray. The camera faced the wall. Then she heard the freezer door open and the discussion before she and the group left for the bar.

Delanie fast forwarded again and saw the purse rise. The picture tilted and jerked, and she saw Gwen walk out to the car with her. It captured their conversation, and then the camera went black again, but she could hear traffic and her car radio in the background.

She picked the pursecam off the floor. The red light was still on. "This thing has taken a beating," she said to herself, turning off the camera and setting it on her table.

Delanie scooted her laptop closer and rewatched hours of footage. Then she played it again at a faster speed, frame after frame of people coming and going. Her eyes stung from staring at the laptop screen. Shutting off the video viewer, Delanie opened her notes.

Last night, she'd talked to Hector, Gwen, Easton, Sven, and Violet. A guy who wore heavy cologne or body spray threw her in the freezer when the lights went out. So, someone had to turn off the lights and get to the kitchen where she was. Or he was working with a partner. It's too much of a coincidence for the lights to go out as some random guy was stalking her in the kitchen. The mechanical closet was in the hallway, so it wasn't that much of a stretch that the guy could have seen her, killed the lights, and ran into the kitchen. He would have had to have known she was there and an idea of the kitchen layout because it was pitch black. *Think, Delanie. What else besides he was taller than me and wore that stinky cologne?*

She sighed and saved her notes. Delanie stretched. Seven-thirty in the morning. Probably still too early for Marco, but she sent a text anyway.

Good morning. Did your cameras pick up anything last night at the CM after closing?

At the gym now. Wanna meet me at the Treasure Chest at 9?

Perfect. See you then.

Maybe a hot shower would help her wake up. After drying off, she glanced in the mirror. The pulsing water felt good, but it didn't do anything for the bags under her eyes. At least, the bruise from the chick fight had started to fade slightly. Heavy foundation made it almost disappear. At least there were no other visible injuries from her time at the Cheeky Monkey.

After pulling on jeans and a pink sweater, she had time for peanut butter toast and another mug of coffee before she packed up her gear and headed downtown. Fishing her sunglasses out of the car's console, she hoped they'd block the unseasonably bright rays and her raccoon eyes.

After cruising through a warren of narrow downtown streets, Delanie had her choice of parking spaces at Chaz's Treasure Chest.

She climbed out of her Mustang, and Marco popped out of the side door. "It's good to see you. Gwen said you had a freezer incident last night. You doing okay?"

"Hi. I'm fine. Thanks for checking. I got surprised when the lights went out. Not sure who grabbed me. I was hoping your cameras caught more than mine did. It's time we find out who this guy is." She stepped through the doorway and took the hallway toward the office. Marco followed.

"Steve's in the security office," Marco said as she stopped in front of the closed door.

Marco knocked several times with his knuckle and then opened the door.

A pale guy with shaggy hair looked up from behind a bank of computer monitors. "Hey." He reached over and removed a stack of papers and magazines from the guest chair next to him. "Sorry. It's a mess in here. I've been going through last night's footage," Steve said.

"Find anything?" Marco asked.

"Nope. Javi, Hector, and Sven were doing a lot of running around. Right before the power went out, those two went up and down the hall several times. Violet showed up a couple of times. She kind of paused once, and then she went to her office. That's her walking around in a hoodie," he said, pointing to the monitor. "That's it. Then everything plunged into darkness."

Violet in a hoodie?

"My hidden camera captured Hector, Sven, Gwen, Easton, and Violet too when I was trapped in the freezer. There's no video after the lights went out. The camera was slung up against a wall, but you can hear the audio of the scuffle."

"This is getting out of hand," Steve said. "They aren't pranks anymore."

"I think we're putting the pressure on someone," Delanie said.

"That could be a good thing. I'm hoping he'll slip up. And like I told Chaz, I think all of the other stuff is cover for something bigger, a distraction, so something won't be noticed."

Marco raised an eyebrow. "I couldn't figure out why stupid pranks kept happening unless they were to annoy someone or get one of the staff in trouble."

"I don't think all the things that happened were aimed at the club. I think the creepy doll was a coincidence. And the couple of incidents that were directed at me were because I was poking around and asking questions."

"Good point," Steve said. "I've got nothing here on any of my feeds except staff running in and out of the camera shot."

"Thanks for checking on it. I'm going to keep my hidden camera on while I'm there. Who knows? Maybe something will appear, or he will trip up."

"You need to talk to Chaz?" Marco asked. "He usually doesn't come in until lunch time."

"I'll call him later. I'm going to head out. I've got some things to do," Delanie said.

She followed Marco down the hallway. From behind, his shoulders looked like they almost brushed the walls. When he opened the metal door, he said, "I want to you be careful and keep Gwen in the loop on everything you do there. I'm going to show up randomly, too."

Delanie patted his massive bicep. "I will. And I appreciate you looking after me. We're going to get this guy. It's definitely personal now."

He cracked a smile that showed his gold tooth. "Get 'em, tiger."

Delanie had every intention of doing so.

She zoomed home to get some sleep before another round at the Cheeky Monkey.

§

DELANIE FELT BETTER when her alarm beeped at four o'clock. Sleep, a shower, and a double espresso made a world of difference. She stopped for a drive-thru dinner and headed over to the club to see what she might find this evening. Convinced it was one of the staff, she decided to focus on the back office, bar, and kitchen. This guy can't be lucky all the time.

Parking near a light, she locked her car and activated her pursecam. Shouting and sounds of chairs scooting across the laminate floor broke her chain of thought. She rushed toward the bar.

Diego faced the stage and waved his arms around. "No. No. Not in this lifetime. Not ever. It's a stupid idea."

Stone, standing on the stage with legs spread apart and hand on his hips, rolled his eyes like a petulant child. "You never let us have any input. This would be so much better if we exited on either side after that number and then raced back with cap guns blazing. The surprise effect is great for an audience. You never listen to anything I have to say." His attitude increased with every sentence.

Jayden and Bruce distanced themselves from the fracas. Jayden tapped on his phone, but he looked up every few seconds.

Stone's ears reddened. Delanie stared as he mocked Diego's gestures and made faces.

"This discussion is over," Diego said. "You're unprofessional. We do the number like we rehearsed it, or you don't do it at all. I can find another waiter," Diego said.

"I. Am. An. Entertainer." Stone spat out the words. He vaulted off the stage and ran toward Diego.

Diego tensed and stepped closer to the approaching dancer.

Hesitating for a moment, Stone glared at Diego. Then he looked around the room. "I can't stay where I am not appreciated. I quit." He stormed down the hallway. A door slammed a few seconds later.

Diego pulled out his phone and tapped a contact. "Hey, man. How's it going? I have a shift opening tonight. Can you fill in? We're rehearsing now." After a pause, he continued, "Great. I appreciate it."

He disconnected and slid the phone in his pocket. "You guys take a break. Maybe get food. Eliot will be here soon. We'll go through it one more time. I need to go talk to Violet." He strode down the hall.

Delanie followed casually, pretending to check her phone.

Stone's loud voice boomed from inside of Violet's office. Diego stuck his head in the doorway. "I need to talk with you."

Violet said something that Delanie couldn't hear.

"We're talking in here," Stone yelled. "Get out."

Violet said something else indistinguishable. Then Stone swished out, shoving Diego as he passed.

Diego put both hands in the air. "You both are my witness. He assaulted me. I didn't touch him."

Delanie almost cracked a smile. Her camera would back up his story if it turned into anything.

Stone brushed past her with a huff. She shifted slightly to make sure to capture his exit on her pursecam footage.

"Diego, have a seat." Violet pointed inside her office and then jogged toward the dressing room. "I'll be back in a minute."

"Does this happen often?" Delanie stood in the doorway as Diego settled in Violet's guest chair.

"More often than you'd think. We have some temperamental folks who can't take direction. It's a team thing. Some people don't get that."

"Do you think he would be vindictive?" She looked over her shoulder.

"You never know. But I don't think so. He's usually all bluster. He'll calm down and call me next week to apologize, and he'll want his job back. He's left before."

Voices boomed from the other end of the hallway.

Delanie raised her eyebrows. "I hope you're right. I'm going to go see what's going on over there."

Inside the dressing room, Stone threw clothes and toiletries into a gym bag while Jayden and Bruce watched from across the room. "This is too freakin' much. I can't take it anymore. It's for the best." He crammed everything in the bag and struggled with the zipper. "I'm outta here. Good luck, Violet. You've always been a good friend. Ciao, babies." Stone waved over his shoulder and strode out.

Violet followed as Jayden returned to his phone.

"Is there a lot of employee turnover?" Delanie asked.

Jayden shrugged. "Enough, I guess. You have strong personalities with lots of creative ideas. It's a lot of sour grapes. He never got over Diego getting picked for the choreographer job."

Bruce nodded. "Most of us have been together since the beginning.

We had about three or four other guys who didn't stay long for whatever reason."

"You like working here?" Delanie watched their facial expressions and listened to see if any of their stories varied from their previous conversations.

Jayden looked at Bruce. "I like the people. For the most part, everyone is good to work with."

Bruce laughed. "I needed a job. But it's a good environment, and the tips are better than other places. And we have a fan club now." He smiled, and Jayden nodded.

Delanie stepped closer and took a good sniff. She got back scents of several different colognes. *I'm not having much success with finding the owner of the musky body spray.*

"Any reason to think any one of your team would be trying to sabotage the show? Anybody not happy?"

Both men shook their heads. "The entertainers are a pretty close, knit team. We hang out after work," Bruce said.

"We go to the gym together, eat dinner at each other's houses. You know, stuff like that. Eliot's even dating Bruce's sister."

"Yup," Bruce added. "I don't suspect any of the dancers. You?"

"Nah, man. I trust this team. Diego gets on his high horse sometimes, but he's a good guy. He wants us to put on a decent show. He grows on you. If it's anybody on staff, it's someone in the kitchen or at the bar."

"Why?" Delanie asked.

"They're jealous of us. We bring in the crowds and get the killer tips. The money's lopsided. They know we're the golden boys," Jayden said.

"Anything else I should know?" Delanie asked.

"You busy Friday night?" Jayden raised one eyebrow.

"Thanks for the offer, but there's someone waiting for me after work. I'll see you both around. If you think of anything else, let me know."

"My heart is broken," Jayden said, clutching his chest. "Let him know he's a lucky man."

Delanie smiled and walked past the offices. Easton's door was closed, and Gwen and Violet's spaces were dark. She strolled around the bar and the stage where she found Gwen leaning on the counter in the lobby, listening to Violet. Delanie moved in close enough to hear, too.

"He stays out this time," Violet said. "As much as I like him, he stirs the stink. And we have enough chaos around here. He doesn't come back to visit or see friends. I'll mail him his last check, so there shouldn't be any reason for him to return."

"Got it. I'll let the rest of the door staff know," Gwen said. "Hey, Delanie. What's up?"

"Fine. Just checking in. How are you all doing?" Delanie asked.

"As well as can be expected. It seems like a new crisis each day." Violet's sensible shoes squeaked on the floor as she retreated to her office.

"Anything else going on?" Delanie said in a low tone.

Gwen shook her head. "But the night's young. A creepy stalker running loose is enough. At first the pranks were kinda funny, but I'm afraid he's braver now, and someone's going to get hurt. Let me know if you need backup. Marco's added extra security, so I'll be around more."

"Will do. Hopefully, Stone's departure won't cause too much of an issue with the entertainment," Delanie said.

"Doubtful. He's always been the mouthy one. At least it should be quieter around here."

"Have you seen Easton lately?" Delanie scanned the doorway to see who was near the stage. Diego, Jayden, Eliot, and Bruce milled around nearby.

"He's holed up in his office making phone calls. Not sure what's up with him. He was in a foul mood when he came in."

"I'm going to camp out and lurk. Let me know if I can help with anything," Delanie said.

"Marco said that I should stick to you like glue." She winked.

"We're going to catch this guy." Delanie headed for the bar. Finding an out-of-the-way table, Delanie settled in. She made sure her pursecam had a good view of the nearby hallways and all the staff action in the background.

Delanie killed time answering what felt like fifty emails. She pocketed her phone when Easton stepped under the spotlight and repeated his spiel to get the show started. He waved and blew kisses as he bounded off the stage and zeroed in on Delanie.

Pulling out the chair across from her, he ran his hands through his dark hair. "Hey, there. You doing okay?" He unbuttoned his jacket and fanned himself with the lapels. "It's hot under those lights. Can I get you a refill?"

Delanie shook her head.

He popped up and headed for the bar, returning a few minutes later with two frosty beers and a ginger ale. "Here. I couldn't remember what you said. So what's shaking?"

"Thanks," she said, pushing the drink toward her empty glass. "It's been pretty normal here tonight. It looks like Eliot blended right in with the routine as rehearsals were wrapping up. Nobody even noticed that Stone is gone."

"Good riddance. Definitely too temperamental," he said in hushed tones.

"Everything okay with you?" She asked leaning forward to hear him better over the music and crowd noise.

"Hey, you want to go somewhere later to talk. Maybe we could do breakfast after the club closes. I know an all-night diner down the street. The food's pretty good."

"What's up?"

"I want to run something by you," he said. "I had an idea, and I want your opinion. You know, to see if it might work."

She hoped she didn't grimace. "Sure."

"Great. I'll meet you in the lobby at the end of the show." Easton disappeared in a crowd of women.

Delanie sighed. She really needed a good night's sleep, but maybe she'd learn something that could help her.

About one-thirty, she drifted to the lobby and leaned on the host station. The crowd that wasn't taking pictures with the dancers had started to file out, and Gwen's hired guard held the door for them.

Before she could come up with an excuse to back out of breakfast with Chaz's cousin, Easton materialized beside her and latched on to her elbow. "Hey. You ready. Do you want me to drive?"

"I'm kinda tired. I think I'll leave straight from the restaurant to go home. I'll follow you."

"Okay. I'm the Audi out back. We're going to the 24-7 Diner about three miles east of here on Broad Street. I hope you can keep up."

"I know where it is," she said. "I'll see you there." *I hope you can keep up.*

Delanie filed in behind the women streaming out the door. By the time she got to her car and blasted the heat, the traffic had thinned out considerably. She headed to the restaurant. Her stomach growled at the thought of pancakes or French toast.

Fifteen minutes later, the hostess seated Delanie in an aqua blue and silver booth near the front windows. She clicked on her pursecam and flipped through the menu.

"Coffee?" the waitress asked.

"Yes, please. I'll order when my friend gets here." Delanie glanced around the restaurant. The after-clubbing crowd streamed in in small groups.

"Gotcha," she replied, snapping her gum.

Easton drifted in and shrugged out of his overcoat. Tossing it on his side of the booth, he slid in the seat across from her. "Sorry. I got stuck in the club traffic. Some of those women are crazy."

The waitress reappeared with Delanie's mug. "Hey, sweetie," she said to Easton. "What can I get you?"

"Coffee's fine."

"Yes, it is." The waitress winked at Delanie. "What will you have?"

"I'll have the French toast breakfast with extra crispy bacon."

"You want the hash browns?"

Delanie shook her head.

"And what about you, handsome?"

Easton turned on his megawatt smile. "I'll have the western omelet with sausage links, hash browns, and the biscuits."

"Sure thing. I'll be back in a flash." She picked up the menus and winked at Easton.

"You've got a fan," Delanie said.

He shrugged. "It happens a lot. Hey, I wanted to talk to you about something."

The waitress returned with Easton's coffee, and she lingered a few moments too long. When she finally moved on to another table, he leaned forward. "I got an opportunity from one of my friends in Arizona. It's business. A chance of a lifetime, you know. It's a chance to get in on a company at the ground level. I need to put a group of friends together to act as investors. I'm a little short, and I thought maybe you as a business owner would be looking for an opportunity to diversify. I'm getting in on this one. I've got all the paperwork and the business plan if you're interested."

"What kind of investment?"

"It's cash for the start up and expansion. Have you seen *Shark Tank*? It's kind of like that. It's a group of investors that agree to fund good ideas that need help. But we've got to have the liquidity to get it off the ground."

"What kind of money are you talking about? I talk all decisions over with my partner."

"I need an answer like now." Easton's eyes darted around the room. "I'd hate for you to miss out because you and your partner couldn't decide."

"How much?" she asked again, louder.

"We have two types of investors. Friends are about the five thousand range, and Angels are at the ten thousand range. We have different plans with different risks. It's an opportunity of a lifetime. Plus, you'd be helping small entrepreneurs get their start. Whatta ya think?"

"It sounds altruistic. But I need to talk it over with Duncan. Can you send me the business plan to review? It may take me a few days to look though everything, but I'll let you know."

Easton made a face.

The waitress interrupted with large steaming platters, loaded with breakfast.

"Here you go, y'all. Watch these plates. They're really hot." She looked at Easton. "Ketchup's over there. Do you need anything? I'll be right back with refills for your coffee."

Easton waved a fork in Delanie's direction. "Don't wait too long. I kinda need an answer now. Somebody may grab your spot if you don't commit. I can promise you your money will double in the first quarter."

Delanie raised one eyebrow and poured hot maple syrup on her French toast. "Really. That sounds like a great opportunity. Guaranteed?"

"Uh-huh," he said, stuffing egg and biscuit in his mouth.

"I'll let you know."

"Okay, but don't wait too long. I'd hate for you to get locked out. And even if he wasn't interested, you should think about it. Everybody needs to diversify their investments. And it's never too late to add another income stream."

They ate in silence except for the times the waitress checked back in and flirted with Easton.

Delanie took another bite of bacon and dropped her napkin on her plate. "This was good. Thank you. I need to head out. I have an early morning." As Delanie rose, the waitress returned for what seemed like the fifth time. *Excellent customer service here.*

"Bye, Delanie. Let me know about my proposition. Don't miss out."

"What proposition?" the waitress asked, topping off his coffee.

She heard him turn on the charm and rewind his spiel for the waitress. Delanie took that opportunity to escape before she had to hear any more of his hard-sell tactics. Maybe her footage had caught something she hadn't noticed in person. She needed a break in this case. Lately, everything seemed like an endless loop of watching the club and combing through video footage.

Chapter Twenty-One

Delanie rolled over and blinked. She hopped out of bed and stretched. It was time to shake things up some more at the Cheeky Monkey.

After a long, hot shower and a coffee, Delanie settled in at her kitchen table to watch last night's recording. Again, lots of people moving in and out of the shot. No one did anything mildly fishy. She blew out a sigh that made her bangs flutter.

Her phone dinged several times with a series of texts.

Good morning, sunshine.

Coming to the club tonight?

Given any thought to my offer? Time's running out. It's a great investment.

Delanie hesitated before she responded to Easton. She listened to the audio of their conversation twice. He knew how to turn on the charm. She wondered if the waitress fell for his smarmy offer.

She tapped her response. **Good morning. Need more information before I can commit.**

Her phone dinged again with an immediate response. **Lunch today? My treat. I think this is right up your alley. 12?**

Sounds good. Where? She replied.

Meet me at Leonardo's on W. Broad.

See you then. Setting her phone on the table, Delanie let out another heavy sigh. She knew she was in for another sell job and chided herself for agreeing to meet him again. But there was something odd about him that she couldn't quite put her finger on. She wanted another chance to keep him talking.

Glancing at the clock on her microwave, she needed to get dressed and head out if she planned to make it to the restaurant by noon.

About an hour later, Delanie slid in a booth that faced the front door and accepted the menu from the hostess.

A young woman with a nose and lip ring approached the table. "Hi, I'm Chelsea. Can I get you something to drink?"

"Iced tea, please." Delanie said.

The bells on the door chimed, and Delanie looked up to see Easton. He waved and zeroed in on her table.

"Hope you haven't been waiting long," he said.

"Just got here."

"You look good. I like your uh, green sweater." He smiled, and it reminded Delanie of one of those cartoon characters with a sparkly grin.

Before Delanie could answer, Chelsea returned with the iced tea. "I see your friend has joined you. What can I get you to drink?"

"Sweet tea," he said, taking the menu she offered and brushing Chelsea's hand.

"Be right back." Chelsea smiled, letting her hand linger for a moment.

Wow. Always the charmer.

"So, what do you do on your time away from the club?" Delanie asked.

"I like sports. I probably watch too much TV. And I'm a photographer. Always looking for new stuff to capture. You should come by one day and see my work."

Delanie nodded. *Not a chance.*

Chelsea reappeared with Easton's drink. "What can I get you all for lunch?" she asked, looking at Delanie's lunch companion.

"I'll have the Italian sub heated with everything and fries."

"Ma'am?" Chelsea asked.

"I'll have the turkey sub. No mayo, onions, or tomatoes with the steak fries." She handed Chelsea the menu. "And a box for what I'll take home."

"Be back soon." Chelsea's smiled curled upward into a sly grin.

"Have you had any more thoughts on my offer last night?" Easton leaned forward and stared at her.

"I never received any documentation from you like the business plan." She paused and looked him in the eye. "I don't want to make a huge commitment right now because we're expanding our business."

"But you can always invest personally at a lower amount. I don't want you to miss out on an opportunity to exponentially increase your wealth with a sure thing. We always need to think about our future. And I like helping my friends." His dazzling smile rivaled anything in a toothpaste commercial.

"That is true. But nothing is ever guaranteed. I love owning my own business, but it's more work than a regular job."

"Wouldn't that mean you should be even more interested in making an investment in your future? Let someone else do all the work and you reap the financial benefits." He turned up his megawatt smile.

Chelsea interrupted with two plates. "The ketchup is over there. You all need anything else? If not, I'll be back soon to check on you. Oh, and I'll bring your box."

Easton reached for the ketchup and blanketed his fries. "You'll kick yourself if you don't get in on this."

Delanie took a bite of her sandwich and chewed slowly. *He doesn't give up.*

She reached for the ketchup and stalled for a few minutes more. "It sounds like a wonderful opportunity, and I appreciate you thinking of me. But I need to pull up with my accountant and discuss my strategy before I commit, and I'm afraid that won't happen in the timeframe that you need. Maybe next time."

A dark look crossed Easton's face. "Sure, but I really think you should reconsider. This is the ground floor of something big. I don't want you to regret your decision."

Delanie took another nibble of her sandwich. *He really doesn't quit.*

"I brought refills," Chelsea said, setting two glasses in front of them. "Can I get you all anything else?" They both shook their heads. "Okay, then. Make sure you save room for our gourmet cheesecake."

Delanie's phone dinged several times and then rang. She fished through her purse and pressed the green button to answer Gwen's call.

"Hey. We've had another situation here. My overnight guard was found in the alley when Javi and Hector arrived. The ambulance just left."

"What happened?" Delanie asked.

"They thought he was sleeping, but someone had konked him on the head. I hope he pulls through. The police left a few minutes ago. Violet and I are here. Easton's not answering his phone, but that's not unusual."

"See you in a few," Delanie said, turning to Easton. "I'm sorry. I have to rush off. Thank you for lunch." Delanie took a swig of her tea and rose.

"I usually don't have that effect on women, but I understand that you're a busy professional."

"You might want to check your phone. Gwen's trying to reach you." Delanie hurried out as Chelsea swooped in.

Thanks to her Mustang, Delanie made it to the club in minutes. She drove behind the building where the dumpster stood alone in the empty space. No open doors or signs that anything was wrong. She looped around and parked out front. Delanie tapped on the glass door. Peering inside the dark lobby, she saw movement. Gwen approached and unlocked the door.

"You've had a busy morning," Delanie said.

"The guard's got a concussion, a broken jaw, and a long recovery, but thankfully, he's going to make it. I'm so relieved. I wasn't too sure earlier. The police think he was ambushed and tussled with his attacker when he was doing his rounds outside early this morning. Hopefully, when he feels like it, he can tell the detective what happened."

Delanie had flashbacks to her attack. The guy had tried to frighten her twice. Maybe three times if the road-rager is the same guy. *What is behind all this? Thankfully, I only ended up with a few bruises and a dented ego. But the acts have amped up and become more violent.*

Gwen locked the door behind them, and the pair walked toward the bar. Violet, Hector, Javi, Diego, and another guard sat around a table near the stage. The group turned as she and Gwen approached.

"Did you hear about the guard? He got clobbered pretty bad. He was covered in blood," Hector said.

"Did you all see anything that might give a clue about who did this?" Delanie asked. She scanned the faces around the table and paused when she got to Violet, who wore a navy hoodie over her blouse. *Odd. It didn't feel that cold in here.*

Javi shook his head. "Hector called me when he got here around eight, I guess. The police searched inside and around the building. It looked like the guard got jumped on one of his patrols. I wish the cameras were working." His voice trailed off.

"I talked to Marco this morning," Gwen said. "We're increasing security here for the time being. We'll have at least four guards on duty when we're open and a pair after hours. Instead of one," Gwen said. "I suggest that the staff do the buddy system, too. Nobody should be in the building by him or herself."

Delanie scanned the table for reactions. Most of the team nodded. *No movement from Violet and Javi. Was she reading into their lack of reaction? Maybe they were just bored with rehashing this same conversation over and over.*

"We're behind on prep for tonight," Javi said. "If you'll excuse us, Hector and I will be in the kitchen." They rose as Easton strolled in from the lobby.

"Hey, guys. What's going on? Sorry I was out of pocket, and I missed your calls." Easton took Javi's seat and glared at Delanie.

"The guys need to get back to work. I'll catch you up," Violet said, pointing to the hallway that led to her office.

Before anyone moved, a high-pitched squeal echoed from the back, followed by a crash and a string of obscenities.

The group rushed to the kitchen. A crate of broken glasses covered the floor, and a pale Hector stood near the table.

"Are you okay?" Violet demanded more than asked.

"There are rats in the pantry. I saw two skitter around and run back in there." Hector pointed toward the open door. "They're weird looking. White with pink eyes. Kinda ghost-like. Not like the kind that hang out in the alleys."

Javi moved closer and flicked the light on. Something moved, and he tensed. "We need to find a way to trap them. There are two that I saw. Hand me one of those plastic baskets."

Violet sighed and reached for the container. "What next?"

"I'll take care of it." Easton pushed his way through the crowd into the pantry that was about the size of a walk-in closet.

They heard scuffles and Easton stomping. "Come here, you. What are you doing in here?" After a few minutes, he yelled, "Gotcha." He stepped into the kitchen, holding two white rats.

"Those look like lab rats or pets," Gwen said. "How did they get in here? Are there any others?"

"I only saw two," Hector said.

Violet shuddered as she glanced at the rats. "I'll call someone to check the place over." Violet shuddered as she glanced at the rats.

"Can we open on time?" Javi asked, eyeing the wiggling rodents in each of Easton's hands.

"I need a box or something. Gwen? Diego?" Easton tightened his grip on the squirming animals.

Diego disappeared and returned with a cardboard box. The rats weren't keen on being trapped. They scrabbled and shook the container.

"I'm going to take this in my office and seal it. But don't worry, I'll poke holes in it. Then I'll figure out what to do with them," Easton said.

"I need to report this," Violet said.

"You're not going to call the health inspector, are you?" Easton asked, picking up the cardboard box and holding the lid shut with his hands. "We don't need that right now. Not with everything else going on."

"I kinda have to." Violet glared at him.

"No, you don't. These aren't vermin. These are someone's pets that got loose. It was probably too cold outside for them. I'll take care of it.

I had a hamster once as a kid. It escaped. They found it at the old lady's house next door. She screamed her head off when she saw it in her kitchen. It happens. It'll be okay. I've got this."

Violet frowned. "We should be okay to open, but I'm still going to make some calls."

"And we'll get this mess cleaned up in the meantime," Javi said, handing Hector a broom and a dustpan.

"That's enough excitement for today," Gwen said.

Delanie followed Gwen to the lobby. "I'm going to head out. I'll be back later this evening. Do you know where the ambulance took your guard?"

"Probably to VCU's Medical Center. It was a trauma wound," Gwen said.

"Can you get a copy of the police report?"

"Here's what the officer gave me." Gwen pulled a yellow sheet of paper from her back pocket.

Delanie unfolded it and spread it out on the counter. She snapped a photo. "Thanks. Any updates on the guard?"

Gwen pulled out her phone and made a call. "This is Gwen at the Cheeky Monkey. Is Rob there?"

A few minutes later, Delanie heard Gwen's half of the conversation that included mostly "un-huhs" and "yeses." Gwen disconnected and said, "He's at VCU. He's regained consciousness, but they've wired his jaw shut, and he's sedated. He's going to be out of work for some time."

"Hopefully, he'll be able to tell them what happened when he's able to communicate. He's going to be in pain for a while," Delanie said.

"I'm going to try to get over there and check on him later today or tomorrow," Gwen said.

"I'll let you know if I find out anything. See ya," Delanie said.

Delanie looked at the copy of the police report on her phone before backing out of the parking space. The guard's name was Arnie Baskerville. Maybe she'd get lucky and be able to see the wounded man.

About a half hour later, Delanie rode the elevator to the trauma center on the ninth floor. When the doors swished open, she made her way to the nurse's station.

"Good afternoon, I'm Delanie Fitzgerald, and I'm here to see my coworker, Arnie Baskerville. He was admitted early this morning."

"Mr. Baskerville has been moved to the fourth floor."

"Thank you," Delanie said.

She repeated her story at the nurse's station on the fourth floor.

"Mr. Baskerville is recovering, and he can only receive family. One person at a time. Friends and coworkers will have to wait," the nurse at the desk said.

"Thank you. If I want to send him a card or flowers, how would I address it?" Delanie asked.

The nurse picked up a business card and wrote something on the back. "Here is his patient number. Include that and his name, and it will get to him."

Delanie pocketed the card and returned to the bank of elevators. *It was worth a try. She'd have to find another way to contact him.*

When she retrieved her car from the large parking deck, she paused and scanned through her photos and stared at the one of the latest police report. She punched in the number for the Goochland Sheriff's office.

After four or five rings, she said, "This is Delanie Fitzgerald. Is Deputy Hudson available, please?"

"He is on the road right now. May I take a message?"

Delanie gave her phone number and headed for her office. *Something has to break soon in this case. The stunts have gotten out of hand.*

When she crossed the Powhite Bridge, her phone rang. "Hello, this is Delanie."

"Ms. Fitzgerald. This is Deputy Mark Hudson with the Goochland Sheriff's office. I'm returning your call."

"Thank you for calling me back so quickly. I'm a private investigator, and I'm working for the owner of the Cheeky Monkey. I was calling about a situation you worked there this morning. I was hoping you could tell me what you found when you arrived."

"I can't go into too much detail, but we received a call around eight-thirty this morning about a security guard who was unresponsive near the dumpster. The ambulance got there around the same time I did. The patient was transported to VCU, and the case is still open."

"I'm hoping that Mr. Baskerville will be able to identify his attacker when he's able to communicate," Delanie said.

"You think he knew his attacker?"

"My client, the owner of the Cheeky Monkey, hired me to get to the bottom of a series of pranks that have been affecting his business. This seems to be another in a string of incidents."

"Interesting. I know the gal in charge of security said they were having trouble with their cameras. Like I said, the investigation is active. If you encounter anything related, I'd appreciate if you let me know."

"Will do. Thank you for your time."

At least if she didn't have any leads, maybe she could offer the deputy more options than just a random mugging.

Chapter Twenty-Two

Delanie paid the clerk at the drive-thru coffee shop and took a long sip of her white chocolate iced mocha. She needed the jolt this morning to help her look again at all the pieces of random information and the timeline. She had to have missed something. Sadly, this was her mantra lately.

She pulled in her usual parking space at the office as her phone binged. **Something weird's going on. Got the prints back. Meet me at the office?**

I'll bring the bagels, Duncan added a few seconds later.

Delanie settled in the conference room. She opened her file and added the attack on the security guard and the pet rats to her list. Then she added all the names of those who were there.

The front door slammed, and Duncan and Margaret padded down the hall. "Good morning," he announced, setting a box of bagels and cream cheese spreads on the table. "Margaret wanted something different for breakfast this morning."

Delanie reached down and patted the dog's boxy head. "Yum. Good choice, y'all."

"So, what's been going on lately? I peeked at some of your camera footage."

"That purse camera is durable. It's been dropped, thrown, and smacked against attackers, and it still keeps on working. Unfortunately, it hasn't revealed any secrets."

Duncan paused and stared at her.

"All in a day's work. Let's see. Easton is trying to get me to buy into his latest fool proof, get-rich-quick scheme. He took me out twice to convince me I had to do this. He's really pushing hard to get me to pay up. Then I got a call from Gwen that they had found one of the guards behind the building. He's going to be okay after a lot of recuperation. Someone attacked him on his rounds and broke his jaw. And then the kitchen staff found two white rats in the pantry."

"The kind you'd find at a pet store?"

Delanie nodded. "Someone put them in there deliberately. I'm going to check the pet stores today and see if they've sold any recently. Just a hunch. What did you find? Your text sounded juicy."

"I'm not sure what it is exactly. The prints came back on the glass you nabbed for Easton. They weren't his. Not sure where the mix up happened. Do you think you could get another sample and put it immediately in a bag?"

Butterflies flitted around her stomach. *A crack in the case?*

"Sure. That's odd. The other two samples were fine," Delanie said. "Could it have been the lab?"

"Doubtful. My friend works at a prestigious lab that does DNA for private industry and several law enforcement agencies. His lab is at a major university on the East Coast. I did some cyber work for him, and he's returning the favor."

"He slips your stuff in and nobody cares?"

Duncan shrugged his shoulders. "I didn't ask. But I know it's quality work and not some of these flim flam offers on the internet."

"I'll figure out how to get a new sample tonight." She jotted a note on the back of a receipt along with a reminder to talk to Gwen about the guard and Violet about her hunch of the prankster's identity.

"Send me the link to your timeline. I want to mull it over to see if I come up with any ideas. The pet shop research sounds like a good idea," he said.

Delanie tapped on her computer. "I sent you the link." She settled in her chair and searched for pet stores in a fifty-mile radius of the Cheeky Monkey.

After calling fifteen of the twenty-two stores listed, Delanie stretched. "Not many rat sales this week in RVA. I'll keep at it." She punched in the next number. After four rings, a young guy answered, "Animal House. How can I help you find your next pet?"

"Hi, my name is Delanie, and my boyfriend bought a pair of rats somewhere in town last week. He didn't get enough rat food."

"That might be me. I sold two white rats last week to a guy who only bought a carrier and a tiny bag of food."

"Tall guy?" Delanie asked. *Most of the guys at the Cheeky Monkey are tall.*

"Yep. With dark brown hair. He liked to talk. A lot."

"Yep, that's him. I see you're located on Broad Street. How late are you open tonight?"

"I may be able to save you a trip," the guy said. "Your boyfriend brought them back yesterday. He said you didn't like them."

"Oh, he did?"

"I got a long song and dance about how he had to return them, or his girlfriend was going to break up with him. I felt bad for the rats. I wanted them to go to a better home. I was annoyed that you didn't like the pets."

"That wasn't me. I thought they were kinda cute. Now I'm curious why he returned them..."

"That makes me feel better about you," the man said.

"Hmmm. We're going to have an interesting dinner conversation tonight, especially if there's another girlfriend. Thanks for your help."

The man laughed. "I'd ask you if you were interested in the rats, but I sold them to a family for their son's birthday already."

"I'm glad they went to a good home. Thanks again." Delanie disconnected and shifted to face Duncan.

"It seems my boyfriend returned the rats. I'm going to take some photos by the store to try to figure out who my guy is. I should be able to pull stills from the videos."

"Already done. I emailed you a few." Duncan looked up from his laptop. "Let me know if I left anyone out. I think I got all the key players."

"If it's someone on the staff, then that explains why they're always on camera." She picked up her phone and punched in Chaz's number.

"Hey, there. How's it going?"

"Good. How are you faring?" she asked.

"Things are going okay here. You need more money?"

"No, your advance covered it. I had a couple of questions for you if you have a few minutes," she said.

"Anything to help catch this guy. How about if we meet for lunch? I've got a hankering for hot dogs. Wanna meet me at City Dogs on Cary Street say around twelve-thirty?"

"I'll see you there." Delanie disconnected the call.

"Lunch date with Chaz?" Duncan asked.

Delanie smiled. "Yep. I need to talk to him about his cousin. I still don't have a good sense about their relationship."

"He's family," Duncan said.

She gathered her things and packed her messenger bag. "Let me know if anything in my notes jumps out at you. I've been staring at it for days."

"I'm going to go back and look at all the footage again. Say hi to Chaz for us," he said.

Margaret looked up from her napping spot near Duncan's chair to see if there were any opportunities to score food. When none materialized, she rolled over for more sleep.

Delanie plugged the address of the Animal House in her GPS and followed its bossy directions to the interstate. She liked open stretches of road where she could let the Mustang run. The smooth ride gave her time to think. *What is behind all of the attacks and the chaos?*

She took the Broad Street exit and followed the directions to an older strip mall near Staples Mill Road. The one-story brick building, divided into four tiny stores, had a flat roof and a design from the 1970s. She dodged cars and pedestrians and located a parking spot. Tall, plate- glass windows sported animal posters that had started to fade and curl.

As she walked through the door, an electronic squeal announced her entrance, and a thirty-something guy with a man-bun looked up from the counter. "Hi, welcome to the Animal House."

"Hey," she said, looking around. "Neat stuff you have here." The large area with aquariums filled with snakes gave her flashbacks to the case she'd had last fall where a pet shop owner was killed by an illegal snake. Then she thought of the giant snake that had escaped and took up residence in the ceiling of her office. She shook off the heebie jeebies and wandered to the other side of the store, filled with different sized tanks full of exotic fish and turtles. The seahorse tank fascinated her. She'd love to have a pet, but it wouldn't be fair to leave a dog or cat home alone so much. *Maybe a turtle?*

She pushed pet thoughts to the back of her mind and headed to the counter. "I'm Delanie Fitzgerald, and I'm looking for some information on a guy who bought two rats here last week. I was hoping you could help me."

"You the girlfriend?" he asked, staring at her.

She smiled. "No. Would you mind looking at some pictures?" Delanie showed him her phone.

He stared at her phone. She scrolled through pictures of all the key players.

"Wait. Go back. That one. That might be him. He wore a dark hoodie. And he had sunglasses on. Yep. That might be him. I couldn't see his eyes or his hair. I think the hair was dark, but I don't really remember. Go back a couple. It might be that guy, too." The man squinted and rubbed his chin. "Go back to the other one." He leaned on the counter and stared at her phone.

"Hey, I'm not one hundred percent sure. He came in here with a long, sad story that his girlfriend didn't like his decision. I gave him a refund because I didn't want the animals to suffer. Animals aren't toys or things you can throw in the closet when you're tired of them." He shook his head.

Delanie nodded. "Do you remember what he was wearing when he returned the rats?"

"Over dressed, sort of. He had on a dress shirt with suit pants and shiny shoes. But he had that black hoodie on again. Oh, and the sunglasses, too. It looked weird with the hood up with dress clothes."

"I appreciate it. And thanks for the information." He had zeroed in on photos of Sven and Easton.

Delanie returned to her car and glanced at the dash clock. Plenty of time to get downtown and find parking for her lunch meeting.

After circling the block twice, she zipped in a recently vacated spot and adjusted the Mustang in the tiny space. The book display in the window of Fountain Bookstore drew her inside like a magnet. She waved at the gal at the counter and browsed the local book section and all the bookish gifts. Picking up a pair of Nancy Drew socks, she looked at the pins and other jewelry.

"Finding everything okay?" the bookseller asked.

"Always. I'll take these." Delanie handed her the socks and her credit card. Then she turned and picked up a pair of Baby Yoda socks for Duncan. "And these."

"Here you go." The woman handed her a bag and a receipt to sign.

"Thanks." Delanie dropped the paper bag and the receipt in her purse.

The crisp winter air caused her to blink when she stepped out on the sidewalk. Hugging her coat closer to her, she hiked up the street to City Dogs.

Once inside the small restaurant, Delanie glanced around for Chaz. Not seeing him, she claimed a table and slid in the seat facing the door. She wiggled out of her coat but kept it wrapped around her shoulders.

Before she finished checking her email, a cold blast filled the restaurant. She looked up and spotted Chaz holding open the door. He arrived with his overcoat hanging open and his shiny purple suit. A black dress shirt gaped at the collar, revealing a thick gold chain. Chaz's style was always befitting the hipster generation, which he had aged out of several decades ago.

"Hey there," he waved as he approached her seat. "It's colder than the... North Pole out there. I'll be glad when spring gets here. Have you ordered yet?"

Delanie shook her head and rose. She followed Chaz to the counter where they placed their orders. Chili and onion smells filled the small space and made Delanie's stomach growl.

When they returned to the table, Chaz shook off his black wool coat and draped it over the back of the seat. "How are things going?" He rubbed his hands together and blew on them. "I heard about the freezer incident. You okay?" He stared at her with concerned eyes.

"I'm fine. I wasn't in there long. Gwen and Violet were quick to react. It happened so fast."

The guy in the white sweatshirt behind the counter called out, "Numbers thirteen, fourteen, and seventeen. Orders up."

The pair rose and headed back to the counter to retrieve their orders. Delanie's mouth watered when she smelled the Hormel hotdogs, hers slathered in mustard, and Chaz's covered in chili, onions, and jalapenos.

Once settled at their table, Delanie took a sip of her iced tea and looked at Chaz. "I know we've talked about your cousin, but can you give me a few more details about Easton?" She watched his face closely for any of his tells.

Chaz's eyes widened. "You're not still thinking about dating him, are you?" Chaz's eyes widened.

Delanie shook her head. "No. I want to know how deep are the ties. Blood is thicker than water."

"Nah, it's not like that at all. I haven't seen him in years. When he approached me with his sad tale, I decided to give him a chance. He was in a really bad place. But if it turns out that he's not working out, he's gone like anyone else would be. I don't treat him any different. He was a little kid when I was younger. We were never that close. Why?"

"He keeps showing up in all the video clips. I see him and Violet everywhere. I mean, I guess it's expected, but they are in almost every shot." Chaz scrunched his nose like something smelled bad, and she continued, "Like yesterday, after the guard was injured and when Hector found two rats in the pantry."

"I heard the big guy screamed like a little girl." Chaz chuckled.

Delanie's eyebrows shot up under her bangs, and she continued, "I would have freaked too especially when you're not expecting for them to jump out at you at work. They weren't alley rats. Their beady eyes and scurrying gave me the creeps. Easton scooped them up and took them out. Later that afternoon, I was wondering about the rats, so I called some pet shops. One of the clerks said some guy bought and returned a pair of rats. He thought the guy was either Easton or Sven. He said the guy wore a hoodie. He remembers him because he brought them back the next day."

Chaz stopped eating and froze for a second. "I've known Sven for years." He paused and checked his phone. "Sorry, I had to look at something. You said earlier that the pranks might be a diversion, so I had my CPA go over everything with a fine-tooth comb. He's one of those brainiacs. You know the kind. He's like your partner's bulldog with a bone. Anyway, after combing through data, he noticed some odd charges on some of the corporate credit cards. They were small at first like you said. Then they got bigger. It's on an account that Javi, Violet, and Easton have access to." Chaz returned to his hot dog.

"I'm going back tonight to poke around and to see if I shake out any other information."

"Be careful. You seem to be a target lately." Chaz slurped his drink. "Don't say anything to anyone about the credit card thing yet. I want to watch the accounts to see if anything else appears, and then I'll call the police. I want to see if there's a bigger plot. I'm not ready to tip off anyone just yet," Chaz said.

"Any word on the investigation about the assault on the guard?" she asked.

Chaz shook his head. "Haven't heard anything. Most of the early stuff was pranks. It didn't hurt anyone but me, but the attacks on you and the guard are different. And the fire..." Chaz paused and his face reddened. "Whoever's doing it is going down. And I don't care if it is family. This is a betrayal." He pounded his fist on the table and stuffed the rest of his chili dog in his mouth. Chili and onions dripped down his chin, and Delanie handed him a napkin.

"I want to give it a couple of more days," Chaz said. "I'm following my gut on this one."

"I had an interesting conversation with Easton last night. He approached me about investing in a new business he's starting. He really wants to give me the opportunity to get in on the ground floor of something big." Delanie took a long sip of her drink.

"Whadya say?"

"I played it off like I needed my CPA to look into it. He kept harping on what a deal it was. It was like he couldn't let it go. Kept saying it's really important that I commit soon, and he doesn't want me to miss out."

"How much?"

"At first, he was looking for angel investors. Then he backed off on the money amounts. I'm surprised he didn't approach you," she said.

Chaz made a harrumphing sound. "He knows better. My money goes into my businesses and real estate. I don't do get-rich-quick stuff. I learned that early on in my career. Speaking of that, I have meeting in a few. It's been great to see you. Keep me posted on what you find, and we'll figure out this credit card thing. I don't want you to put yourself in harm's way for me."

"Thanks, Chaz. I'll be fine." Delanie patted his arm and gathered the trash they had scattered on the table.

Chaz stood and pulled his designer sunglasses from his jacket pocket. "See ya around." He saluted with two fingers.

Too early to arrive at the Cheeky Monkey, Delanie drove through town to Maymont. She pulled into a narrow lot off of Hampton Street next to the row of stately trees that bordered a stone arch at the entrance. A brisk walk in the sun would clear her head. Her thoughts were full of way too many facts that bounced off of each other. And none of them seemed to fit together, but one person kept coming up over and over.

Delanie strolled through the gate and down the walkway. Ducking down a path through the Italian gardens.

She descended the stone steps that led to stepping stones across the pond in the Japanese gardens. The giant lily pads in the water garden provided the perfect backdrop for Delanie to think about all the random clues that were starting to form a larger picture. Even in winter, the evergreen trees provided enough greenery to make the place look enchanted. Breathing in the woodsy smells brought an immediate calming effect.

She strolled through the gardens and took a path by the river where two American black bears lazed on the rocks in their enclosure. She snapped pictures of them. *They have the right idea. I've been working too much lately. Maybe after this case, I'll take a vacation.*

She formulated a plan for tonight. She would focus on Easton and Sven. Sven had worked for Chaz for years. What would cause him to run a swindle on his employer now? And what about Easton? Would he scam his cousin who gave him a job when he needed it most?

Chapter Twenty-Three

Delanie took one last bite of her granola bar and balled up the wrapper with one hand. She changed lanes on Route 288. Last night's time at the Cheeky Monkey had been a bust. Easton stayed holed up in his office all evening, and the staff scurried to get out of the way of Violet's foul mood. She yelled and slammed doors more than once. And all Sven did was serve drinks from behind the bar. On the bright side, no other incidents happened. But that also meant there were no other opportunities to nail the culprit.

She pulled into the front lot and smiled when she spotted the creepy doll, still standing guard in front of Chaz's sign. It looked like he was hugging the leg of the monkey. To date, no one had reported any other new dolls in town.

Grabbing her spy purse and phone, she locked her every-day purse and her coat in the Mustang and jogged to the front door. Clicking the button on her pursecam, Delanie approached the bar that was a hive of activity. Sven stocked bottles on the mirrored shelves while Hector loaded glasses under the counter.

"Hi, y'all," Delanie said. "Anything interesting going on? I thought you were locking up the bottles."

Sven shot her a sideways glance. "That lasted all of two days."

Hector laughed. "Change is the only constant, and it's always a barrel of monkeys around here."

Sven blew out a heavy breath. "Actually, it hasn't been that much fun lately. Everyone's grouchy all the time." He frowned and wiped off fingerprints from the glass shelf.

"You should hang out in the kitchen. We always laugh." Hector hefted five empty plastic crates and disappeared in the back.

"Lately, I can't wait to get out of here." Sven busied himself with arranging items on the counter. "I dread coming back. All Violet does is yell."

"Have you thought of going back to the Treasure Chest if you were happier there?" Delanie hopped onto one of the barstools in front of him.

"This was a promotion. Plus, Chaz asked me if I'd do it. I don't want to let him down. I need to think about what I really want to do. The tips are way better here than the Treasure Chest." His voice faded as he set a ginger ale in front of her.

"Thanks. Maybe things will calm down around here."

He shrugged. "Maybe, I'll join Hector in the kitchen for laughs." He almost cracked a smile.

"What do you think is going on around here?"

"I think someone's trying to ruin the business." He looked around to see if anyone else was in the dining room. I think it's sabotage," Sven whispered.

"Any ideas?"

He shook his head. "Nah, if I did have one, I'd do something about it." He balled his hands into fists. He hastily turned and busied himself with the tray of garnishes.

Delanie picked up her drink and wandered to the edge of the stage where Jayden drug out a rolling plastic bin. C. J. bounded on stage with pieces of split-rail fencing. They placed fake cacti in front of the fence. Diego reached into the bin and pulled out several hats and lassos. He draped them on random fence posts and stepped back to survey the look.

Eliot, C. J., Bruce, and Jayden found their marks on stage as Diego hopped off the stage and headed to the sound room. Lights flashed and danced as a country medley boomed from the speakers, and the guys stepped through two numbers.

"Again," Diego yelled from the back, and the group repeated the same routine.

After the third time with the same song, Delanie picked up her drink and wandered down the hall past Gwen and Violet's empty offices. Heavy metal music blared from Easton's open door.

Delanie took another swig of her drink like it was something stronger and steeled herself for another investment conversation with Easton.

She stepped through the doorway. "Hi, there," she announced, probably louder than she anticipated.

Easton startled and then recovered. He switched to his super smiling mode and stood to greet her. "Delanie, it's so good to see you. We didn't get to chat much last night. I was running around putting out fires."

"Real fires?"

He laughed. "Of course not. We had credit card reader issues, a missing purse, and a couple of drunk bridesmaids who needed an Uber. I saw you come in last night, but by the time I finished with all the issues, you'd already left. Have you given any more thought to my proposition? You missed the deadline, but I still may be able to help you out." His smile shifted to a mischievous grin.

Before she could comment, he continued, "With this project, we're skipping the part where the entrepreneurs have to pitch ideas. We're seeking a select group to do the funding. I've handpicked everyone. It's an opportunity for you all to make some serious money, but it benefits the guy or gal with the idea. Everybody wins. So whaddya think?" He stepped around his desk and into her personal space.

Delanie shifted her weight to her other foot and leaned against the doorjamb. "I think I'm going to have to pass right now. I'm sure you know as a businessman that liquidity is key for small business owners. Business is good, but I need to keep a cushion in case the economy turns, or work dries up. For now, I need to cheer you all on from the sidelines."

"Think about it. I'd hate for you to miss this chance. It's another source of revenue. I don't want you to kick yourself later. I don't want you to have regrets."

Delanie closed her eyes for a couple of seconds.

He continued, "How about this? You sleep on it and call me tomorrow. You might want to change your mind. Who wouldn't want me as a partner?" He snickered and sobered his expression when she didn't respond.

Delanie fidgeted and looked at her shoes.

"Have you eaten? I missed dinner. Let's pop in and see what Javi's got on the menu tonight." He put his hand on her shoulder and guided her to the main room "Grab a table, and I'll see what I can rustle up for two hungry cowpokes." *At least the food will be better than the company. He's definitely heavy handed with the sell job.*

The main room was packed as usual with hundreds of women hooting and hollering at the bare-chested dancers in chaps and cowboy hats. Diego took center stage and did a routine with a lasso. The crowd went wild.

After several bows, the music shifted to a medley of older country songs, and the routines slowed down.

Easton appeared with several dishes cradled in his arm "Javi had lots of good appetizers on the menu tonight. We'll start with boneless spicy wings, lobster-stuffed mushrooms, and spicy spinach dip. He's going to bring out some sliders when they come out of the oven. I'll be back with another round of drinks. Dig in. Don't let it get cold."

Delanie pulled a dessert plate closer to her and added a dab of spinach dip and a couple of mushrooms. The seasoned tortilla chips paired well with the garlicy dip. She hoped this counted as a vegetable.

Easton returned with two beers and a ginger ale. "Sven said this is what you're drinking. You're always on duty, huh? I won't tell Chaz if you want to cut loose a little." He winked and slid into in the seat across from her.

He stuffed his plate and then his mouth. Delanie took advantage of the lull in conversation to scan the crowd. The women were rowdier tonight than they had been. Gwen and her guards stood quietly on the perimeter of the room in case they were needed to assist with stumbling bridesmaids or tipsy birthday girls.

Delanie adjusted her camera-purse to capture the wild women in the audience and anything Easton decided to share as Javi dropped off two plates of sliders.

"Mmm. These are good. Try one," Easton said with his mouth full of food. "He made burgers, tuna bites, Memphis barbecue, and some kind of cheese thing."

Before Delanie could respond, Violet stormed the table and almost skidded to a stop behind Easton. She hovered like a vampire with bulging eyes. "Easton, if you don't mind. We have a woman in your office who said you booked an appointment with her to plan her divorce party. Why would you book something during a show? It's too noisy in here to pay quality attention to our guests." She huffed and clamped her jaw shut.

"I'll take care of it. Don't worry about it. I got to talking to Delanie, and I lost track of time. I've got this. Just relax." Easton rose and wiped both hands off on a black cloth napkin. He pulled out a breath spray and gave himself a couple of squirts. Running his fingers through his model-perfect hair, he glanced around the room and then disappeared into the throng of women.

Violet's nostrils flared, and she waved her hand in front of her nose. Delanie heard the tap, tap, tap of Violet's foot when the song ended. "I swear. He never follows any protocols. I am always cleaning up after him." She turned and followed the path that Easton took a few minutes before.

Picking up her purse, Delanie dodged tables and guests in the audience to follow Violet to the offices. She slid in behind Violet, who stood in Easton's doorway.

He sat across from a platinum blond whose bangle bracelets jingled as she waved her arms around. "I want this to be a fabulous party. I am celebrating my freedom. Can you accommodate fifty guests?"

"Of course. We can set up the tables in a couple of different arrangements to make your party special." Easton turned on the charm and his toothy grin. "We can make this an event to remember."

"I want it to be better than my wedding reception," the woman announced, leaning forward in her chair and waving her arms wide.

Easton hopped out of his seat and sauntered to the front of his desk inches from the woman's guest chair. He leaned on the desk in an almost a lounging position. "Margot, this will be the party to remember. It's going to be hot, hot, hot," Easton said.

"Fabulous. And I want you to take care of all the details for me."

"Of course. I'm at your service. Anything you need." Easton winked, and Delanie coughed to stifle a laugh.

Violet turned to stare at her, and she almost cracked a smile. She hesitated and then she brushed past Delanie and disappeared into her own office.

Easton leaned closer to Margot and continued his spiel about catering, drink menus, and over-the-top entertainment for her soiree.

When he finally paused, Margot said, "I want to see everything you have to offer."

Easton laughed like a nine-year-old. When Margo didn't react to his fourth-grade humor, he cleared his throat and stood taller. "How about if we tour the club tonight while there's a live audience so you can see it in action, and then we'll make an appointment at your convenience to sample the menus and sign all the paperwork."

"You're such a doll," Margot said in a breathy whisper. "Let's go take a tour, so you can show me what you've got." She rose and put her hand on Easton's shoulder to steady herself. Her tight peach dress crept up her long legs as she balanced on a pair of matching stilettos.

"Right this way." Easton pointed to the door with his open palm. He put his other hand on the small of her back.

Delanie stepped back as the pair sashayed past her. When they disappeared around the corner, she poked her head in Violet's office. "Everything okay?"

"Of course. Busy night, but all is well. Easton still with his special guest?"

"Yep. He's giving her a tour of the place," Delanie said.

Violet looked at the ceiling for a moment. "He's better at the schmoozing part than I am. He's good at booking the large parties. Hopefully, this will be another one." She picked up a handful of folders and glanced at her laptop.

Delanie took that as her dismissal and wandered down the hall to the bar. Easton stood close to Margot near the wall by the stage. If

Delanie hadn't known the woman was a client, she would have thought they were a couple.

Too far away to hear their hushed conversation, Delanie relied on watching the pair's gestures and facial expressions to get a gist of what was happening. Margot smiled quite a bit and touched Easton's bicep every chance she got. As the song ended, the couple walked arm-in-arm around the perimeter of the room to the lobby.

Deciding it was time to head home, Delanie double-timed it in the chilly night air. Pausing, she spotted Easton leaning into the driver's window of a dark Corvette, parked near the curb.

"This is going to be the party that all your friends talk about for years," he said. "After we get all of your planning done, we need to have a dinner where we can talk. I have some ideas for some other projects that you might be interested in."

"Here's my card. Don't be shy." Margot took his hand and held it for a few seconds as she passed her information to him. "I'll be waiting to hear from you. And dinner some time this week would be great. I'm not looking for anything heavy. Just to have fun."

Easton said something as Margot's car engine roared to life. Delanie could only imagine what his response was.

Delanie stepped into the shadows and hurried to her Mustang. Margot rocketed past her.

Her phone dinged, and Delanie resisted the urge to reach for it. At the next stop light, she glanced at the screen.

Duncan had texted, **You found a dead guy's DNA. Going to bed now. I'll call you tomorrow.**

Chapter Twenty-Four

Too amped to sleep when she got home from the Cheeky Monkey, Delanie binge-watched *Reacher* until she finally fell into a fitful sleep on the couch.

After what felt like minutes, she sat up and rubbed her eyes. The sun streamed through the living room window. Ten o'clock. Padding to the kitchen, she fired up the coffee maker and checked her phone. No new updates from Duncan after his cryptic, late-night text.

A hot shower and her coffee helped her mood. But still no updates from Duncan. *Why no details? What is up with him? He's hardly ever off the grid.*

After another mug of coffee and a slice of buttered toast, she checked her phone for what seemed like the fiftieth time, but there was still nothing from her partner. Being too fidgety to concentrate on reading or house cleaning, she slipped on her coat. She'd go through the video feed from the past few nights while she waited for Duncan and Margaret to show up at the office.

Twenty minutes later, she locked the door and opened the blinds behind her desk. Settling in, she watched hours of last night's Cheeky Monkey footage. No plot and not much action. *Maybe Easton found a new investor in Margot. High finance and romance, a dangerous combination.*

To ward off the crick in her neck, she stood and headed to the kitchen for hot tea. The caffeine and sugar would help the dull headache forming behind her eyes. Rooting around in the snack drawer, she scored a bag of salted peanuts. Thoughts of all the hijinks at the Cheeky Monkey bounced around in her head. *What am I missing?* On her way back down the hallway, she heard a noise and a paused. A motorcycle revved outside and zoomed past the building.

No Duncan. No Margaret. *I want details to go with his text. Could this be something that might crack this case wide open?*

Her phone rang and interrupted her thoughts.

"Hey, Delanie. I'm glad I caught you. This is Easton. I'm in a jam. We're having an issue at the club. It's kinda serious, and I need some help before I call Chaz. Can you get here quick? I really need your help."

"Sure. I'm on my way. What's up?" She hoped he didn't hear her sigh. *What else could happen at that club?*

"Meet me around back. I want you to look at something before I start calling people. I'm worried about Violet." Easton cleared his throat and disconnected.

She sighed again and picked up her laptop, pursecam, and coat.

Traffic was light, and she pulled around behind the club in under thirty minutes. Easton stood in the doorway. He dropped a cigarette and crushed it out with his dress shoe when he saw her approach.

"Hi. Thanks for coming so quickly. Come here. I want to show you something." He motioned for her to follow him into the building.

Delanie kept pace with him as he scurried down the dark hallway to the offices. She reached in her purse and activated the camera, hoping there was enough light for the pursecam to work.

"I got a text this morning from Violet," Easton said. "She wanted me to meet her to talk with some vendors. She said I had to be here, so I rushed over. When I arrived, she was nowhere to be found. She's not answering her phone. And I found this." He pushed the door open and stood so Delanie could see.

Papers and files covered the floor and the guest chairs. Violet's chair sat on its side in the corner. Delanie stepped gingerly over the loose papers and peered behind the desk. A pair of rainboots sat next to blue and red Vera Bradley purse with its contents strewn across the floor.

"Then I got this text." He held up his phone. **Something came up. Had to rush home. V.**

Delanie frowned and stared at his phone. She hadn't been around Violet enough, but "V" sounded too casual for the woman who ran this place with an iron fist. *Maybe she and Easton are closer than I thought.*

"I'm worried about her." Easton raked his fingers through his hair. "This place looks like a tornado blew through here. I want to go by her house, but I wanted someone with me. I feel silly calling the cops if she did this. I have gut feeling that something is really wrong." Easton stepped out in the hallway.

"Do we have to wait for your vendors?" Delanie asked.

Easton scowled for a moment and then turned the charm back on. "I don't think so. I've been here for a while, and no one has showed up. Javi will be here soon. He can take care of it if any sales guys turn up. We need to swing by her condo. I'm worried about her. Come on. I'll drive."

Delanie followed him to the back. "Hey, I'm going to follow you. I have some afternoon appointments."

Easton shrugged and trotted toward his Audi. "Suit yourself." He gunned the engine and drove out of the back lot. Delanie floored it to keep up.

He zipped out of the side entrance and dodged cars as he headed toward the city. Having no idea where she was going, Delanie accelerated to keep an eye on him in case he made a quick turn.

Near Staples Mill Road, Easton crossed three lanes and made a left turn at the light. Delanie sped up and hurried through the yellow light to keep the black Audi in sight. He zigzagged through a maze of narrow streets and stopped suddenly in front of a row of colonial townhouses. He stood on the curb near a cluster of mailboxes, waiting for Delanie to park.

When she caught up to him, he said, "Come on. Hers is the third one from the end." He looked at Delanie. "What? We had drinks a couple of times. I took her back to her place."

"Nothing," Delanie said. "I want to make sure she's okay. Violet is not the kind to ditch appointments."

Easton climbed the cement steps two at a time, pushed open the door, and yelled, "Violet, Violet, are you home?"

Inside the dark foyer, Easton peeked in the living room on the right and wandered past what looked to be a closet and a half-bath. He disappeared around the corner. "Violet, it's Easton and Delanie. Violet!"

Delanie inched down the dark hallway. Pulling out her phone, she flipped on the flashlight.

She froze when she saw the den and eat-in kitchen. The table and several chairs, flipped on their sides, lay next to the back door. Books, papers, and contents of the coffee table were strewn across an area rug. One brown loafer sat on the floor near the couch.

When she tapped on her phone, Easton clutched her arm. "Wait. Don't call anyone yet. We need to find Violet. She could be hurt. Let's go upstairs first, and then you can call the police." He tugged on her arm and led her back to the foyer. Not listening to that little voice in her head, Delanie pocketed her phone and crept up the carpeted stairs behind him. Listening for any noises, she held her breath. She heard a faint noise that sounded like a TV or a radio in a distance and the humming of the heating unit.

Easton didn't hesitate. He turned right at the top of the stairs and headed straight for the main bedroom. Delanie followed him into the cozy bedroom decorated with quilts and cat pillows. Enough light seeped in from behind the plantation shutters for the pair to get a view of the room. Easton ducked in the adjoining bathroom while Delanie looked under the bed.

"Nothing in here," he said. "Everything looks fine."

"I'll check the closet," Delanie said, striding across the room to the louvered doors.

Easton swooped in behind her. "Maybe the guy doing all the sabotage got her."

As she reached for the closet door handle, he put his hand on the door. "Let's make sure we're prepared for what we find in here. It could be gruesome, or it could be Violet's shoe collection."

"What?" she muttered. "We need to see if Violet is okay. And what happened to her. Somebody dangerous could be out there." She yanked on the knob.

Easton blocked the door again. "Wait. Are we sure? I mean, are we ready to go to the police and reveal what you've found about the pranks?" His normal voice changed to almost a hiss."

His sudden change in temperament confirmed her hunch.

"Yes, and all the skimming. Get out of the way. She could be hurt." Delanie put both hands on the door.

Easton paused and turned his head slightly.

As she pulled again on the knob, he wrapped his arm around her neck and shoulder and pulled her off balance. "What do you know about the money?"

Delanie elbowed him in the rib cage and swung her pursecam at his head.

Batting it away, he tightened his elbow around her neck and squeezed her wrist. The purse bounced off the wall and landed under the window.

He jerked her arm at an angle behind her back. "What skimming?"

With her free hand, she reached for her cell phone in her back pocket.

Easton grabbed her arm, and her phone flew a few feet, landing under the bed's dust ruffle.

Her heart sank to her stomach and pain shot through her arm. She steeled herself and focused on getting away from him. "Chaz knows about the account skimming about everything. And I know you're not his cousin. Stopping Violet and me isn't going to make it go away."

Easton let out a string of curses and yanked on her arm harder.

Delanie heard a noise. She struggled to wriggle free, but something hit the back of the head. Stars burst in front of her eyes, and her line of vision reduced to a pinpoint.

❧

DELANIE MOVED and blinked in the darkness. Her head pounded, and she took a deep breath to ward off a wave of nausea. *Where am I? The last thing she remembered was fighting with Easton.*

She blinked several times and tried to focus. There was small outline of light ahead of her around the door. Her hands were tied behind her with some kind of cloth, and a gag was wrapped around her mouth.

My phone. Under the bed. Okay, focus. You have to get out of here before he comes back. Is he still here?

Taking several cleansing breaths through her nose, she felt slightly better even though her head still pounded. She moved her wrists back and forth, and her binding moved. Giving her hope, she increased the intensity of the movement. The cloth tie slipped down her wrist. She tugged and tugged with her opposite hand. "Finally!" she exclaimed through the gag when she loosened one wrist. She hastily pulled out the other wrist and removed the gag. Relieved that she was free, she listened closely. No sounds of movement in the townhouse.

But she did hear a raspy noise and a slight groan.

Fear gripped her again. What was in here with her? She swallowed the panic and moved toward the slivers of light. Pushing on the door, it moved and stopped. Something blocked the door.

Delanie sat next to two plastic storage bins. Across from her, a blob with two bare feet lay on a pile of clothes and moaned again.

She blinked several times to clear her vision. Violet. Scrambling up to check on the woman, Delanie gulped in air to fight off the dizziness. Violet's eyes were closed. She couldn't see any visible wounds in the semidarkness. But she was breathing.

I have to get out of here and get help.

Delanie stood. She felt a little shaky in the knees, but so far, no more dizziness. Pushing on the louvered doors with both hands, Delanie shoved until they moved. She repeated the exercise several times, but the door didn't budge enough for space to exit.

Taking a deep breath, she rammed her full body into the doors. A cracking sound echoed in the closet and the doors came off the hinges. Daylight flooded into the closet.

Violet stirred. "You broke my door."

"Sorry about that. Are you okay, Violet? It's me. Delanie."

"I've felt better, but at least that slimy little weasel didn't kill me." Her voice trailed off.

"Violet, Violet. Stay with me," Delanie said, patting the woman's arm. Afraid to move her, Delanie stepped gingerly out of the closet around the broken door and the overturned dresser. She scrambled under the bed and found her phone.

Her call connected with the dispatcher, and she tried to calmly tell her of the situation without sounding like a panicked lunatic.

"Stay on the line," the dispatcher said. "I will send police and rescue. Do you know the address?"

"No." More panic welled up inside. "Wait, let me check something." She held the button on her phone. "Siri, where am I?"

Her phone responded, "You're at 22 Wharfside Road in Henrico County, Virginia." Delanie almost laughed when Siri pronounced it, "Hen-Reeeco" County.

"Got it," the dispatcher said. "Police and rescue are on their way. Are you in a safe place?"

"I think so. I'm here with the other victim. I can't seem to keep her awake. Her name is Violet Martin. I don't know where the guy who attacked us went. He might still be in the house."

"Okay, remain where you are. Help is on the way. I'll stay on the line. They're about two minutes out from your location. You should hear sirens soon."

"I think I hear them," Delanie replied, glancing at the still prone Violet.

Sirens echoed out front.

"Police," someone yelled and pounded on the door.

"We're up here," Delanie yelled. "In the main bedroom."

"I take it they've arrived," the dispatcher said. "They'll take care of you now"

"Thank you very much." Delanie disconnected. "We're in here," she yelled again.

Two police officers rushed in the room, guns drawn. The female officer checked the room and then stepped in the closet with Violet. The other secured the rest of the house.

Delanie fired off a text to Eric and her brother, Steve. Hopefully, one would respond and have some ideas about where to search for Easton. No telling where he was. He had a pretty good head start. At least fifteen minutes by her best guess. Then she fired off texts to Marco, Gwen, Chaz, and Duncan.

A few minutes later, two EMTs carrying what looked like tackle boxes ran up the stairs. One EMT and the officer dragged the dresser out of the way, and they started to work on Violet.

"I'm Officer Allen. What's going on here," the female officer said to Delanie.

"I'm Delanie Fitzgerald, private investigator. My client hired me to get to the bottom of some pranks at his establishment, the Cheeky Monkey. The guy claiming to be the owner's cousin, Easton Marsh, did this. We found that he was skimming from the accounts."

"That doesn't explain why you're here?" Officer Allen asked.

"Easton called me this morning and said something was wrong at the Cheeky Monkey. The club was dark when I arrived. He and I were the only ones there. It looked like there had been a fight in there. He said that he had texts from Violet and wanted to check out her home before he called the police. I followed him here. The door was open, and a lot of the furniture was upended downstairs." Delanie paused and took a couple of deep breaths. "Then he attacked me. I woke up in the closet next to Violet."

The other officer rushed in with two more EMTs, hefting a backboard.

"So, it's a guy impersonating someone named Easton Marsh and he left?"

"Right."

"And where is he now?" the officer asked.

"I assume he escaped," Delanie replied. His black Audi was parked out front in front of my Mustang." She picked up her pursecam and rifled through it. The camera light was still on. *Just like the Energizer Bunny. It doesn't quit.*

"There's only a black Prius in the driveway and a Mustang on the street," the officer said.

"Anything else?" Officer Allen asked Delanie.

Delanie ignored the rapid-fire dings on her phone. "My partner and I did some digging into his background. He's really Darrell Davidson. He was here scamming my client and impersonating his cousin." She scrolled through her phone and showed the screen to the officer. "This is him."

"Send that to me," she said to Delanie.

Delanie handed her the phone, so she could add her contact.

Officer Allen jotted furiously in her notebook as Delanie shared the details. When she finished, she pulled out her radio and gave an abbreviated version of the story to the dispatcher.

"We want to check you out, too," the male officer said to Delanie. The three EMTs and another officer transported Violet down the stairs.

Delanie glanced down at her phone and responded to the string of texts.

The EMT opened his tackle box. "Can you sit over there? I want to check your vitals."

Delanie sat on the edge of Violet's bed while he poked and prodded and looked at her pupils.

"You should get checked out. You've got a bruising on the back of your head. Feeling any dizziness or nausea? What about a headache?"

"My head throbs a bit. The nausea subsided."

"You need to go through the formal concussion check." He packed his gear.

Delanie turned toward the door and the sound of heavy footsteps climbing the stairs. Officer Allen and her partner, along with Eric Ellington strode into Violet's room.

"You doing okay?" Eric asked Delanie as she stepped closer. He kissed her on the top of her head.

"I'm fine. I got konked on the head again." Eric cocked one eyebrow and stared at her. "No comment."

Before Delanie could say anything sassy, Officer Allen said to Eric, "My partner didn't realize he was with you. Sorry about that. He recognized you and thought the feds were taking over the investigation."

Eric cracked a slight smile. "No, I'm here to make her go get checked out. But if you need anything, let me know. You about ready to go?"

Delanie nodded. "Here's my contact information," she said, handing a card to Henrico County officer. "Where did they take Violet?"

She flipped open one of the slots on her Batman utility belt and handed Delanie her card. "St. Mary's Hospital. Call me if you think of anything else." Her radio chirped, and she paused to listen. "They found his car a few blocks over. No sign of him."

"Come on," Eric said, taking her elbow. "Your next stop is the ER."

He followed her down the stairs as the forensic team moved gear into Violet's downstairs. Delanie and Eric picked their way around the boxes, containers, and tripods. Outside, there were enough police vehicles to draw interest from the neighbors.

Delanie ducked under the perimeter tape. "Where are you parked?"

"About a block from your car." Eric pointed down the street.

It was nice of him to show up to check on her. Delanie smiled to herself. He looked good in his black leather jacket and aviator glasses. She took his hand as they strolled past her car.

"Need anything out of your car?"

"Nope. But I'll need a ride back to pick it up," she said.

"We'll take care of that. It'll be fine here. You don't need to be driving right now."

They strolled down the sidewalk to his truck. After they passed her Mustang, he pulled out his truck's key fob.

Delanie paused.

"What's wrong?" he asked.

She hesitated and then stepped next to the back fender of the Mustang.

Eric stopped and looked at her.

Delanie touched the trunk, and it flew up.

Easton vaulted out of the back from a crouched stance. Teetering when he landed, he fell toward Delanie. She didn't have time to get away as he stumbled into her and knocked her down in the grass.

Easton caught her wrist, but she wiggled out from under him and kicked him in the face with her boot. He grunted and dove to protect his nose.

Eric tossed him like a ragdoll into a nearby flowerbed. "Stay down," Eric ordered, reaching for his gun.

Delanie rose and dusted the grass and dirt off her pants. "What were you doing in my car?" she hissed.

"I figured the police would be looking for my car, so it bought me some time," Easton said, holding one arm over his face. "You weren't supposed to figure this out. It was easy money, and I was going to disappear." He rolled over on his side.

"Don't move," Eric ordered.

An officer stepped off of Violet's front porch and approached them. Delanie was sure she saw several curtains move in some of the houses across the street.

"So, Darrell, when did you decide to impersonate Chaz's cousin?" she asked.

"On the long walk to town after the accident. I crawled out of the wreckage. Easton was already dead. The body was charred by the time I left the wreck. I had a lot of debt. The timing was perfect for me. He didn't have any close relatives, and Dare Davidson would be mourned for his tragic life. I closed up shop and headed back east. It was fortunate that Chaz wanted to meet and when I called him. You know the rest." He flopped down on his back in the grass.

Before Delanie could comment, Officer Allen and her partner jogged across the yard. "What's going on?" she yelled.

"He ambushed us from the trunk as we walked past her car." Eric holstered his weapon.

Officer Allen took their statements as her partner handcuffed Dare and moved him to the back of a police cruiser. Two of the forensic technicians descended on Delanie's car.

"Thanks for detaining the suspect," Officer Allen said.

"What about my car?" Delanie asked. "I see the keys in the trunk. He must have taken them from me when he trapped me in the closet."

"We'll call you when they're done processing it," Officer Allen said.

Eric handed the officer his business card. "But for now, we're going to get you checked out."

Delanie followed him to his truck. She had to hold onto the railing to boost herself up to the passenger side.

After several long hours at the hospital, Eric helped Delanie settle on her couch. He ordered a pizza for dinner.

"I'm fine," she said. "I'll keep a check on the bump and look for any concussion signs. The doctor said it wasn't serious."

"Take it easy for a couple of days. You wrapped up your case, so you can take a break."

"Thanks for coming to get me again." She was glad to have Eric around. He sat on the couch next to her and draped his arm around her shoulders. "Any word from the police?" she asked.

"I talked to Officer Allen earlier. They're still piling on the charges for Darrell Davidson. She may contact you with more questions."

Delanie nodded and flipped on the TV. "I'll send Officer Allen my notes."

"What clued you in on the imposter?" Eric pulled her closer, and she muted the TV.

"There were little family details that contradicted what Chaz had told me. I didn't pay much attention at first. Then when we found some old pictures, the hair color was off. Again, people forget details and dye their hair. But the clincher was when Duncan had some DNA tests done. His first sample had problems, and then the second one came back as his deceased partner."

"Good work," he said.

The doorbell rang, and he rose to get the pizza.

She shuffled into the kitchen to get plates and drinks. "Tea, Coke, or orange juice," she yelled.

"Water's fine." Eric closed the door and set the pizza box on the coffee table.

Delanie returned to her spot on the couch as Eric switched the channel from news to sports.

She'd wrap up her report tomorrow, but for now, it was time to hang out with Eric and watch college basketball.

Chapter Twenty-Five

D uncan honked from Delanie's driveway. She slipped into her
coat and pulled the door behind her.

When she opened the passenger door of his Camaro,
Margaret raised her head and glared.

"Come on, baby," Duncan said. "Delanie needs to sit in the front
seat. You can get comfy in the back." The brown and white log with
legs rose reluctantly and took her sweet time climbing into the back
seat, but only with a lot of coaxing and coaching from Duncan.

"Thanks, Margaret," Delanie said, sliding into the passenger seat.
"And thanks for taking me to get my car."

"No problem. Glad you wrapped up the case. How's your head?"

"I'll be fine. It's a bruise. No concussion. Your text about Easton
not being Easton was the missing piece. I realized he was hiding in
plain sight."

Duncan nodded and headed for the Powhite Parkway. "My friend
reported back twice that we'd submitted a sample from a dead guy. I
was scratching my head with the first sample. I figured something
went wrong at the lab. But then it happened again with the same
results."

"Yup. When Easton died in the car crash, Dare decided to assume his identity and start a new life."

"Pretty convenient. Bury the old Dare Davidson with all his debts and problems."

"And head to Virginia to reunite with what was left of Easton's family. A new place, a new scam."

"But what's with all the pranks?" Duncan asked.

"I think some were random and not connected to him like the creepy doll, but the others he did to create confusion," she added. "And part of it may have been his warped sense of humor. He liked the chaos of stirring up stuff. After I get my car, I'm meeting Chaz to catch him up."

"Well done. Another case closed." Duncan glanced in the backseat to check on the snoring Margaret.

On the other side of the river, Delanie directed him through the neighborhood of townhouses to where she had left her car. Violet's house looked dark, with no sign that the police had investigated there the previous day.

While Duncan idled at the curb, Delanie stepped out of the Camaro. "Thanks so much for carting me over here. Will you be in the office tomorrow?"

"Yup. And now Margaret and I are going to grab some lunch. See ya." He revved the engine and disappeared around the corner.

Delanie walked around her car and peeked underneath. She also looked in the back seat before she climbed in and started it. Her other set of keys sat on the passenger seat.

When she parked on the side of the Treasure Chest, she texted Chaz and Marco. Before she had time to check emails, Marco opened the side door and saluted.

"Hey, Marco. How's it going?" Delanie stepped out of her car.

"Good. I'm counting down the days until warmer weather. Anything below seventy-eight degrees is freezing." He shut the door behind her. "He's in his office."

Delanie followed him down the hallway. The bass from the party music thumped through the walls and provided a steady, pulsating background noise.

Marco rapped on the door, and Chaz pulled it open. "Delanie. Thanks so much!" He squeezed her hard enough to make her squeak. "It's great to see you. Come in. I hope you're feeling okay."

Chaz motioned toward the guest chairs. "I'm still totally ticked at Easton or whatever his name was, but I'm glad you got to the bottom of this. I knew you'd figure it out."

"I guess he thought Easton's life was better than what he had as Dare Davidson," she said.

"Thanks for putting an end to this. The detectives came by yesterday. I told them everything. I'm pressing as many charges as I possibly can. He doesn't need to be out scamming more people. I can't stand a liar and a conman."

"I'm glad it all worked out," she said.

"I heard you got knocked around again."

Delanie shrugged. "Sometimes it comes with the job. How's Violet doing?"

"She's still in the hospital. I talked to her earlier. She hopes to go home today. Knowing her, she'll be back to work in a few days. I told her Javi and Gwen have it all under control. Not sure if that made her nervous or not. Here, this is for you. "He handed her a white envelope and pressed it in her hands. "You and Duncan deserve it."

"Thanks so much for always calling Falcon Investigations."

"You're at the top of my speed dial list. I'm going to call you in a week or so. I have an idea for a new project." A grin spread across his face.

Delanie wondered what he had in mind. She offered a smile to her best, cash-paying client. Who knows what Chaz had up his sleeve this time? All Delanie wanted was a little downtime. Maybe Robin and Paisley would want to have a girls' night out at the Cheeky Monkey. *I'm pretty sure I can get good seats. It's nice to have contacts.*

These are Real...

Carytown – This is a specialty shopping district on Cary Street in Richmond, near the museums and the Fan neighborhood. It has trendy shops and restaurants, and it opened in the 1930s. It's an eclectic place to hang out.

Chesterfield County, Virginia – Formed in 1749 and named for the fourth Earl of Chesterfield, the county is south of the capital, Richmond. It is the third most populous county in the Commonwealth of Virginia.

Church Hill – This is an historic neighborhood in Richmond that overlooks the James River. St. John's Church, site of Patrick Henry's "Give me Liberty" speech and Chimborazo Park, the location of the famous Civil War hospital, are historic sites in the area. Chaz Smith has a townhouse here with a great view of the river. It's also home to the Church Hill Tunnel disaster. Check out my story about it called, "Derailed." It explains how Chaz got his teardrop tattoo.

City Dogs – If you visit RVA, you have to stop in City Dogs, a few doors down from Fountain Bookstore. They have the best hot dogs in town.

Edgar Allan Poe – The famous author, poet, literary critic, and father of the modern mystery lived for a time in Richmond, Virginia. After his parents' deaths, he was taken in by wealthy Richmonder, John Allan. As a young man, he held a position at the *Southern Literary Messenger*. Poe's mother is buried at St. John's Church (made famous by Patrick' Henry's "Give me Liberty" speech). I took my own liberties and built Chaz's Treasure Chest on the site of the *Southern Literary Messenger*. And there is a statue of Edgar Allan Poe in Richmond, but it's on the lawn of the Virginia State Capitol. I made up the one on Chaz's property.

Fountain Bookstore – This indie bookstore is located on Cary Street in downtown Richmond. Known for its eclectic collection, I love their section of books by Virginia authors. Kelly and her team of amazing booksellers are so helpful.

Goochland County – Named for Sir William Gooch, Royal Lieutenant Governor, the county formed in 1728 and was originally part of Henrico County.

Henrico County – One of the eight original shires in Virginia, this county surrounds the city of Richmond (which was a part of it until 1842) on the east, west, and north sides.

Leonardo's – This family-owned restaurant near Short Pump is known for its amazing subs and Italian dishes. The steak fries are my favorite.

Little Bookshop – This cozy indie book story is located in the Village in Midlothian. I love the local authors' section, the kids' books, and the great selection of bookish gifts. Mary and her team are so supportive of local authors.

Maymont – This park consists of a mansion from the Gilded Age, an animal sanctuary/nature center, and gardens. It's located in heart of downtown Richmond near Byrd Park. Once the home to financier, James Dooley, the park has a wildlife rehabilitation area, Italian and Japanese gardens, and a petting zoo. The grounds are lovely for a stroll, and it's home to hundreds of weddings and the Richmond Jazz Festival. I always visit the bears when we go to Maymont.

Midlothian – This is a town in Chesterfield County. It was originally a coal mining region and home to Virginia's first railroad.

And the Urban Farmhouse Market and Café is a wonderful place to stop if you're visiting the nearby library.

Monroe Park – This is the city of Richmond's oldest park. Located on the Virginia Commonwealth University campus, it's a hub for city residents and college students. Over the years, the site has been the home to rallies, fairs, and a camp for Civil War soldiers.

Perly's – This is a deli on Grace Street in the heart of the city.

Pickleball – This racquet sport has elements of tennis and badminton. It can be played inside or outside. The court is smaller than a traditional tennis court, and the game has grown in popularity through the years. There are quite a few outdoor courts in Central Virginia.

Poe Museum – Located in the Old Stone House in Richmond, Virginia, it houses a vast collection of Edgar Allan Poe artifacts. The house is near his boyhood home and the *Southern Literary Messenger*, where Poe worked. The museum hosts "unhappy hours" in the garden. Edgar and Pluto are the real museum cats.

Sears Catalog Homes – While there are several Sears Catalog homes in Hopewell, Virginia in the Crescent Hills neighborhood, I moved one to western Chesterfield County for Delanie's residence. The homes were ordered from the Sears and Roebuck catalog and were shipped by rail. Delanie's Yates model dates back to 1939.

Shockoe Slip and Shockoe Bottom – Located in downtown Richmond, this area lies between the financial district and the James River. A lot of the buildings are restored warehouses, and many of the streets and alleys have cobblestones. A lot of Richmond's nightlife is in this part of town. My short story, "Art Attack" in *Deadly Southern Charm* is set in a gallery in one of these warehouses.

Short Pump and the West End – These neighborhoods are west of the city. They were much closer to the city in decades past, but the borders migrated west as the suburbs expanded.

Short Pump Town Center – This is an upscale mall on west Broad Street. The area used to be home to a tavern for travelers between Richmond and points west. Legend has it that the name came from a porch installed over the pump at the tavern. When it blocked the handle, it had to be altered to fit under the new room. After it was cut off, it was a "short pump."

VCU – Virginia Commonwealth University is a public, urban research university in Richmond, Virginia. Its hospital and graduate art programs are renowned. This is Delanie's alma mater. The hospital is now called the VCU Medical Center. It was known locally for years as MCV (Medical College of Virginia).

Acknowledgments

Writing is a long (and often solitary) process, and I'm glad I'm not alone. I want to thank my family and friends who provided all the wonderful support for this book – Stan Weidner for putting up with all my writing adventures, my parents who instilled in me a lifelong love of reading, Cortney Cain for her amazing support, Meagan and Jocelyn Cain, my social media and pop culture experts, and Bill Cain for always keeping everyone entertained.

And I appreciate all the encouragement, love, and support from my Bethia UMC family.

Many thanks to Jessica Mehta and Stephanie Martin for some great advice and to the Chesterfield County Police Department for hosting a wonderful Citizens' Police Academy. We were the Covid Class of 2020. And I appreciate all the time Officer Cristina Allen spent with me on my ride-along. She did a great job of explaining procedures and answering my hundreds of questions.

I am so grateful for my talented Sisters in Crime, Guppy, and James River Writer friends. Your support is amazing, and I am eternally grateful.

Thanks to my critique group: Susan Campbell, Sandie Warwick, Catherine Brennan, Kellie Murphy, Amy Lilly, and Marjorie Bagby for all the great feedback. Jayne Ormerod, you are a wonderful beta reader!

Joy Pfister and her wonderful crew at Studio FBJ are fabulous. Fiona Jayde does a great job on the artwork and covers, and Tina Glasneck makes sure everything is perfect and ready to go. I cannot thank you all enough for turning my words into a book. Tara Marie Kirk for being the wonderful voice of the Delanie books in the audio versions.

And I am so grateful for my readers who share Delanie, Duncan, Margaret, and Chaz's adventures with me.

More Delanie and Duncan (and Margaret and Chaz) ...

Delanie, Duncan, and Margaret also appear in several short stories and a Mutt Mystery. Check out their new cases and antics in *To Fetch a Villain*, *Mystery by the Glass*, and *Virginia is for Mysteries 3*. The short story, "Derailed," in *Virginia is for Mysteries 3* explains how Chaz Wellington Smith, III got his infamous teardrop tattoo.

Tantor Media has released the audio books of the first three book in the Delanie series. Check out the awesome narrations by Tara Marie Kirk.

About the Author

Male Revues and Subterfuge is Heather Weidner's fourth novel in the Delanie Fitzgerald series. Her short stories appear in the *Virginia is for Mysteries* series, *50 Shades of Cabernet*, *Murder by the Glass*, and *Deadly Southern Charm*. Heather also writes the Jules Keene Glamping Mysteries and the Mermaid Bay Christmas Shoppe Mysteries (2023).

She is a member of Sisters in Crime – Central Virginia, Sisters in Crime Chessie, Guppies, International Thriller Writers, and James River Writers.

Originally from Virginia Beach, Heather has been a mystery fan since Scooby-Doo and Nancy Drew. She lives in Central Virginia with her husband and a pair of Jack Russell terriers.

Through the years, she has been a cop's kid, technical writer, editor, college professor, software tester, and IT manager.

www.ingramcontent.com/pod-product-compliance
Lightning Source LLC
Chambersburg PA
CBHW070444120726
47910CB00003B/928